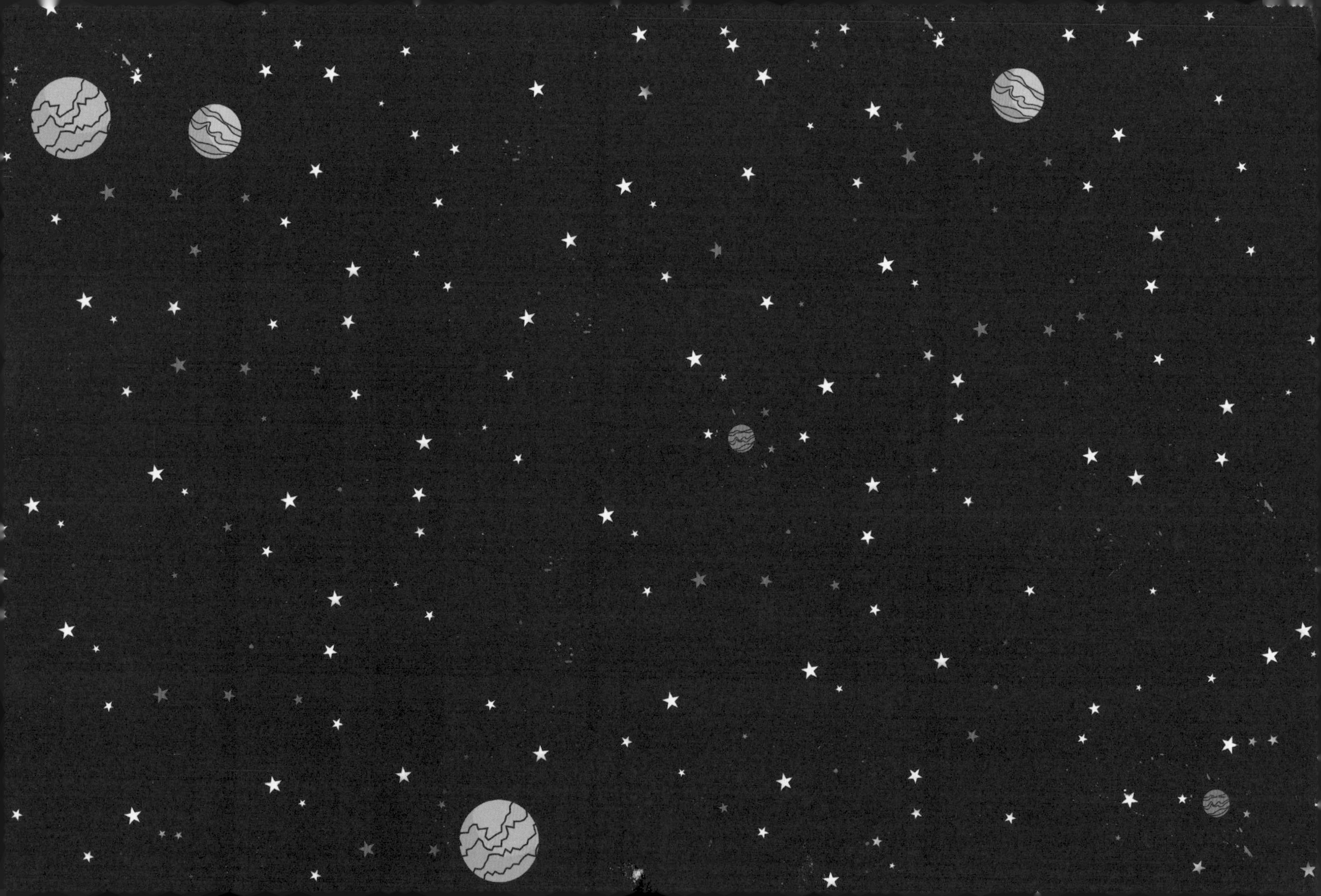

ED'S TERRESTRIALS

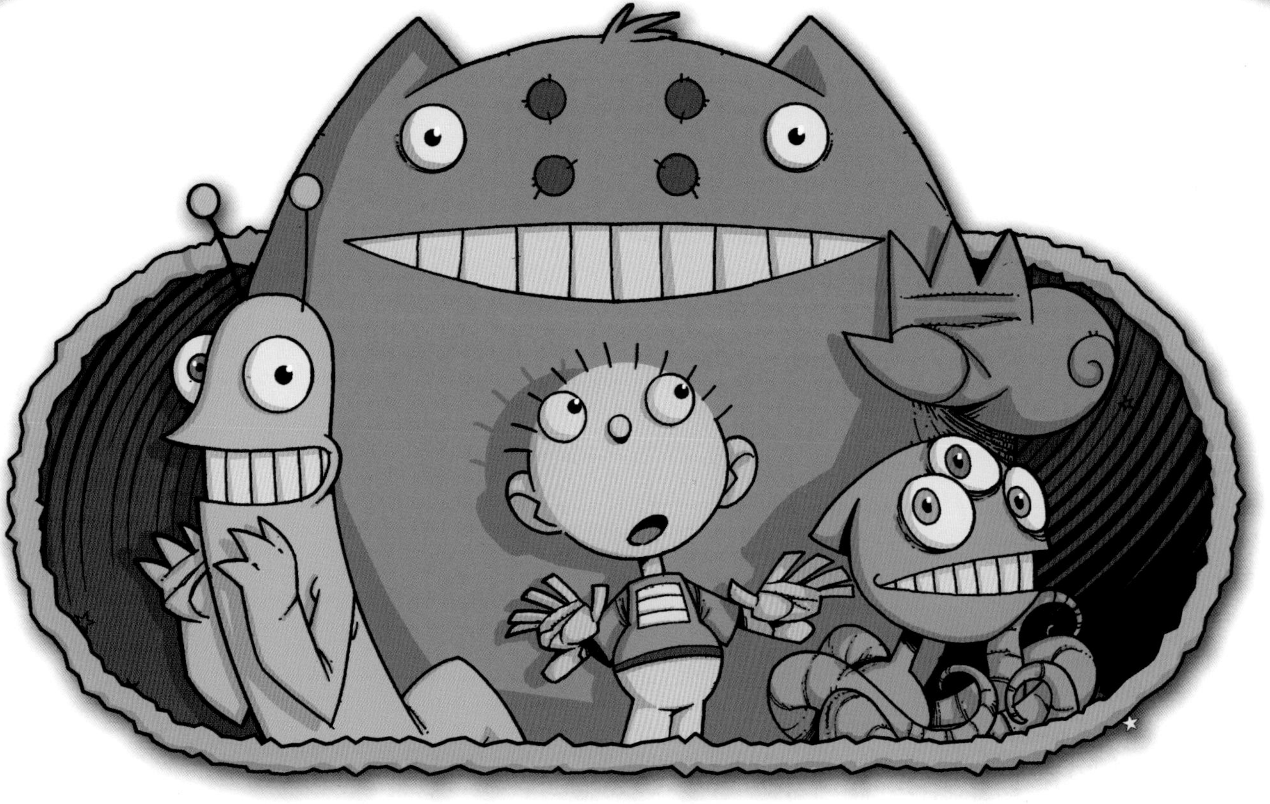

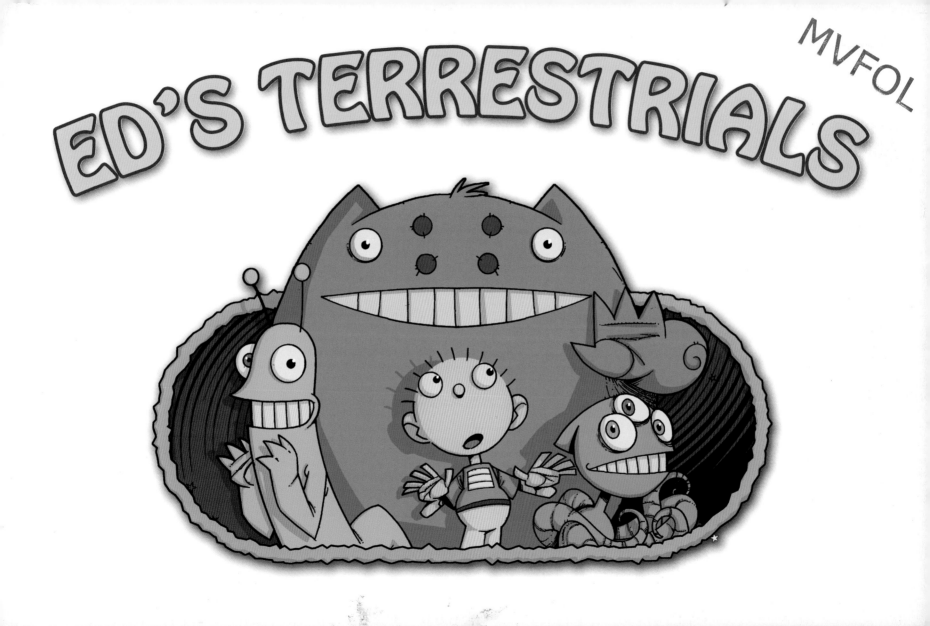

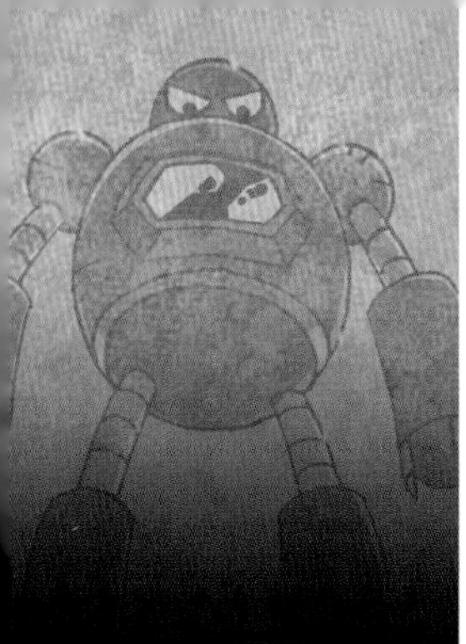

ALIAS

Brett Burner
Publisher

Mike S. Miller
Executive Director

Sean J. Jordan
Managing Editor

Everett Fitzgerald
Production Manager

Steve Gray
Production Artist

Eddie Ostrowski
Web Master

ALIAS *presents...*

ED'S TERRESTRIALS

CREATED & WRITTEN BY:
Scott Christian Sava

ART BY:
Diego Jourdan

COLORS BY:
Frank Villarreal

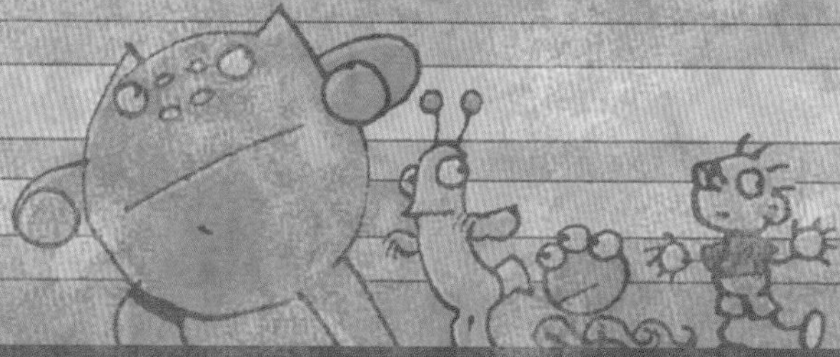

ED'S TERRESTRIALS, July 2005. First Printing. Published by Alias Enterprises LLC. Office of Publication: 8367 Lemon Avenue, La Mesa, CA 91941. Printed in Korea.

WWW.ALIASCOMICS.NET

ED'S TERRESTRIALS

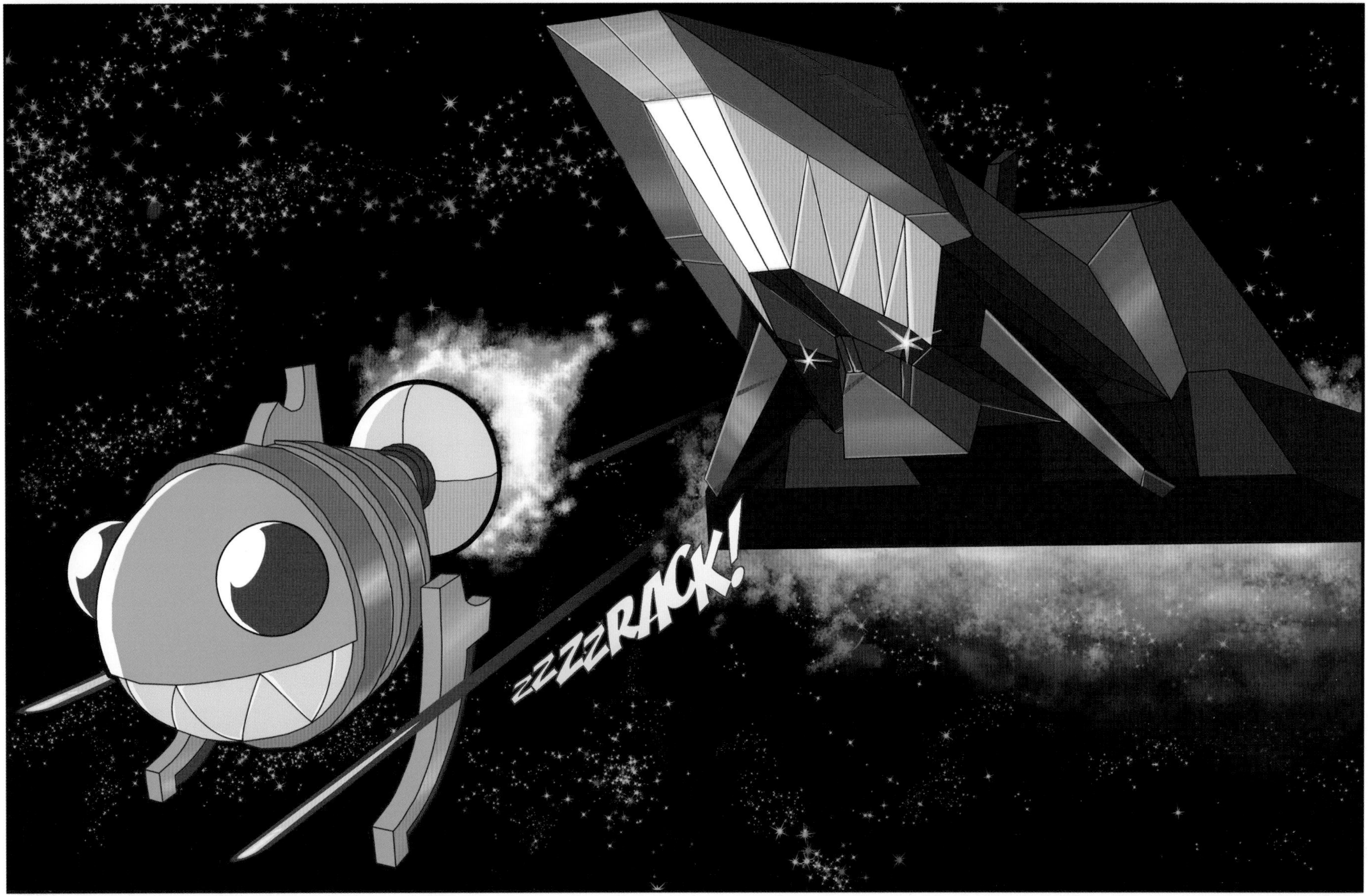
zzzzRACK!

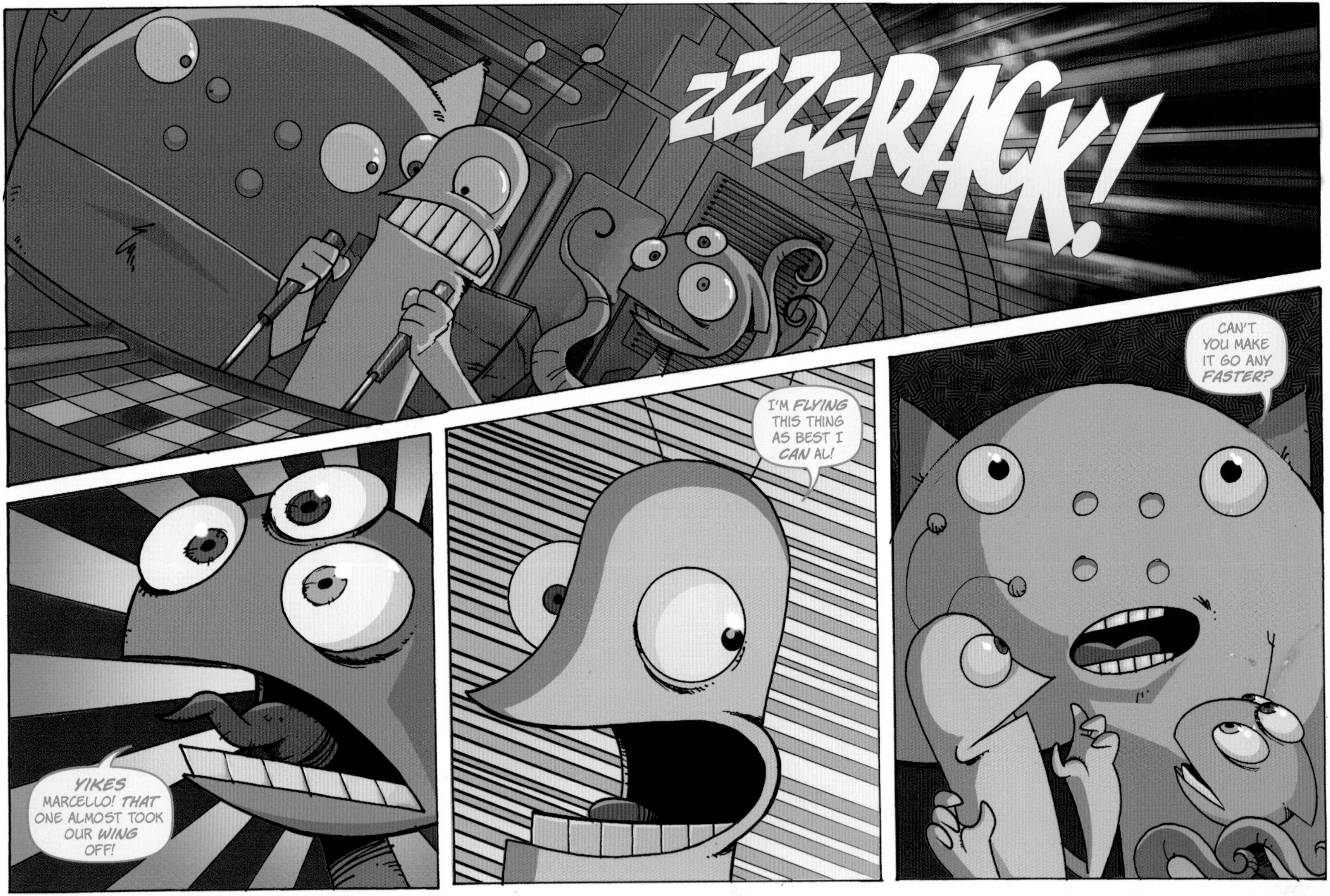
ZZZZRACK!
YIKES MARCELLO! THAT ONE ALMOST TOOK OUR WING OFF!
I'M FLYING THIS THING AS BEST I CAN AL!
CAN'T YOU MAKE IT GO ANY FASTER?

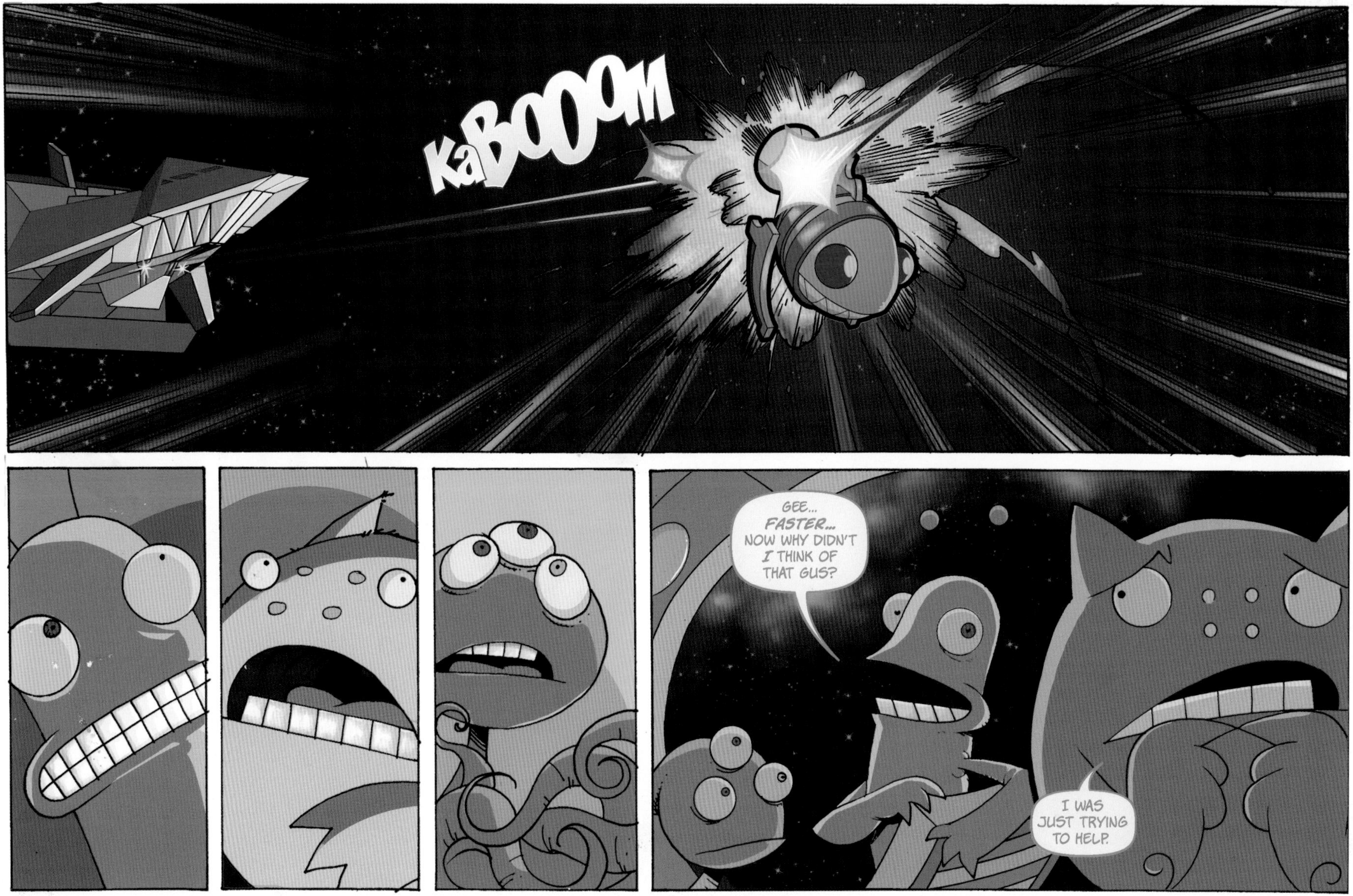
KaBOOOM
GEE... FASTER... NOW WHY DIDN'T I THINK OF THAT GUS?
I WAS JUST TRYING TO HELP.

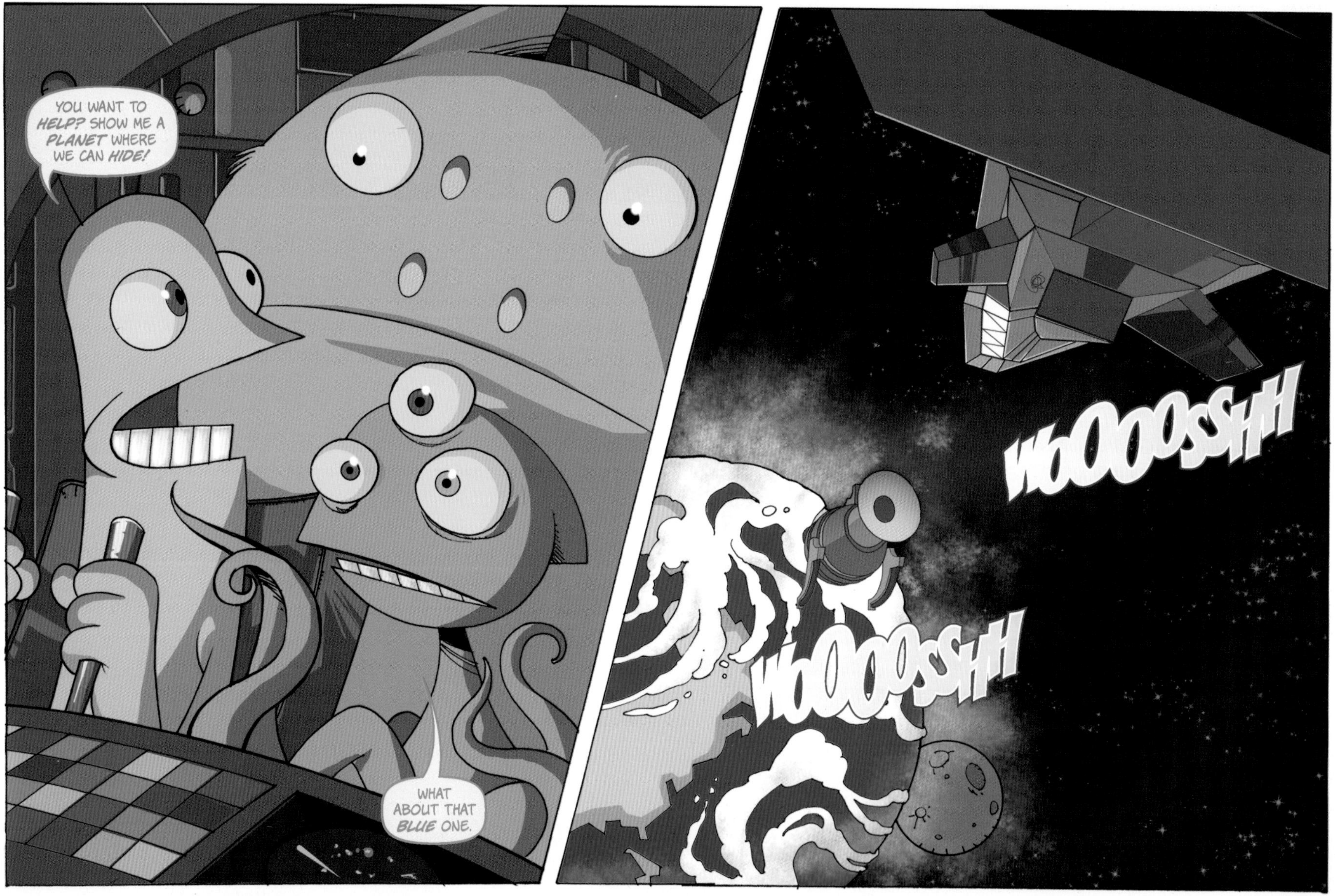
YOU WANT TO HELP? SHOW ME A PLANET WHERE WE CAN HIDE!
WHAT ABOUT THAT BLUE ONE.
WOOOOSSHH
WOOOOSSHH

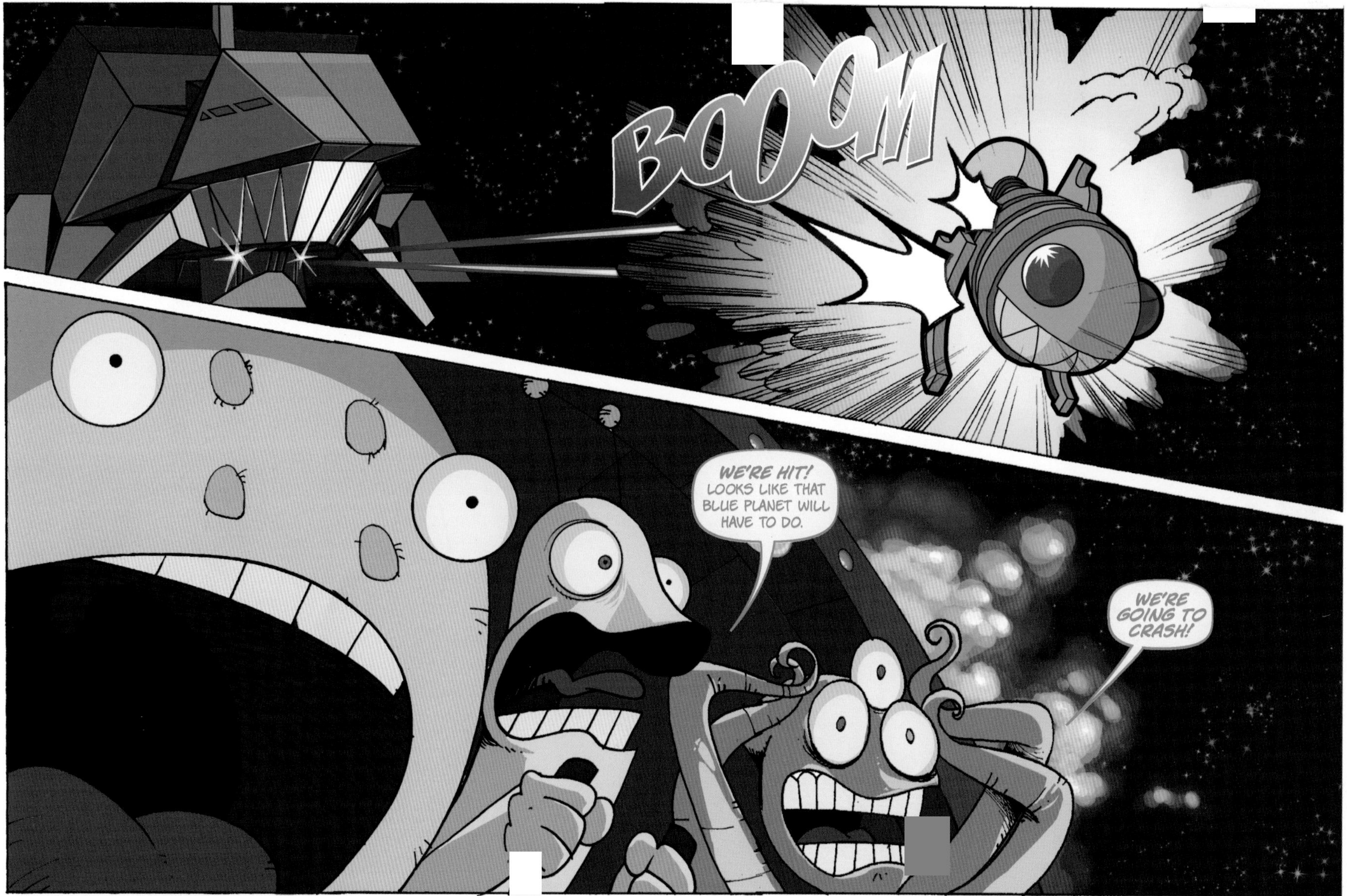

BOOOOM
WE'RE HIT! LOOKS LIKE THAT BLUE PLANET WILL HAVE TO DO.
WE'RE GOING TO CRASH!

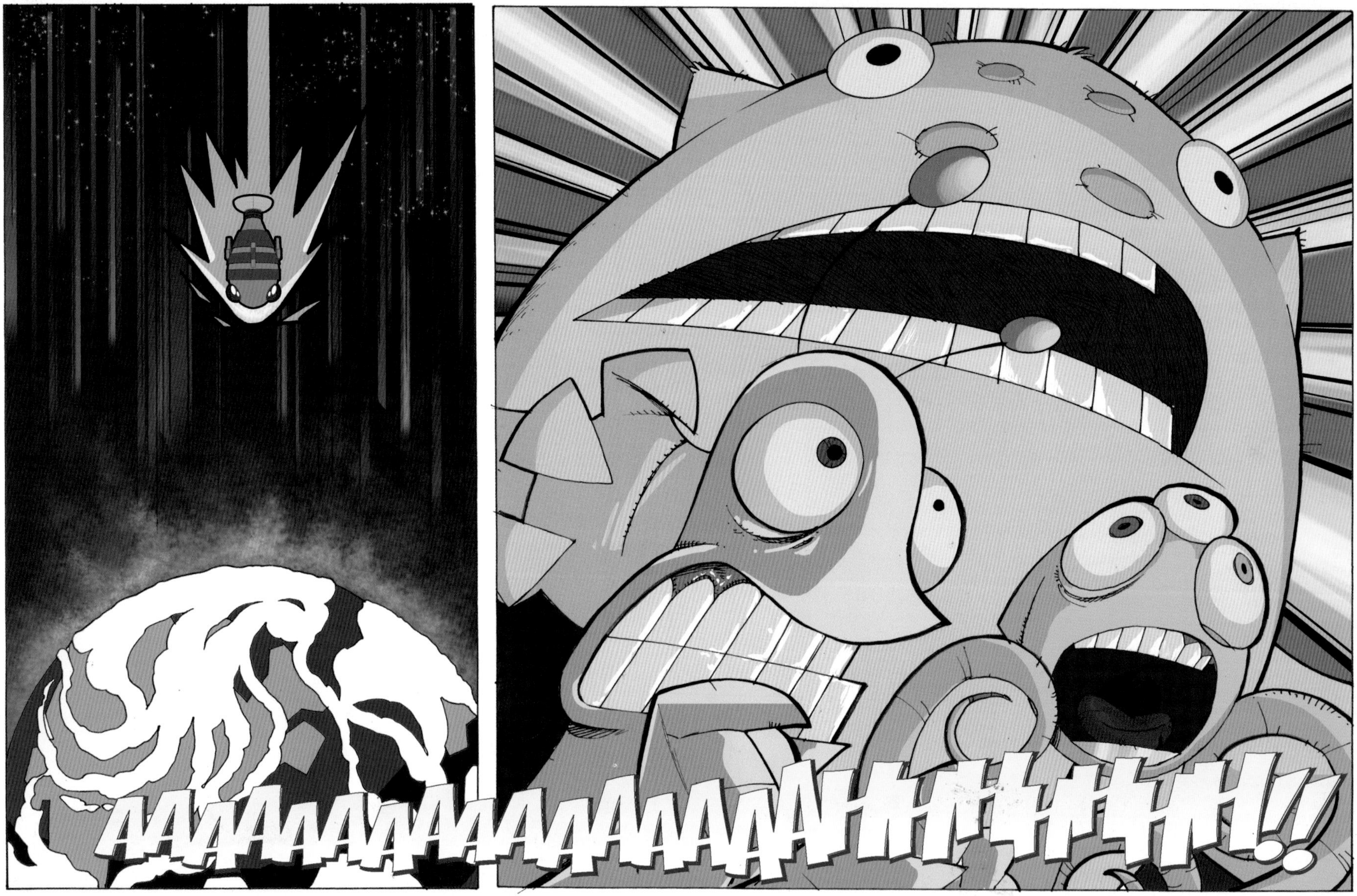
AAAAAAAAAAAAAAAAAAAAHHHHHHHHH!!

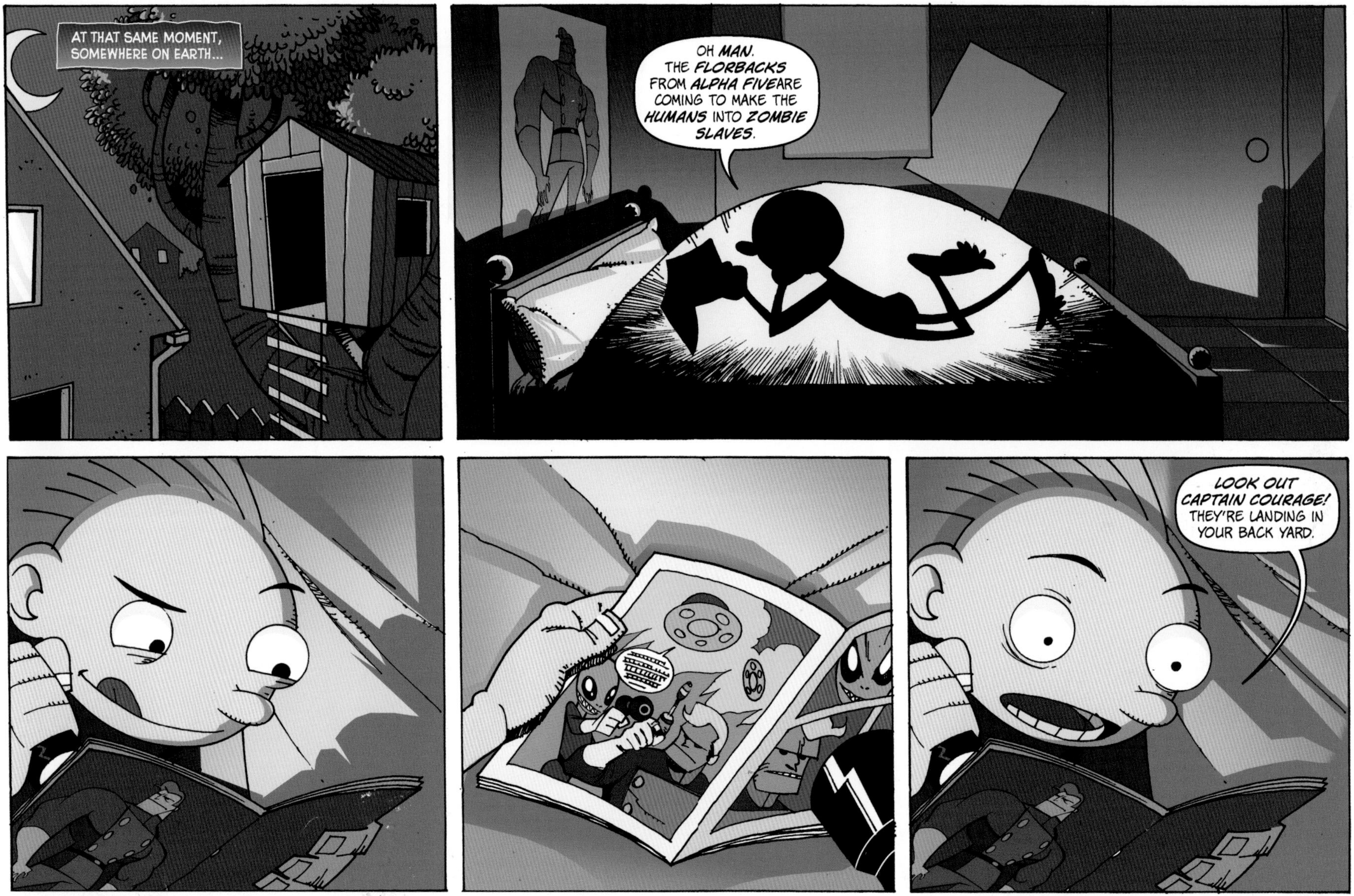
AT THAT SAME MOMENT, SOMEWHERE ON EARTH...
OH MAN. THE FLORBACKS FROM ALPHA FIVEARE COMING TO MAKE THE HUMANS INTO ZOMBIE SLAVES.
LOOK OUT CAPTAIN COURAGE! THEY'RE LANDING IN YOUR BACK YARD.

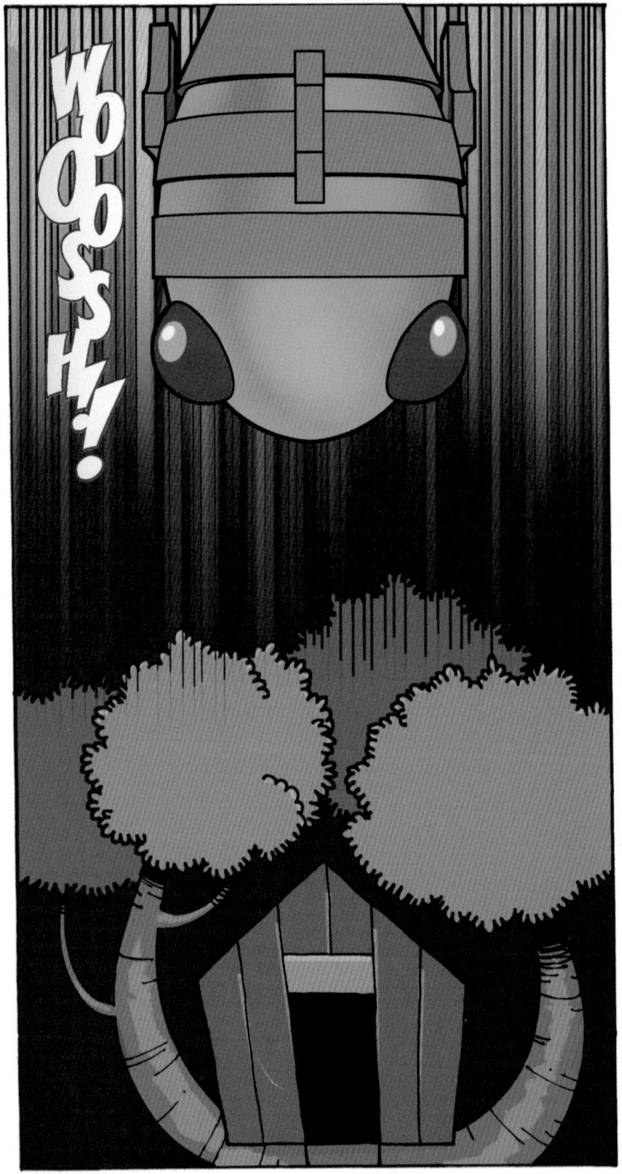
WOOOSSH!!

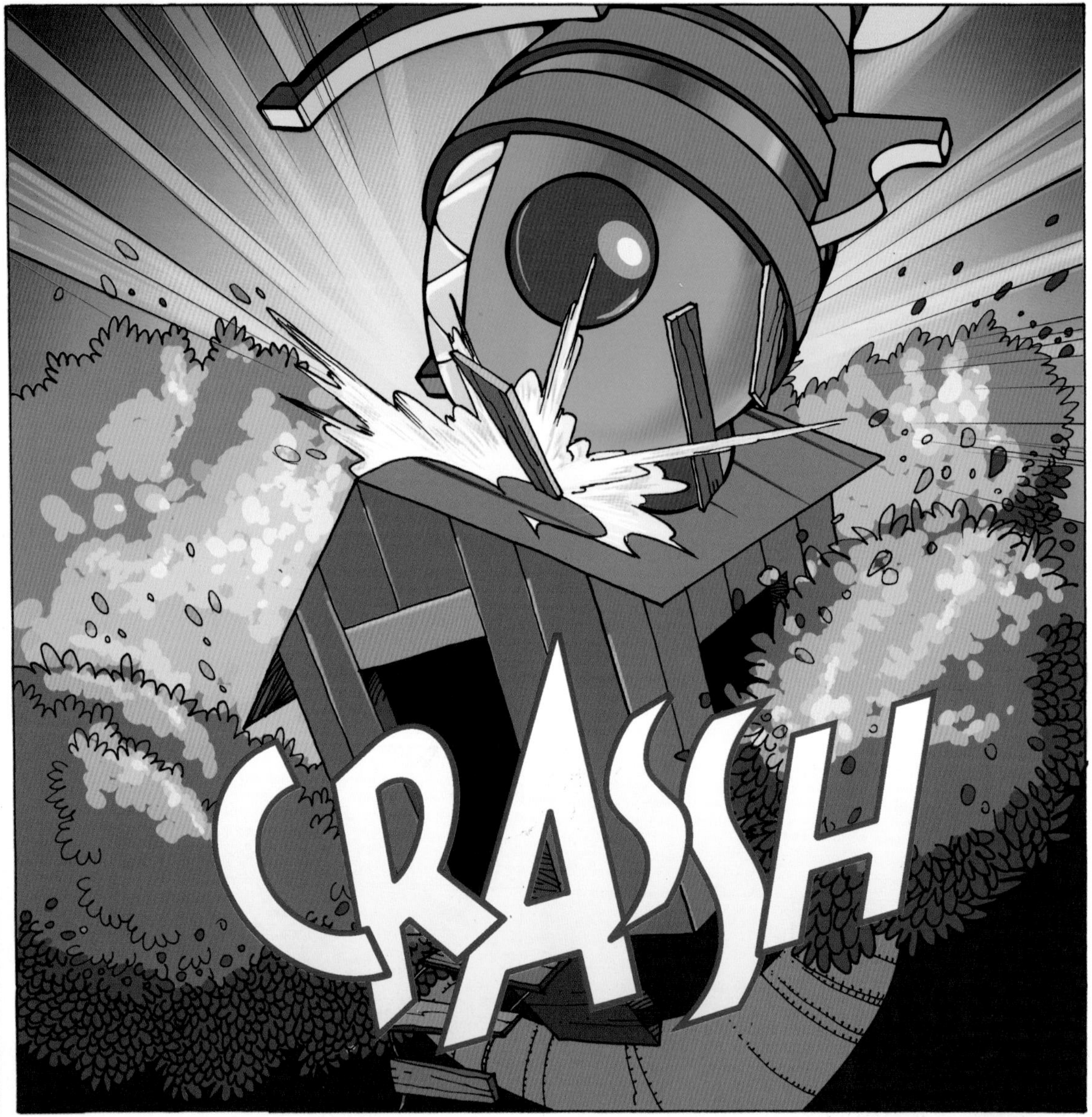
CRASSH

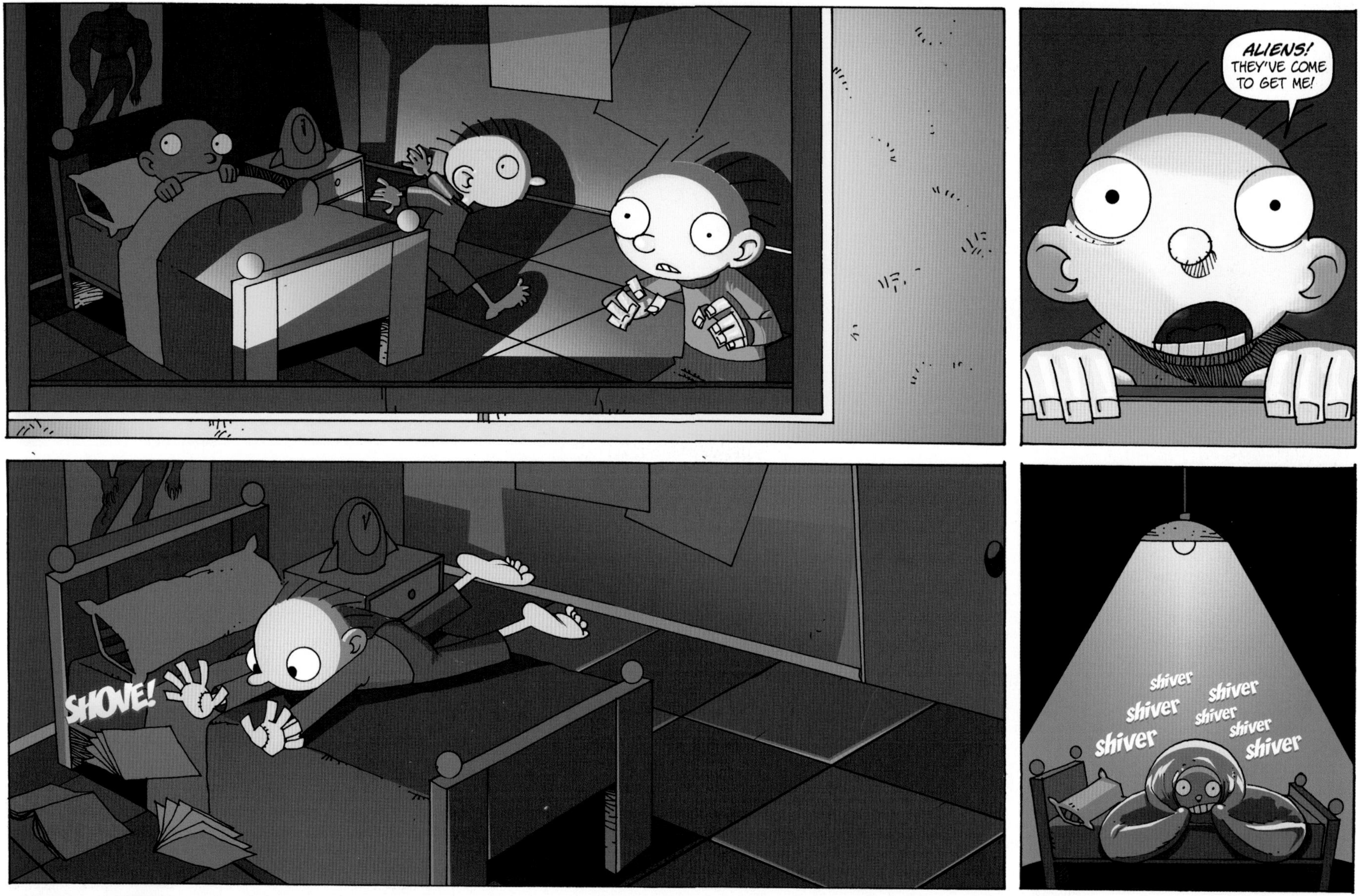
ALIENS! THEY'VE COME TO GET ME!
SHOVE!
shiver
shiver
shiver
shiver
shiver
shiver
shiver

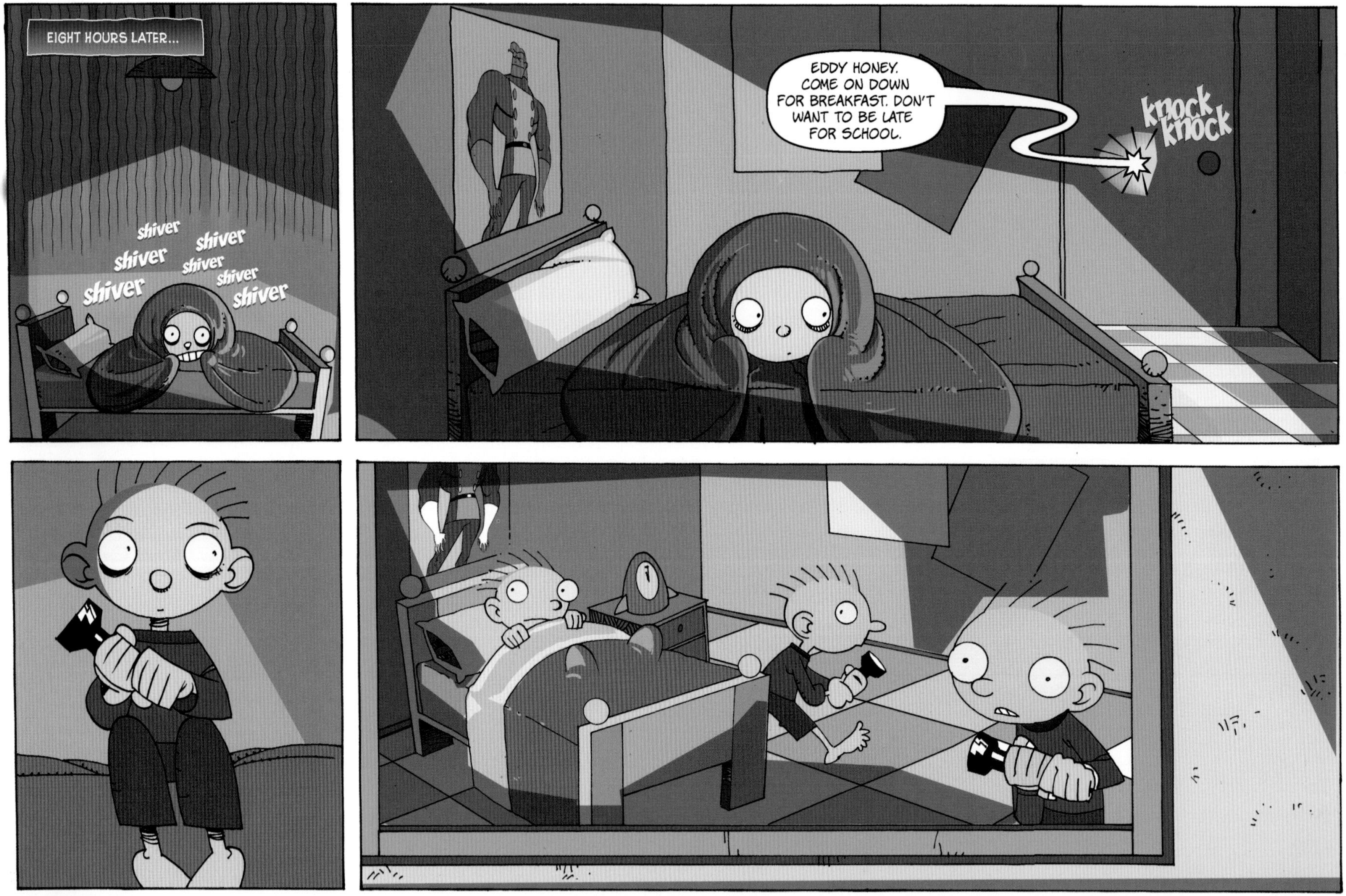
EIGHT HOURS LATER...
shiver
shiver
shiver
shiver
shiver
shiver
shiver
EDDY HONEY. COME ON DOWN FOR BREAKFAST. DON'T WANT TO BE LATE FOR SCHOOL.
knock knock

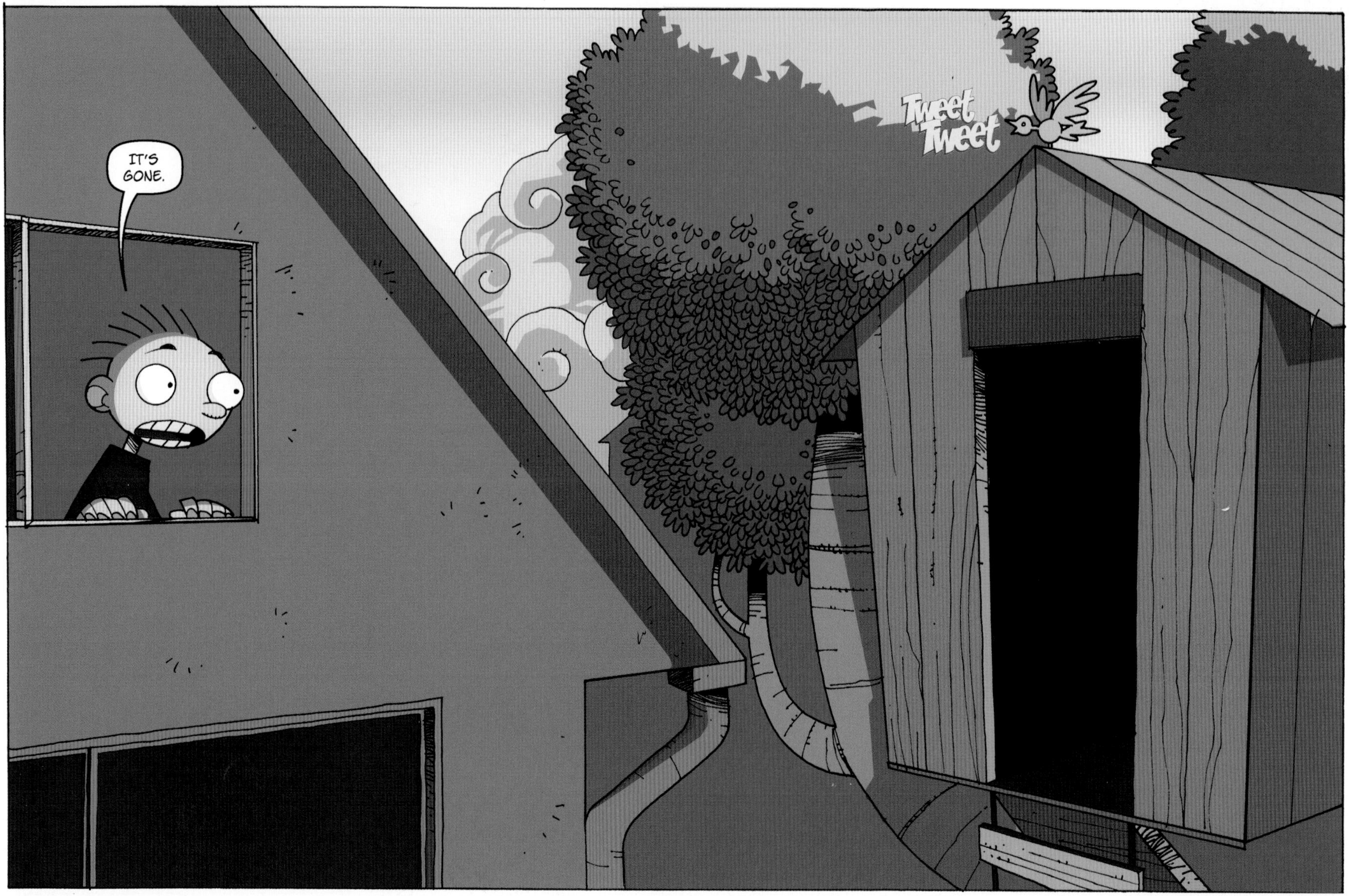

IT'S GONE.
Tweet Tweet

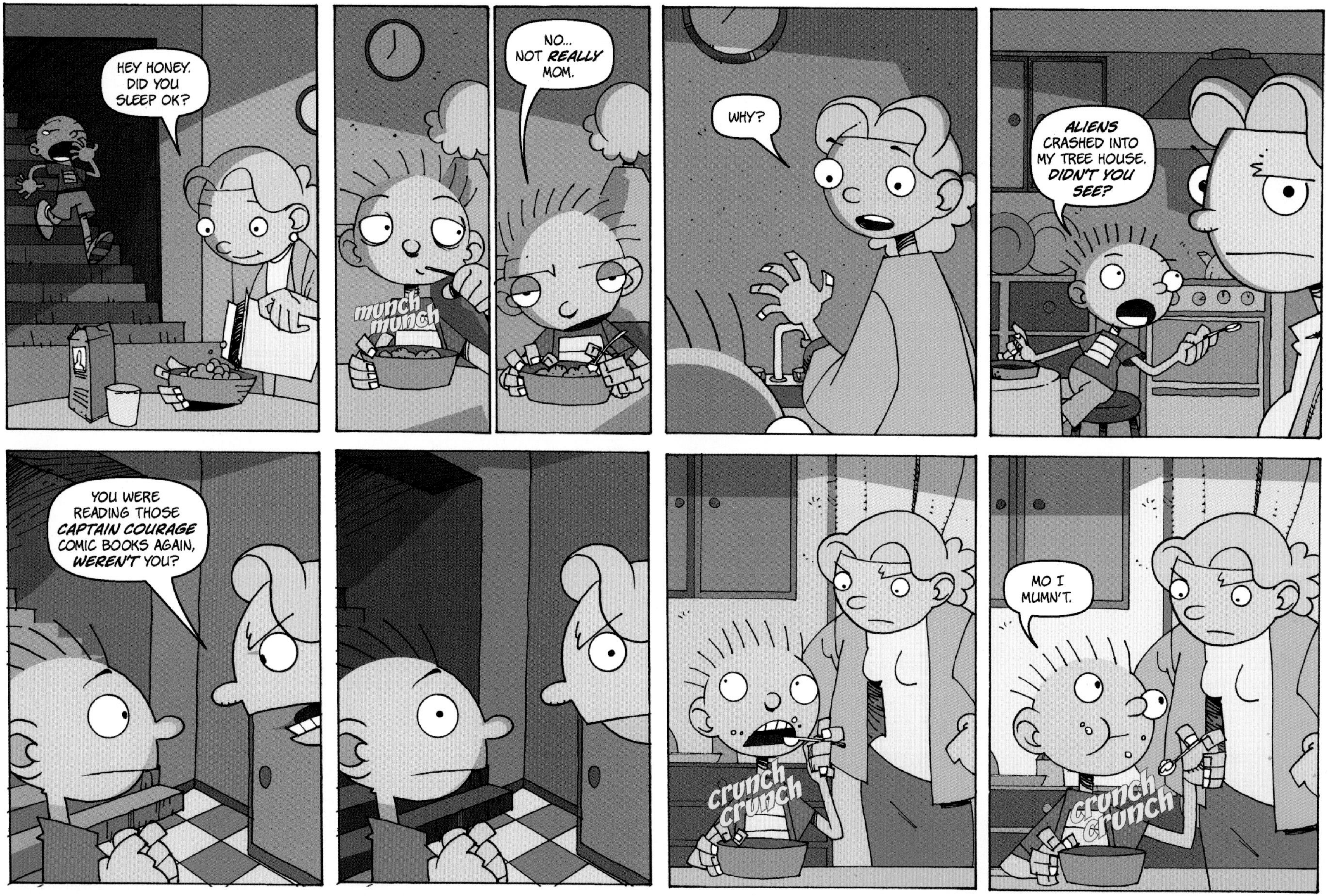
HEY HONEY. DID YOU SLEEP OK?
munch munch
NO... NOT REALLY MOM.
WHY?
ALIENS CRASHED INTO MY TREE HOUSE. DIDN'T YOU SEE?
YOU WERE READING THOSE CAPTAIN COURAGE COMIC BOOKS AGAIN, WEREN'T YOU?
crunch crunch
MO I MUMN'T.
crunch crunch

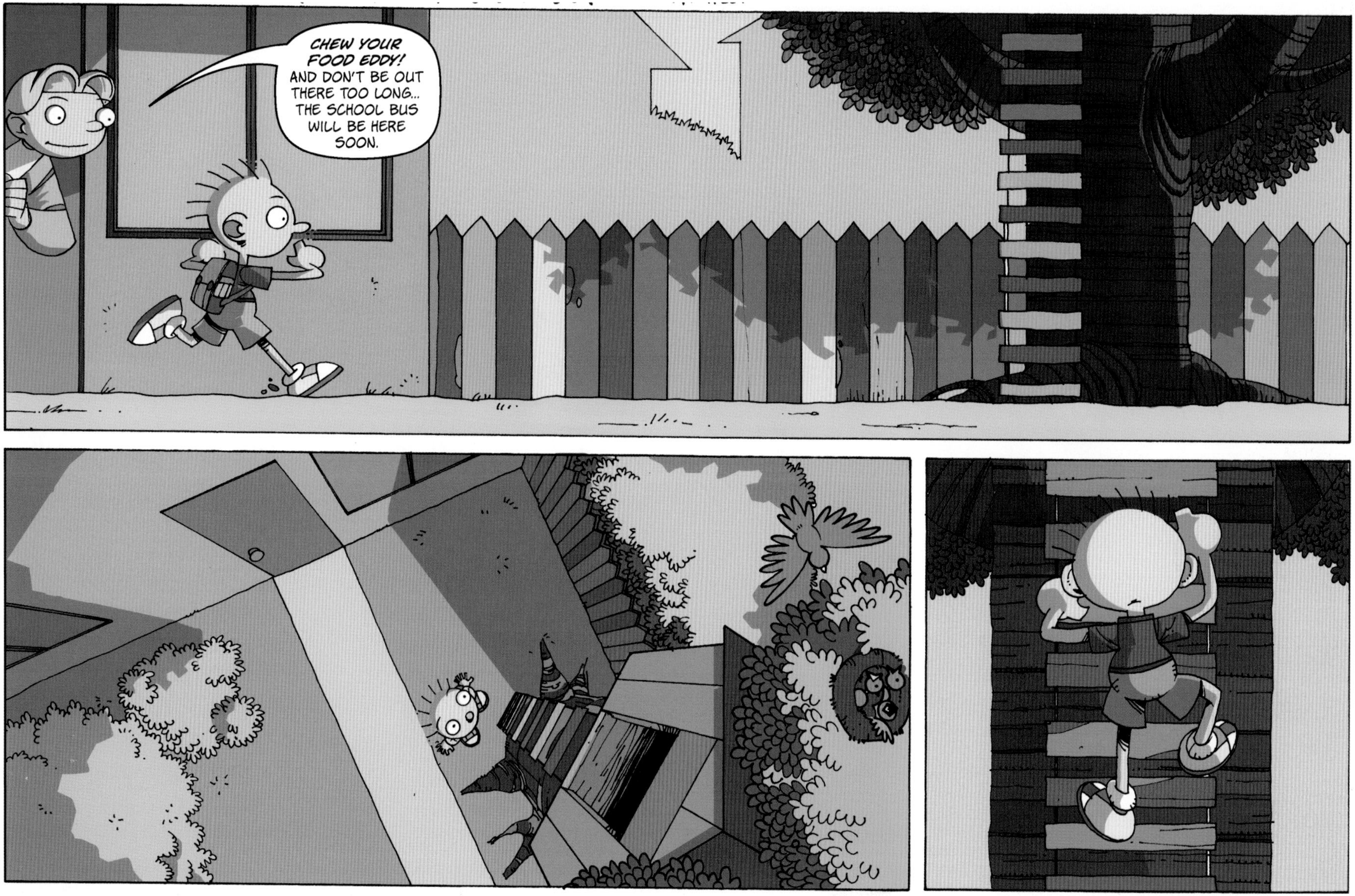
CHEW YOUR FOOD EDDY! AND DON'T BE OUT THERE TOO LONG... THE SCHOOL BUS WILL BE HERE SOON.

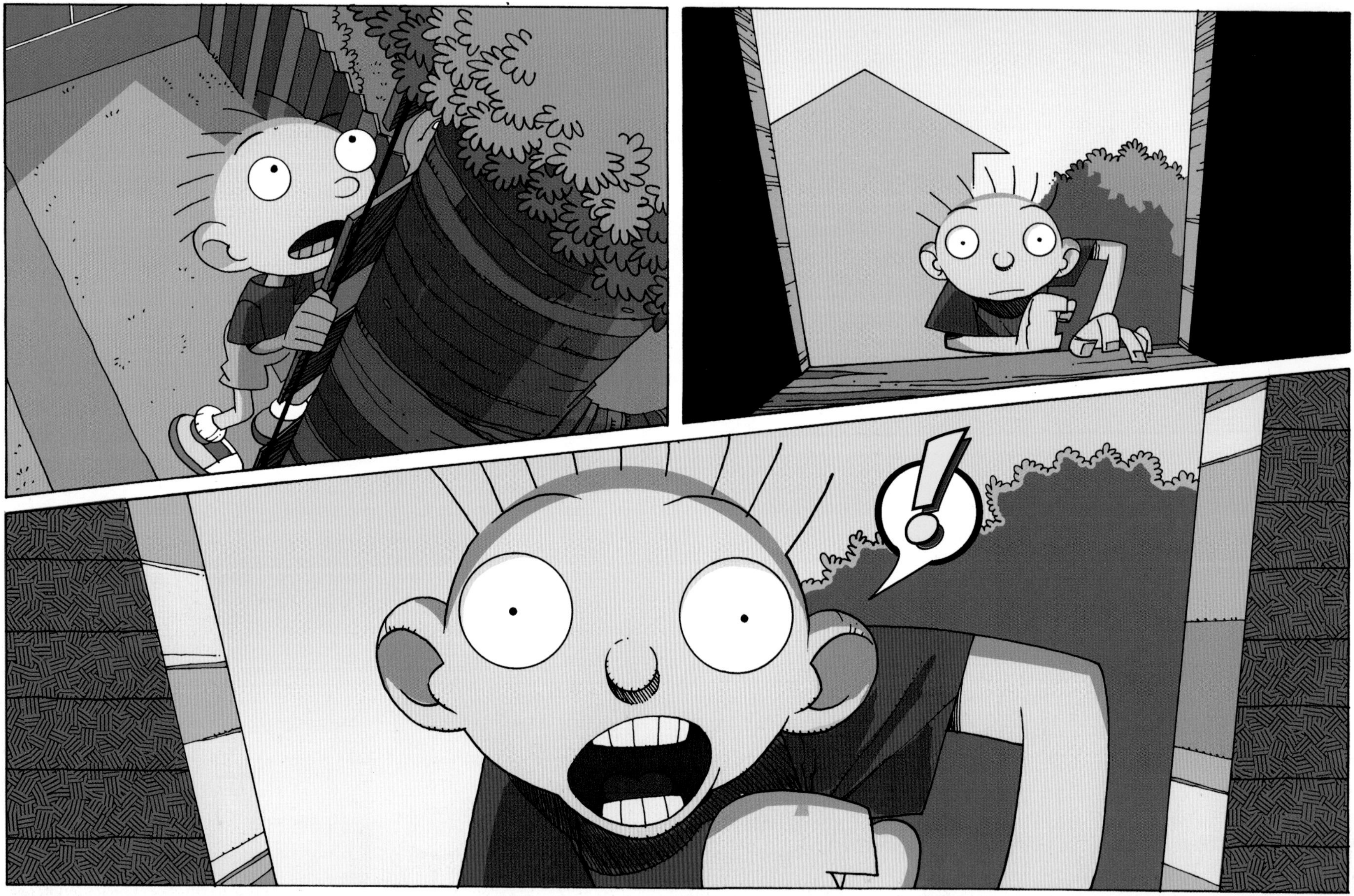
!

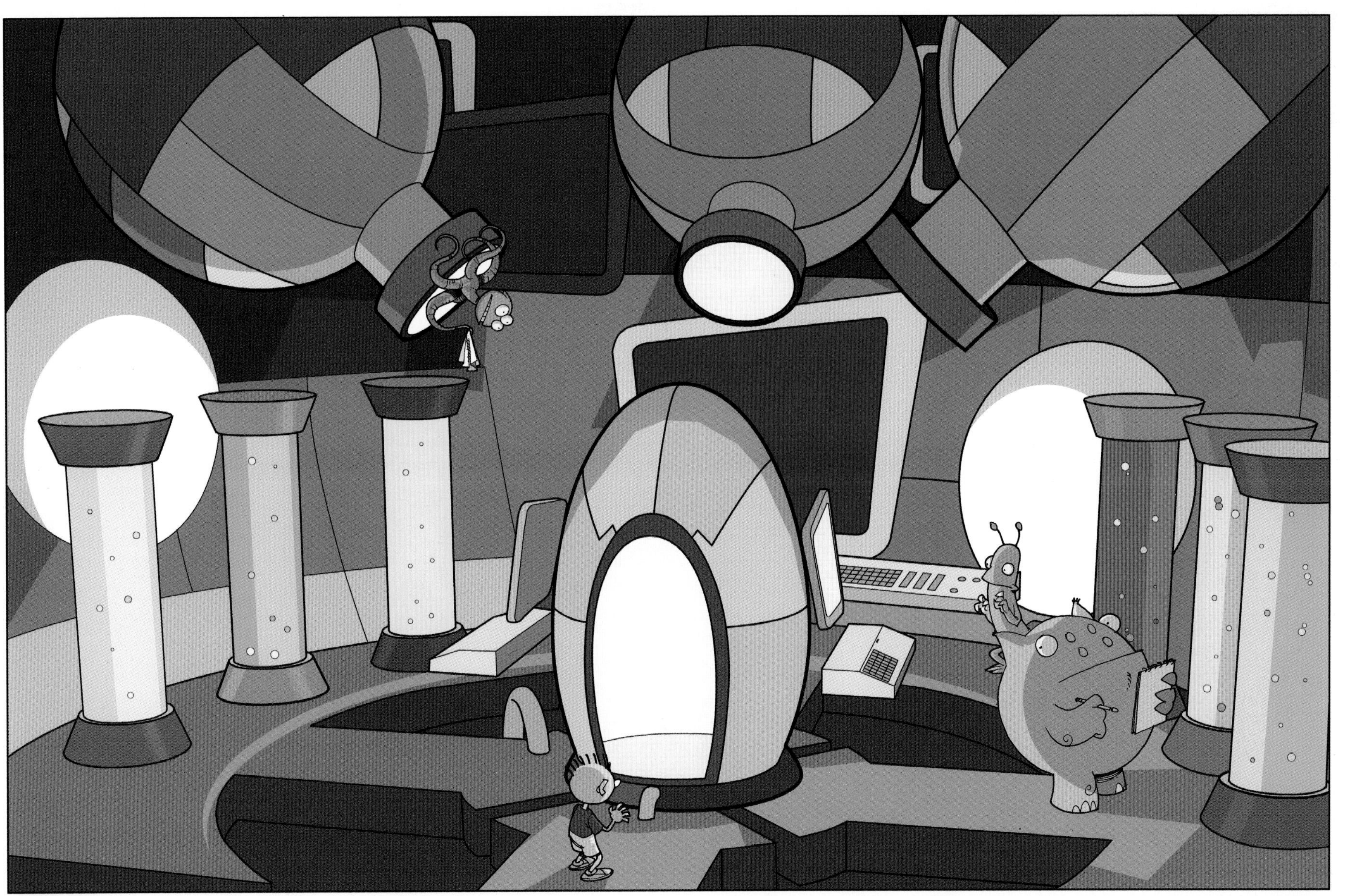

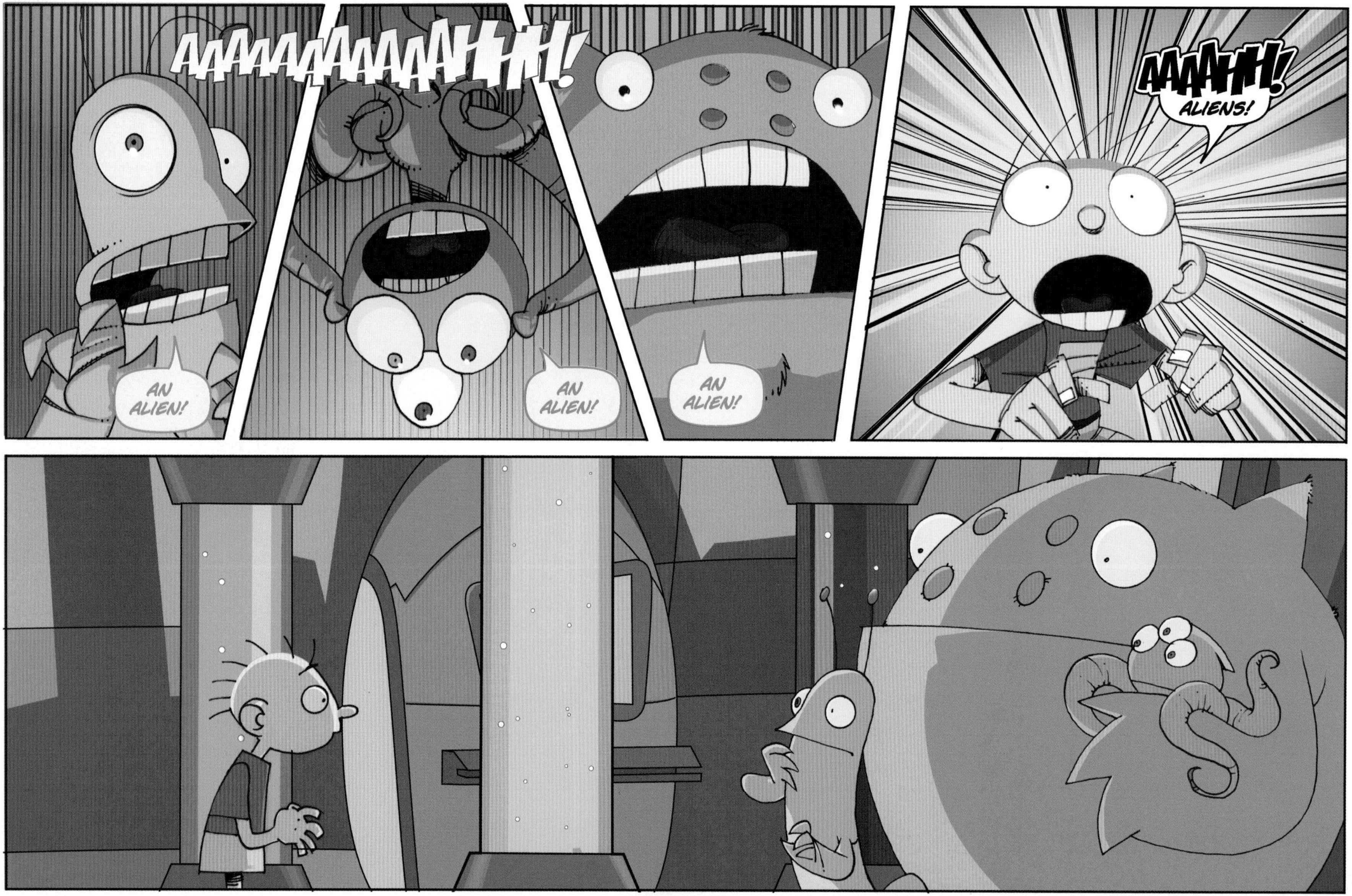
AAAAAAAAAAAAHHHH!
AN ALIEN!
AN ALIEN!
AN ALIEN!
AAAAHH!
ALIENS!

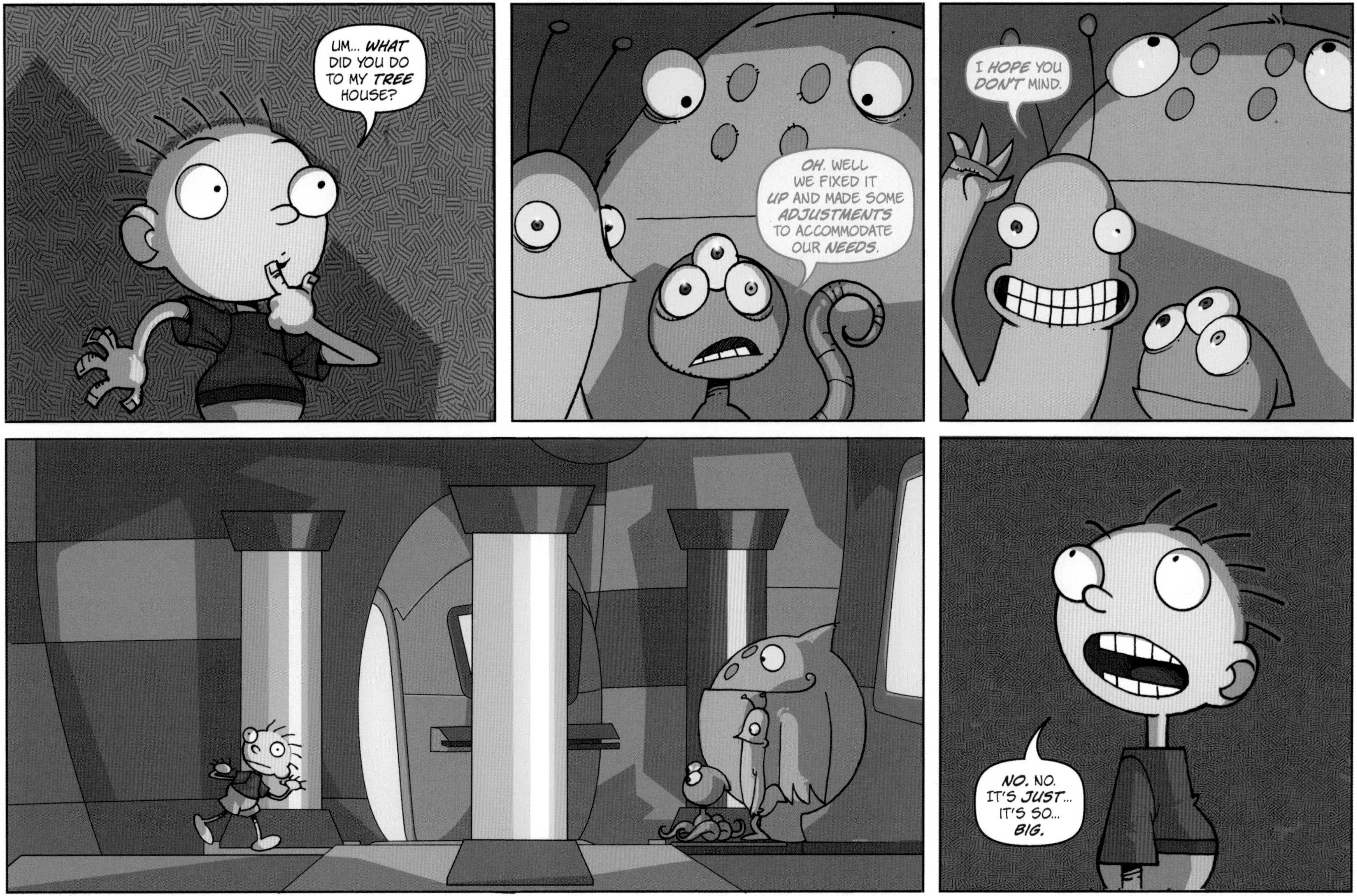
UM... WHAT DID YOU DO TO MY TREE HOUSE?
OH. WELL WE FIXED IT UP AND MADE SOME ADJUSTMENTS TO ACCOMMODATE OUR NEEDS.
I HOPE YOU DON'T MIND.
NO. NO. IT'S JUST... IT'S SO... BIG.

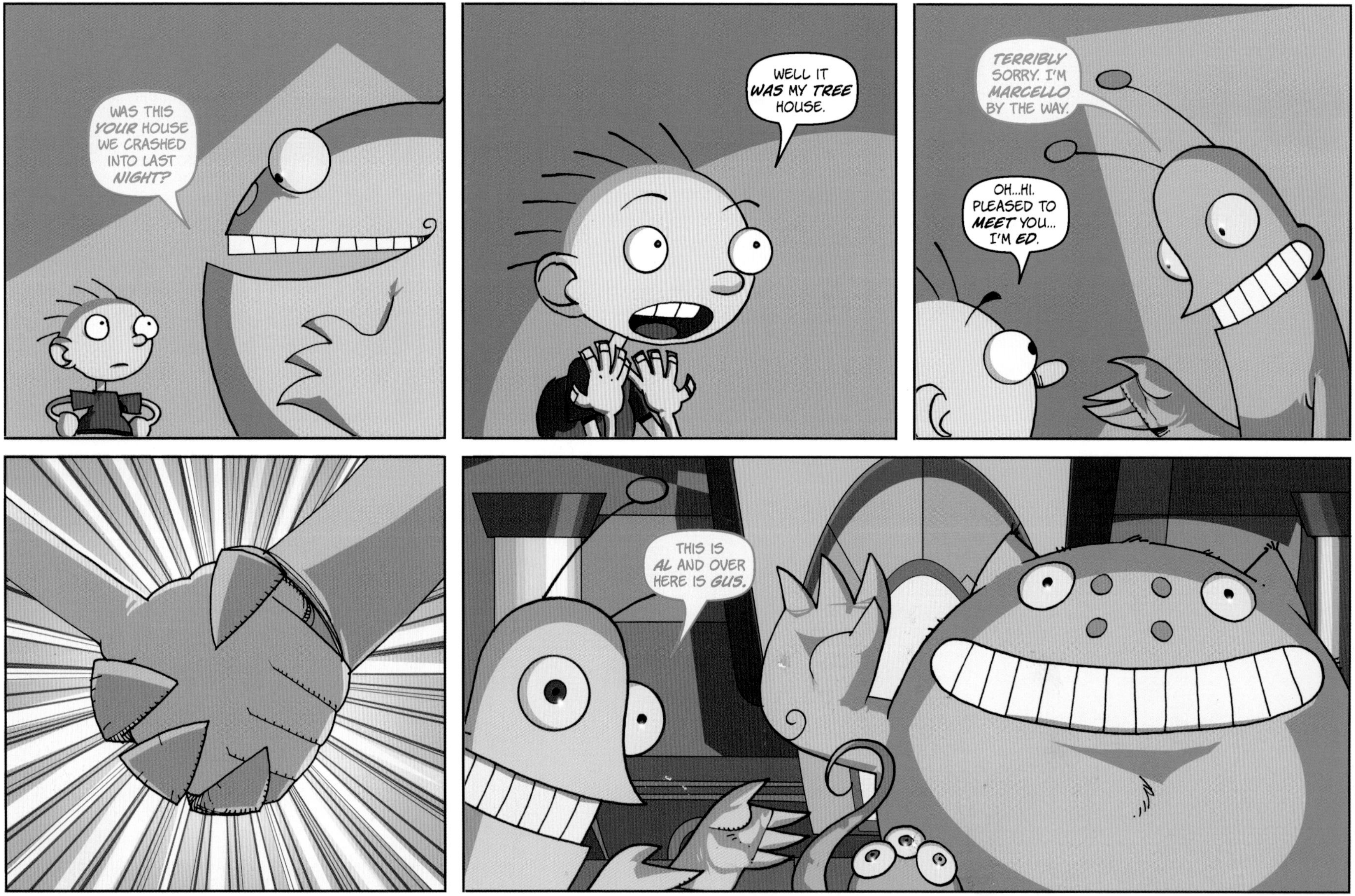
WAS THIS YOUR HOUSE WE CRASHED INTO LAST NIGHT?
WELL IT WAS MY TREE HOUSE.
TERRIBLY SORRY. I'M MARCELLO BY THE WAY.
OH...HI. PLEASED TO MEET YOU... I'M ED.
THIS IS AL AND OVER HERE IS GUS.

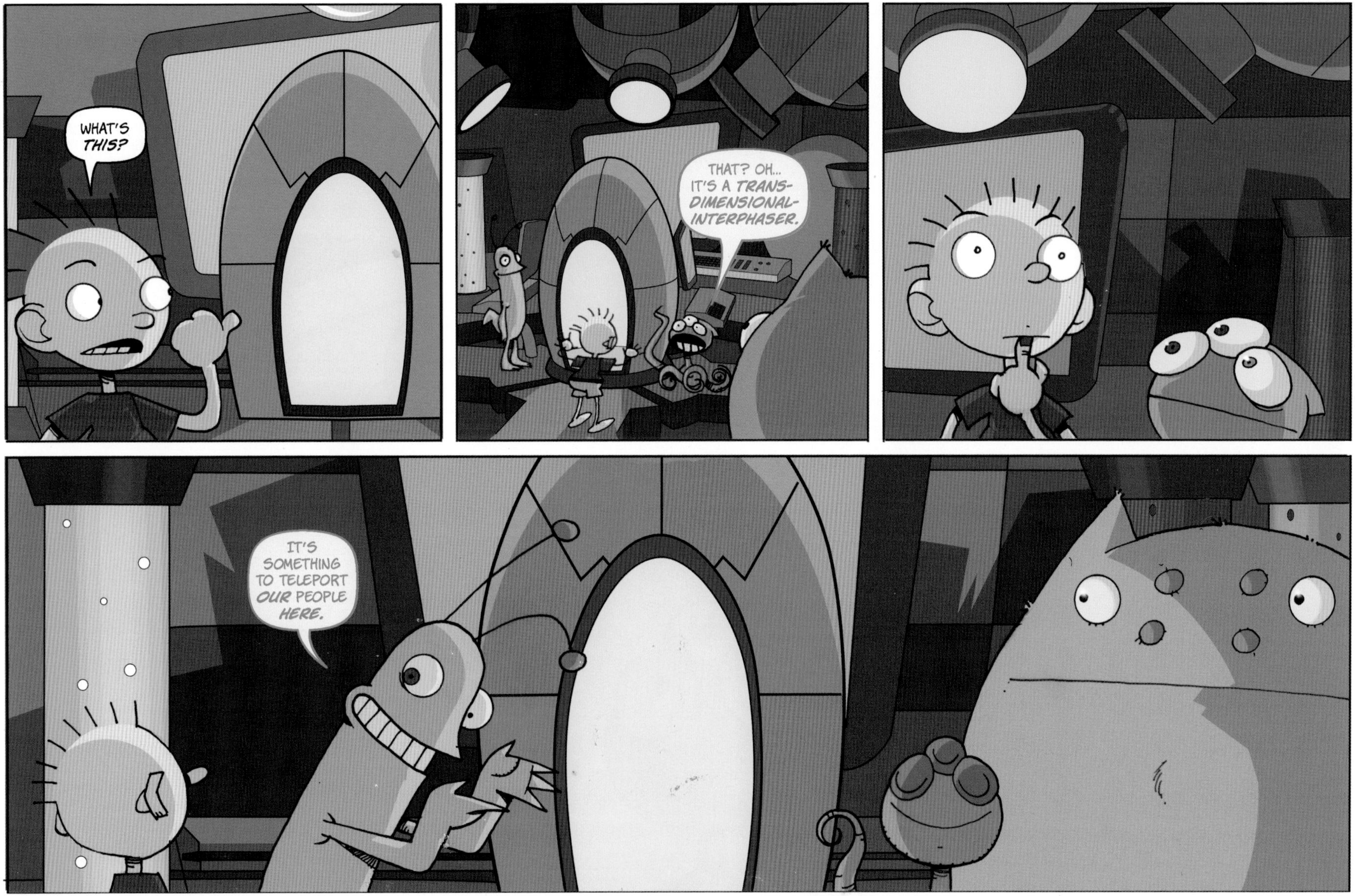
WHAT'S *THIS?*
THAT? OH... IT'S A *TRANS-DIMENSIONAL-INTERPHASER.*
IT'S SOMETHING TO TELEPORT *OUR* PEOPLE *HERE.*

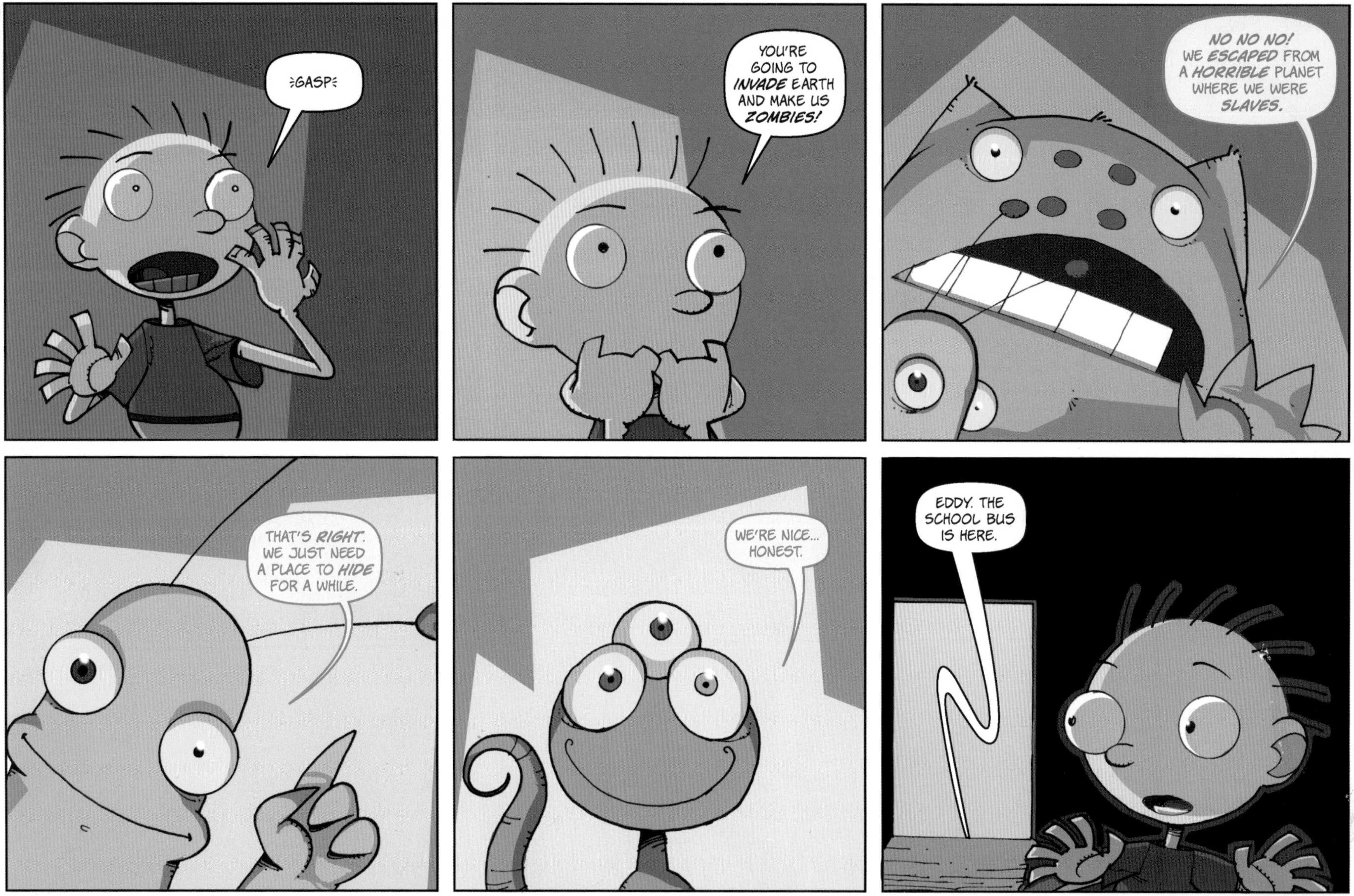

≷GASP≶
YOU'RE GOING TO *INVADE* EARTH AND MAKE US *ZOMBIES!*
NO NO NO! WE *ESCAPED* FROM A *HORRIBLE* PLANET WHERE WE WERE *SLAVES.*
THAT'S *RIGHT.* WE JUST NEED A PLACE TO *HIDE* FOR A WHILE.
WE'RE NICE... HONEST.
EDDY. THE SCHOOL BUS IS HERE.

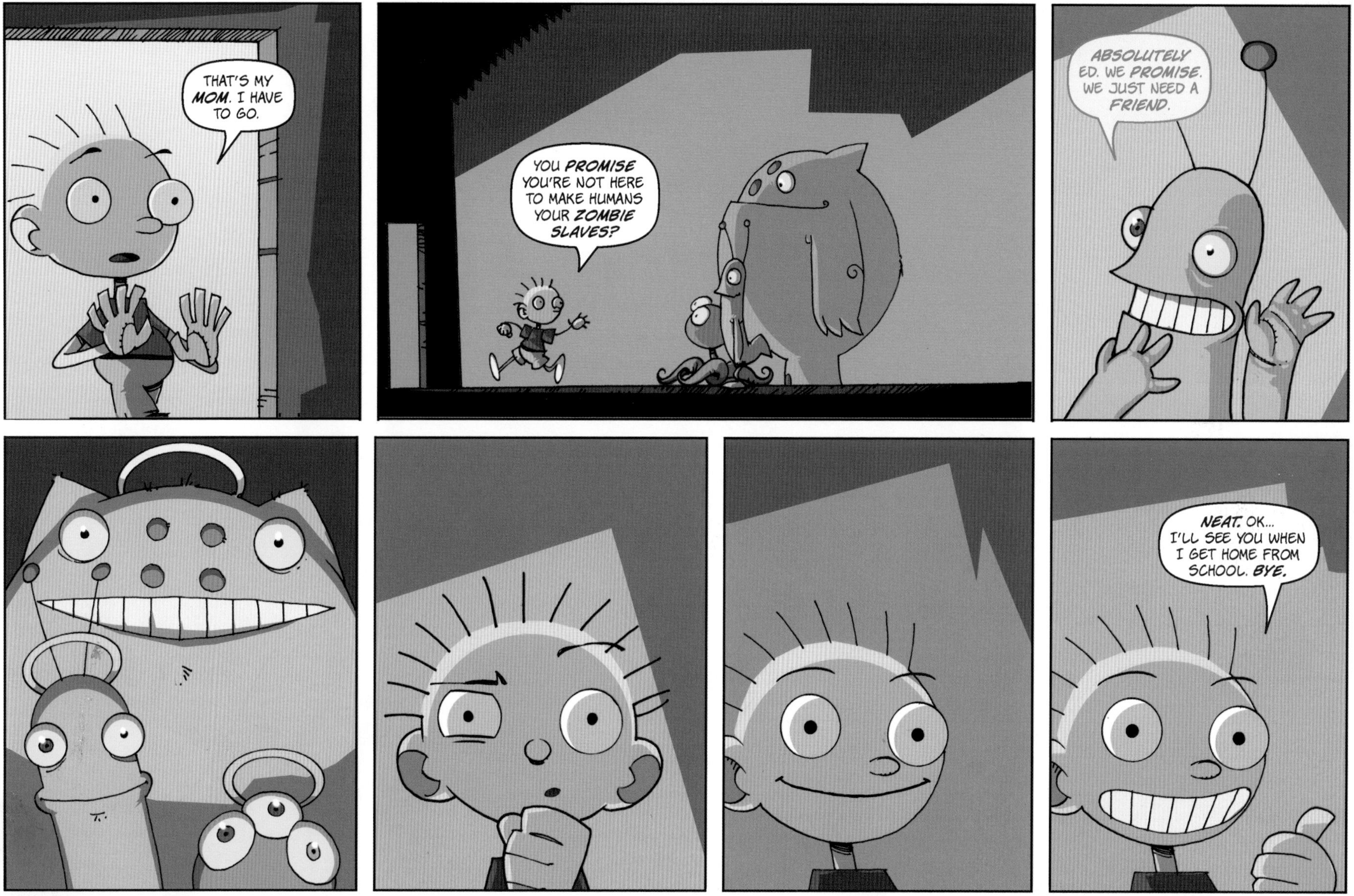
THAT'S MY MOM. I HAVE TO GO.
YOU PROMISE YOU'RE NOT HERE TO MAKE HUMANS YOUR ZOMBIE SLAVES?
ABSOLUTELY ED. WE PROMISE. WE JUST NEED A FRIEND.
NEAT. OK... I'LL SEE YOU WHEN I GET HOME FROM SCHOOL. BYE.

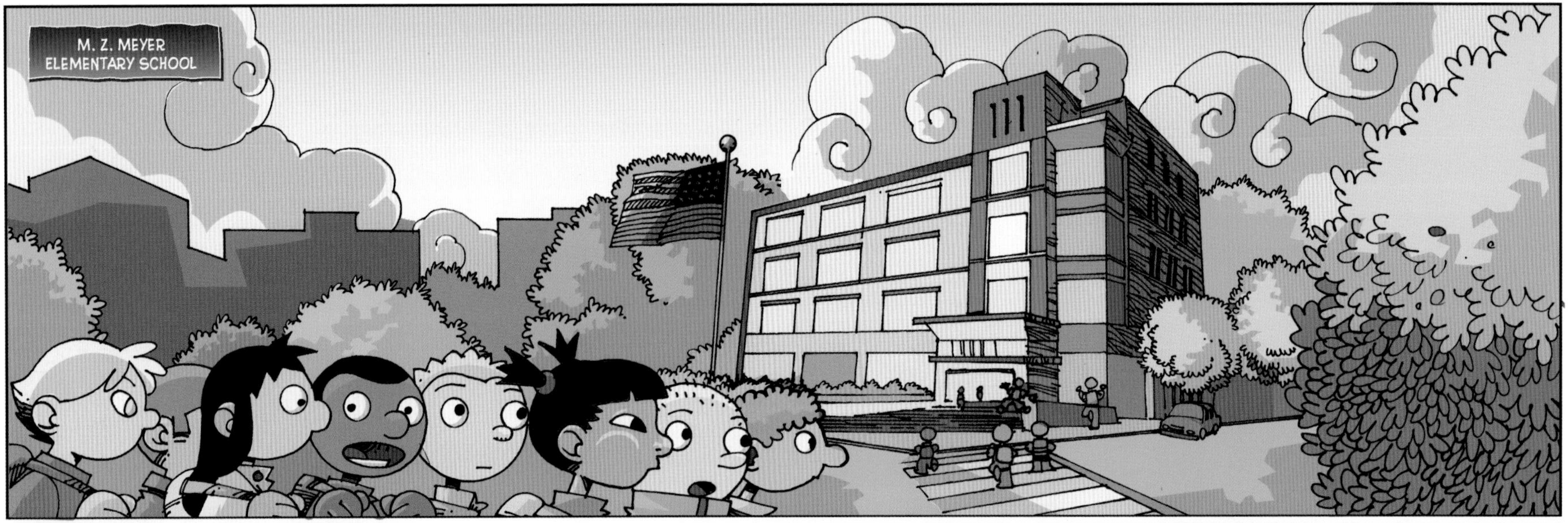
M. Z. MEYER ELEMENTARY SCHOOL

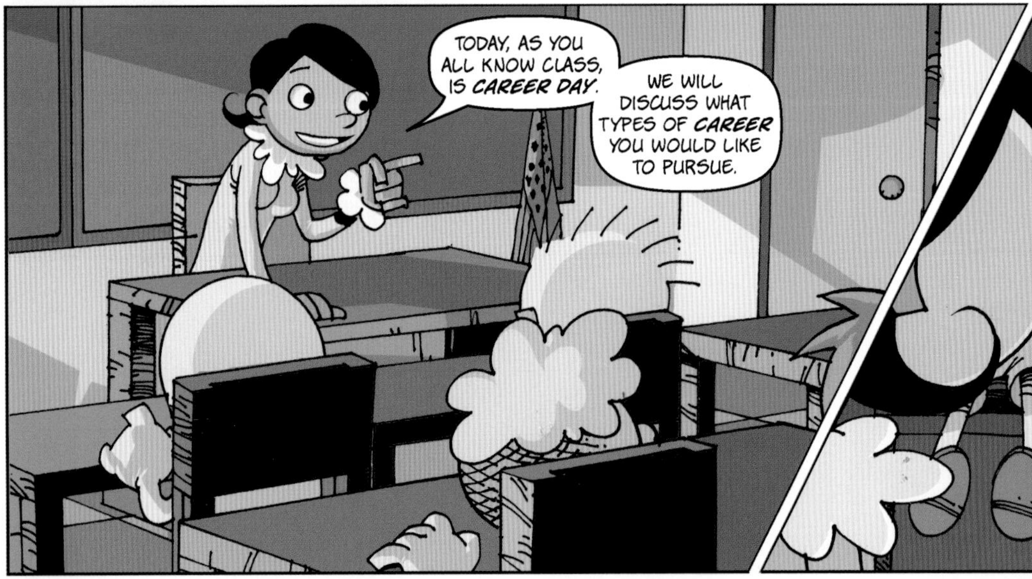
TODAY, AS YOU ALL KNOW CLASS, IS CAREER DAY.
WE WILL DISCUSS WHAT TYPES OF CAREER YOU WOULD LIKE TO PURSUE.

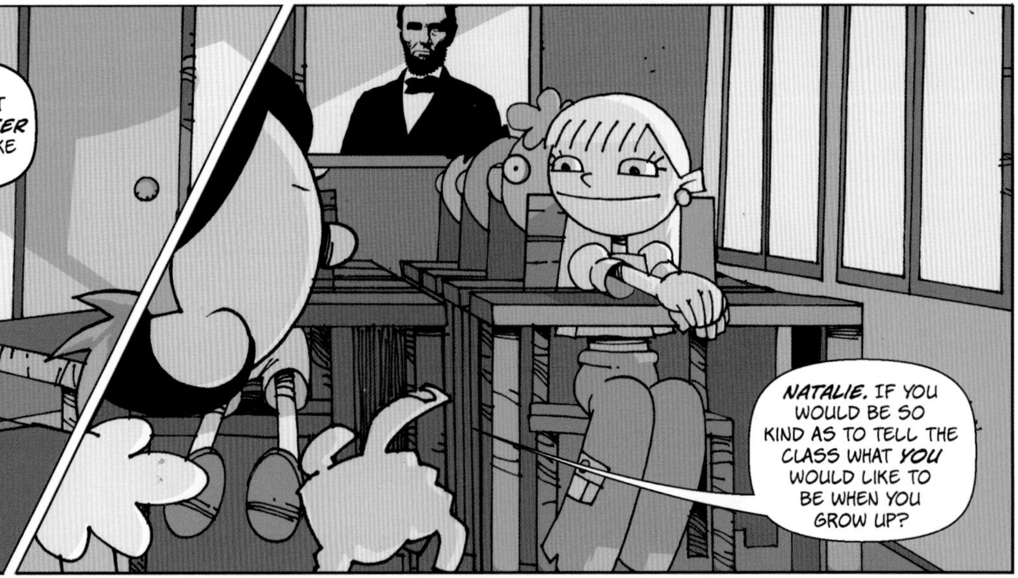
NATALIE. IF YOU WOULD BE SO KIND AS TO TELL THE CLASS WHAT YOU WOULD LIKE TO BE WHEN YOU GROW UP?

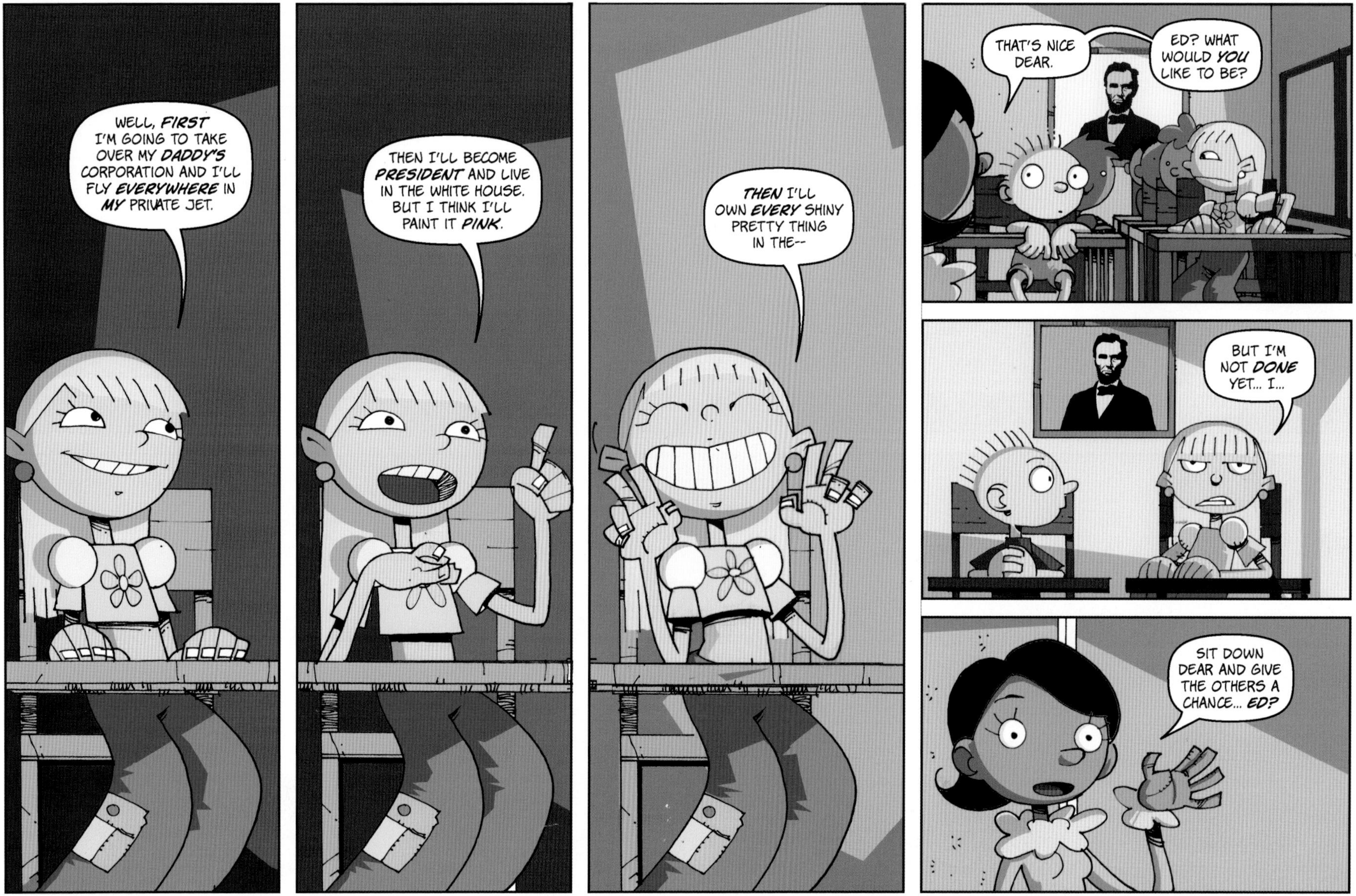
WELL, FIRST I'M GOING TO TAKE OVER MY DADDY'S CORPORATION AND I'LL FLY EVERYWHERE IN MY PRIVATE JET.
THEN I'LL BECOME PRESIDENT AND LIVE IN THE WHITE HOUSE. BUT I THINK I'LL PAINT IT PINK.
THEN I'LL OWN EVERY SHINY PRETTY THING IN THE--
THAT'S NICE DEAR.
ED? WHAT WOULD YOU LIKE TO BE?
BUT I'M NOT DONE YET... I...
SIT DOWN DEAR AND GIVE THE OTHERS A CHANCE... ED?

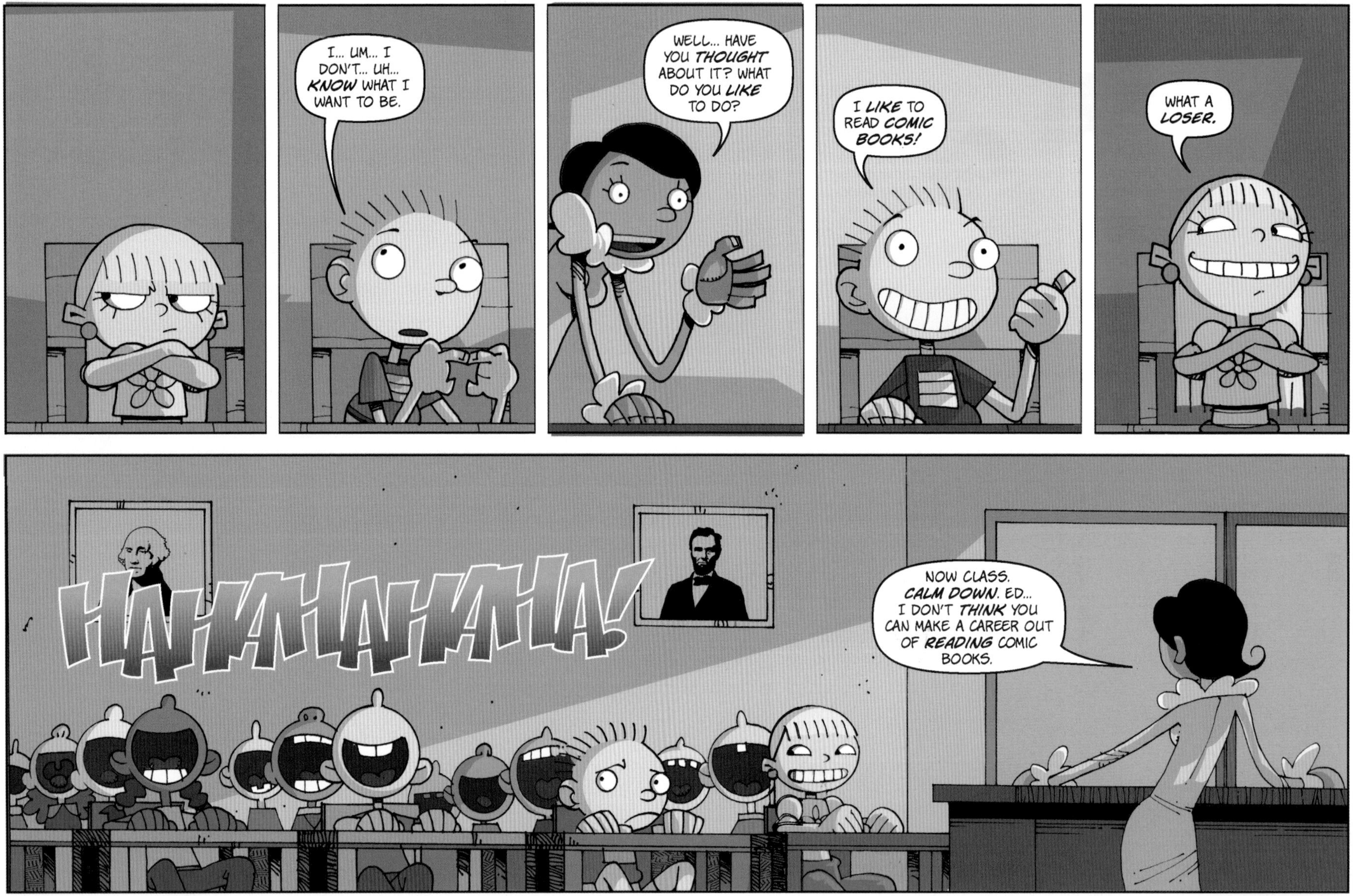

I... UM... I DON'T... UH... KNOW WHAT I WANT TO BE.
WELL... HAVE YOU THOUGHT ABOUT IT? WHAT DO YOU LIKE TO DO?
I LIKE TO READ COMIC BOOKS!
WHAT A LOSER.
HAHAHAHAHAHA!
NOW CLASS. CALM DOWN. ED... I DON'T THINK YOU CAN MAKE A CAREER OUT OF READING COMIC BOOKS.

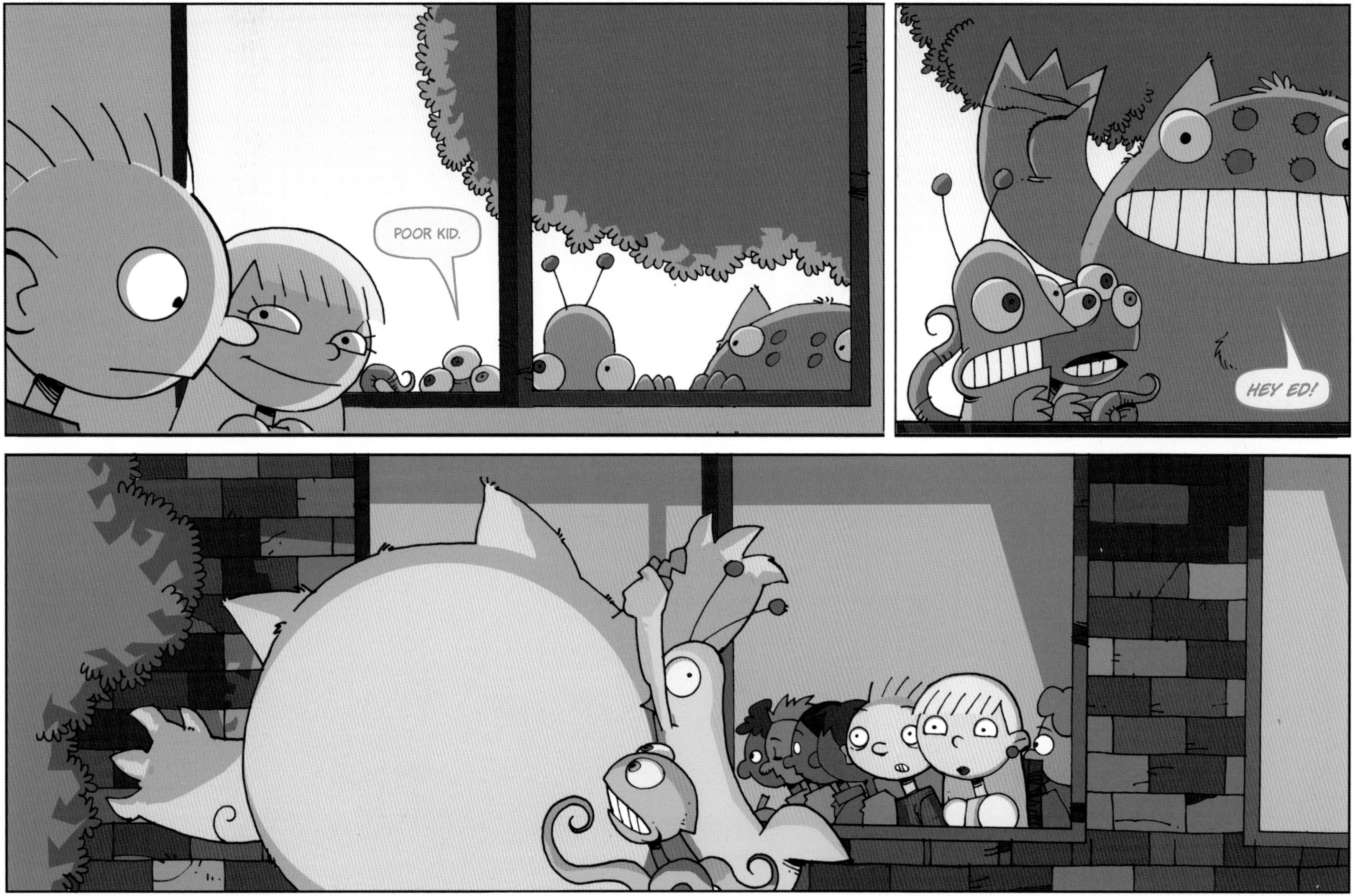
POOR KID.
HEY ED!

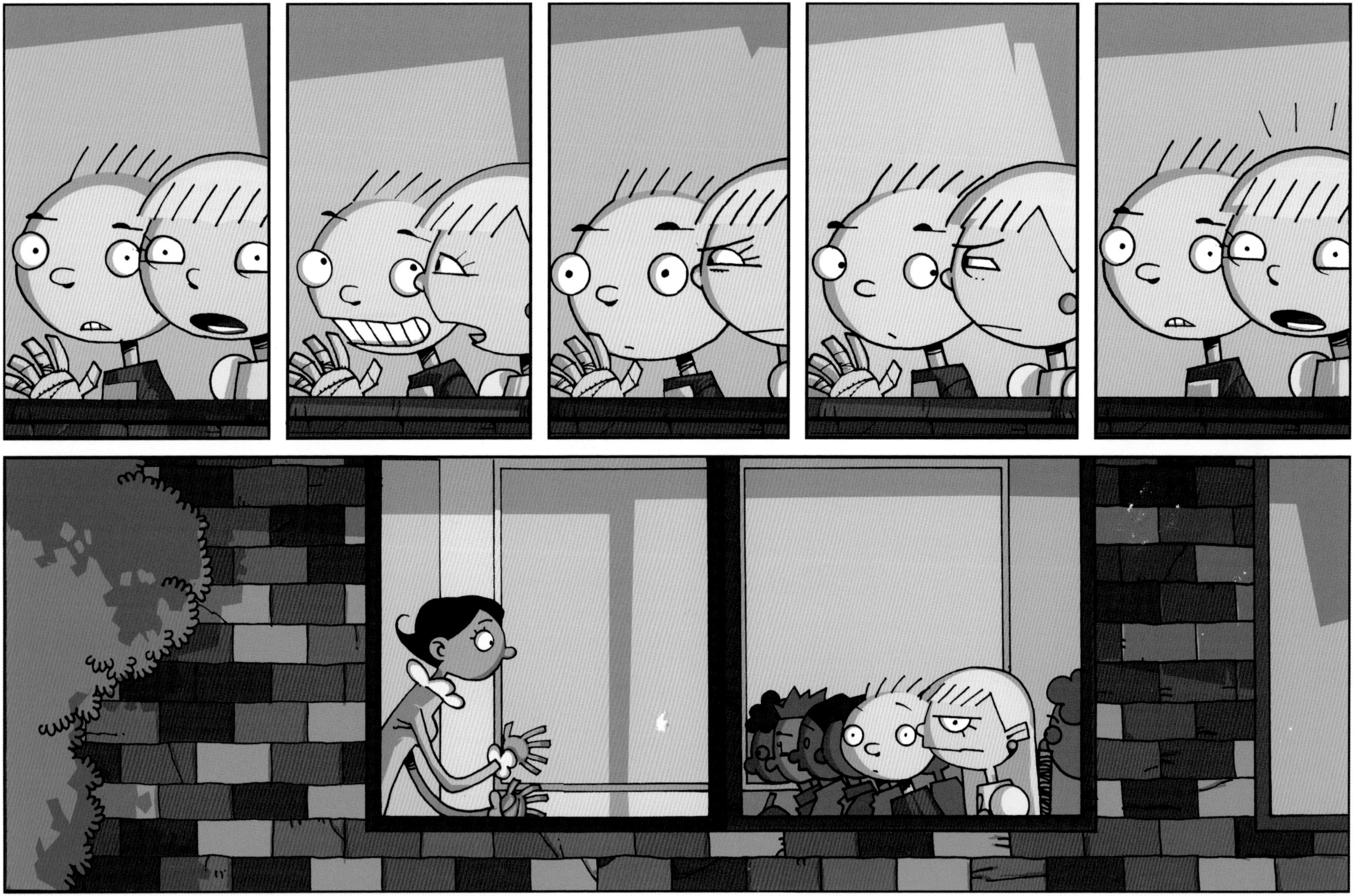

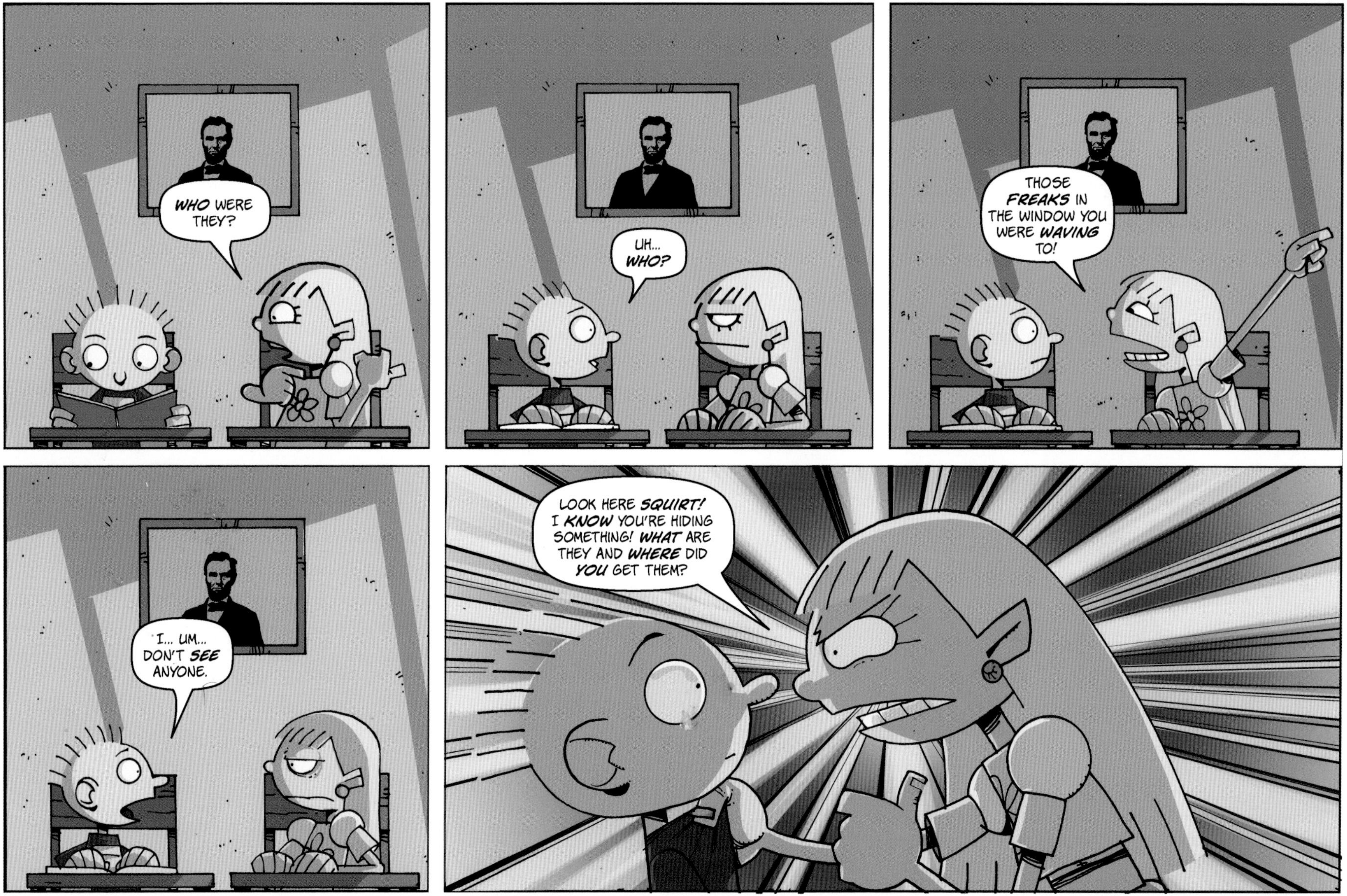
WHO WERE THEY?
UH... WHO?
THOSE FREAKS IN THE WINDOW YOU WERE WAVING TO!
I... UM... DON'T SEE ANYONE.
LOOK HERE SQUIRT! I KNOW YOU'RE HIDING SOMETHING! WHAT ARE THEY AND WHERE DID YOU GET THEM?

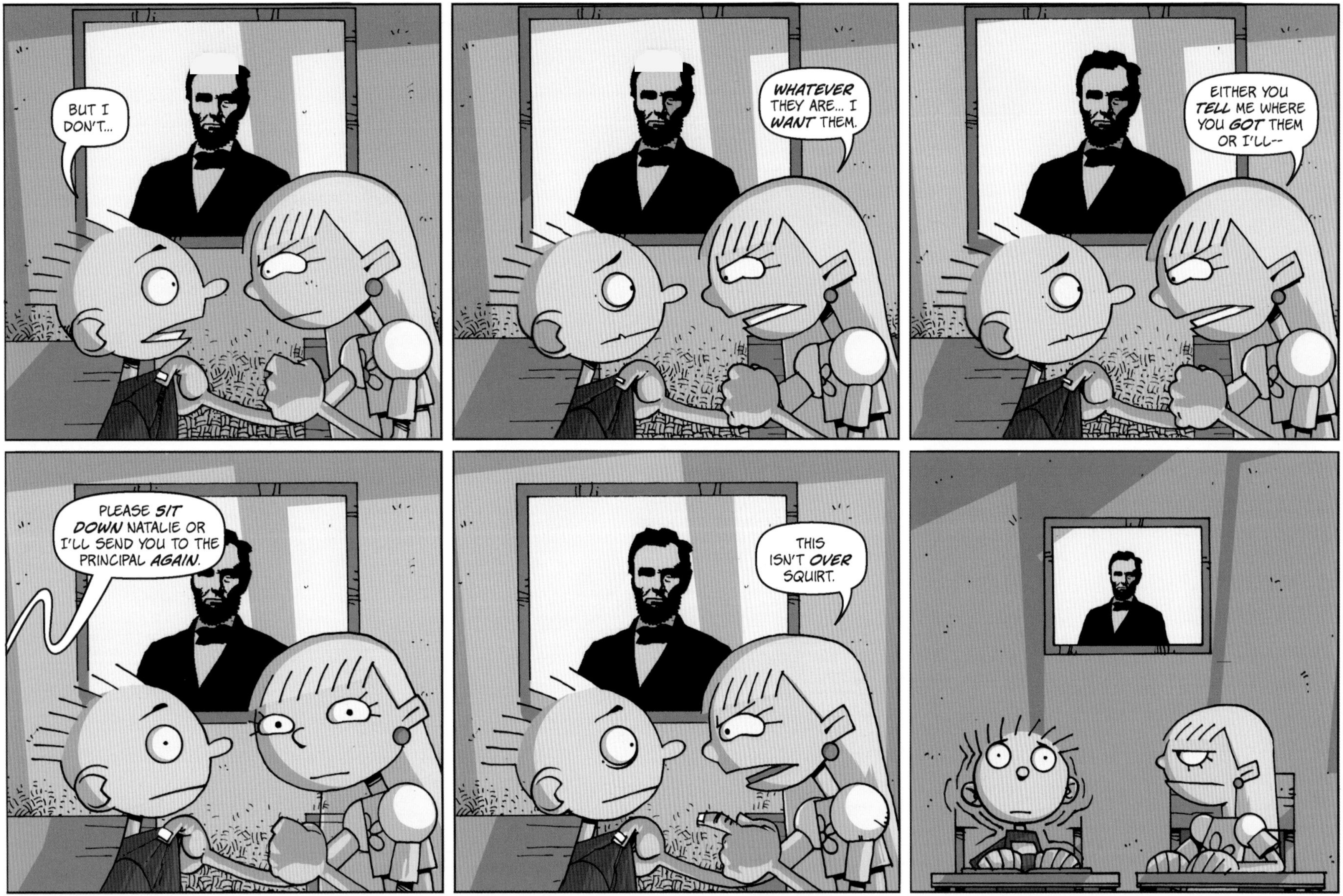
BUT I DON'T...
WHATEVER THEY ARE... I WANT THEM.
EITHER YOU TELL ME WHERE YOU GOT THEM OR I'LL--
PLEASE SIT DOWN NATALIE OR I'LL SEND YOU TO THE PRINCIPAL AGAIN.
THIS ISN'T OVER SQUIRT.

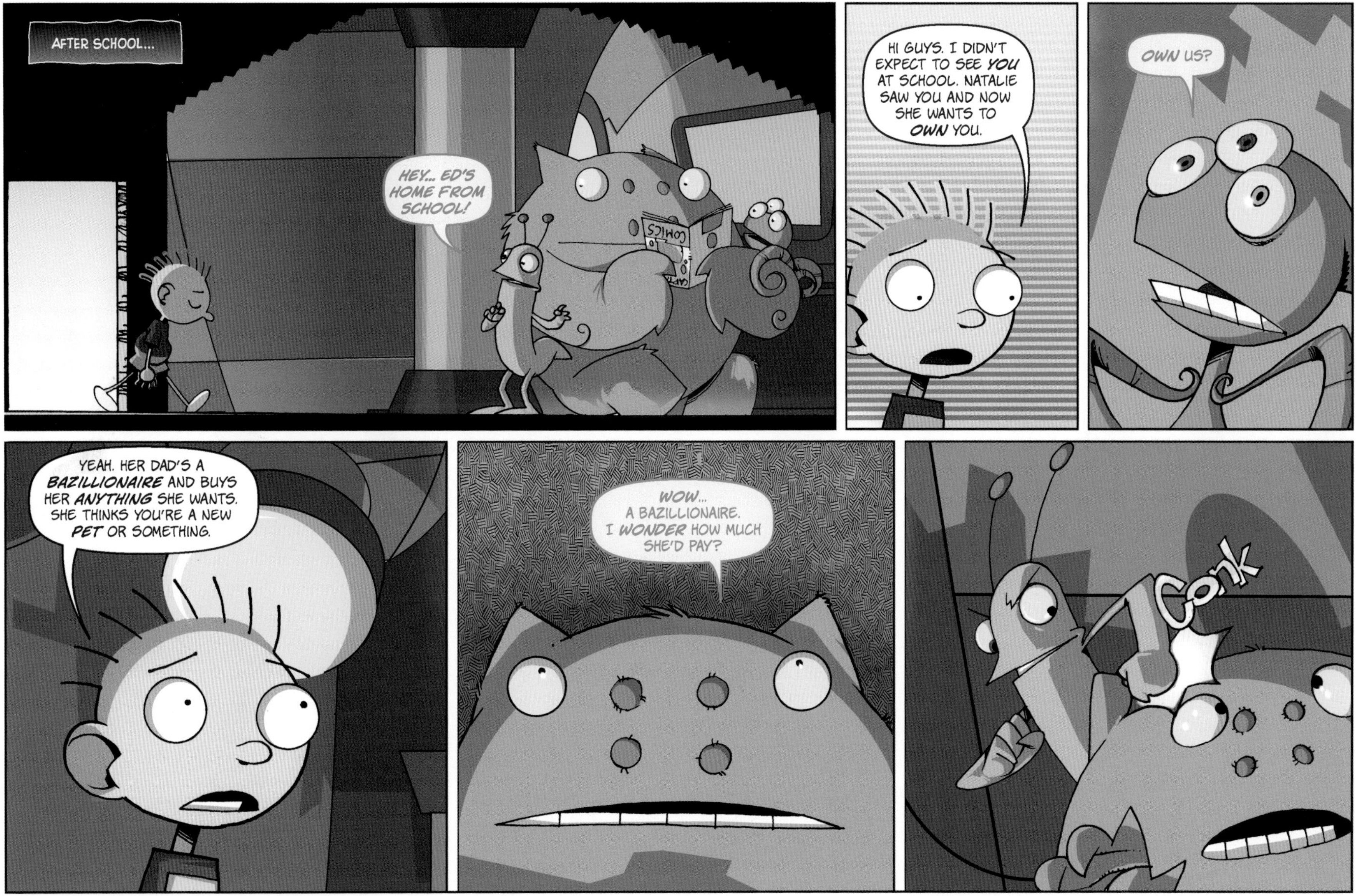

AFTER SCHOOL...
HEY... ED'S HOME FROM SCHOOL!
COMICS
HI GUYS. I DIDN'T EXPECT TO SEE YOU AT SCHOOL. NATALIE SAW YOU AND NOW SHE WANTS TO OWN YOU.
OWN US?
YEAH. HER DAD'S A BAZILLIONAIRE AND BUYS HER ANYTHING SHE WANTS. SHE THINKS YOU'RE A NEW PET OR SOMETHING.
WOW... A BAZILLIONAIRE. I WONDER HOW MUCH SHE'D PAY?
CONK

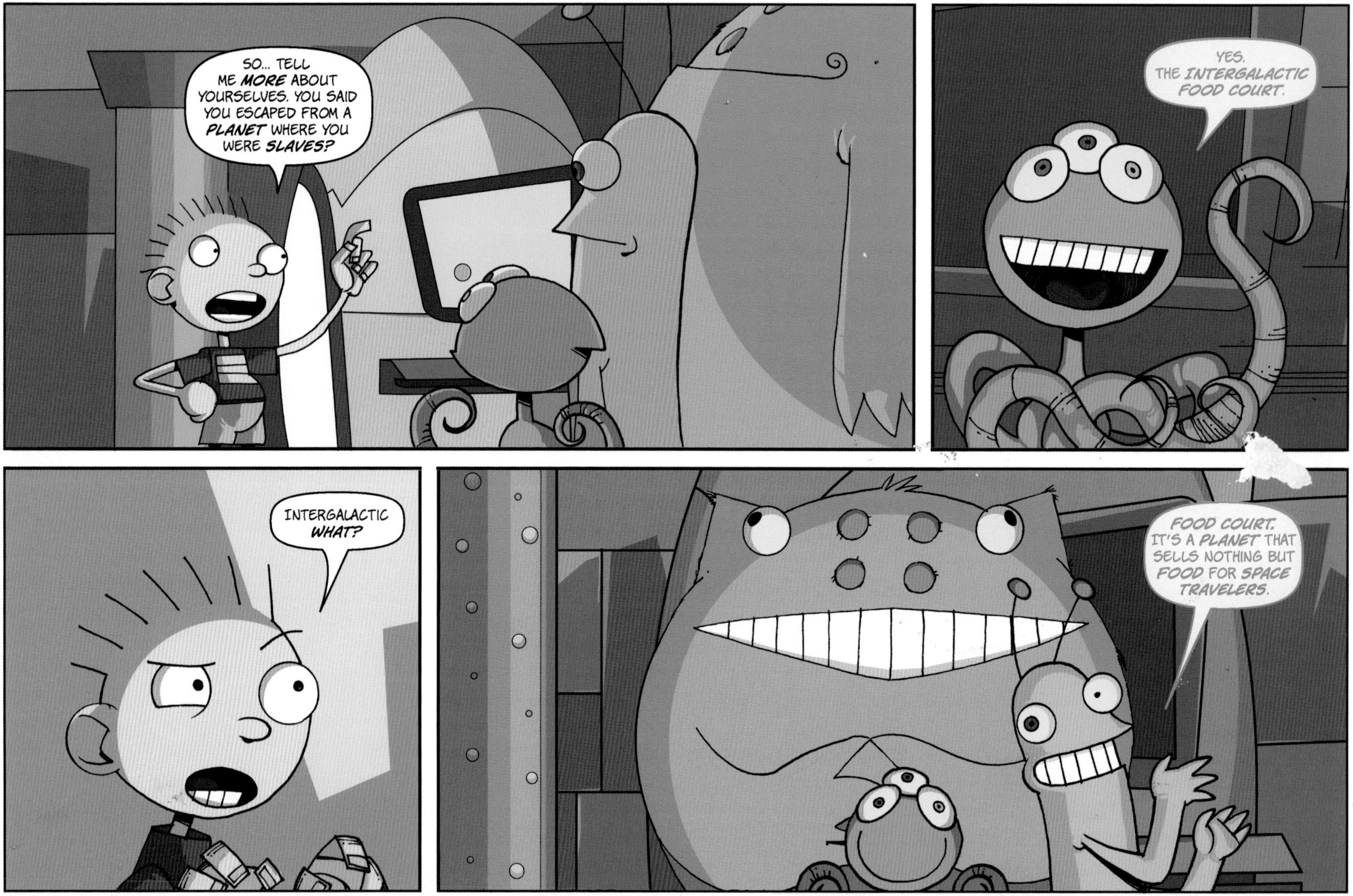
SO... TELL ME MORE ABOUT YOURSELVES. YOU SAID YOU ESCAPED FROM A PLANET WHERE YOU WERE SLAVES?
YES. THE INTERGALACTIC FOOD COURT.
INTERGALACTIC WHAT?
FOOD COURT. IT'S A PLANET THAT SELLS NOTHING BUT FOOD FOR SPACE TRAVELERS.

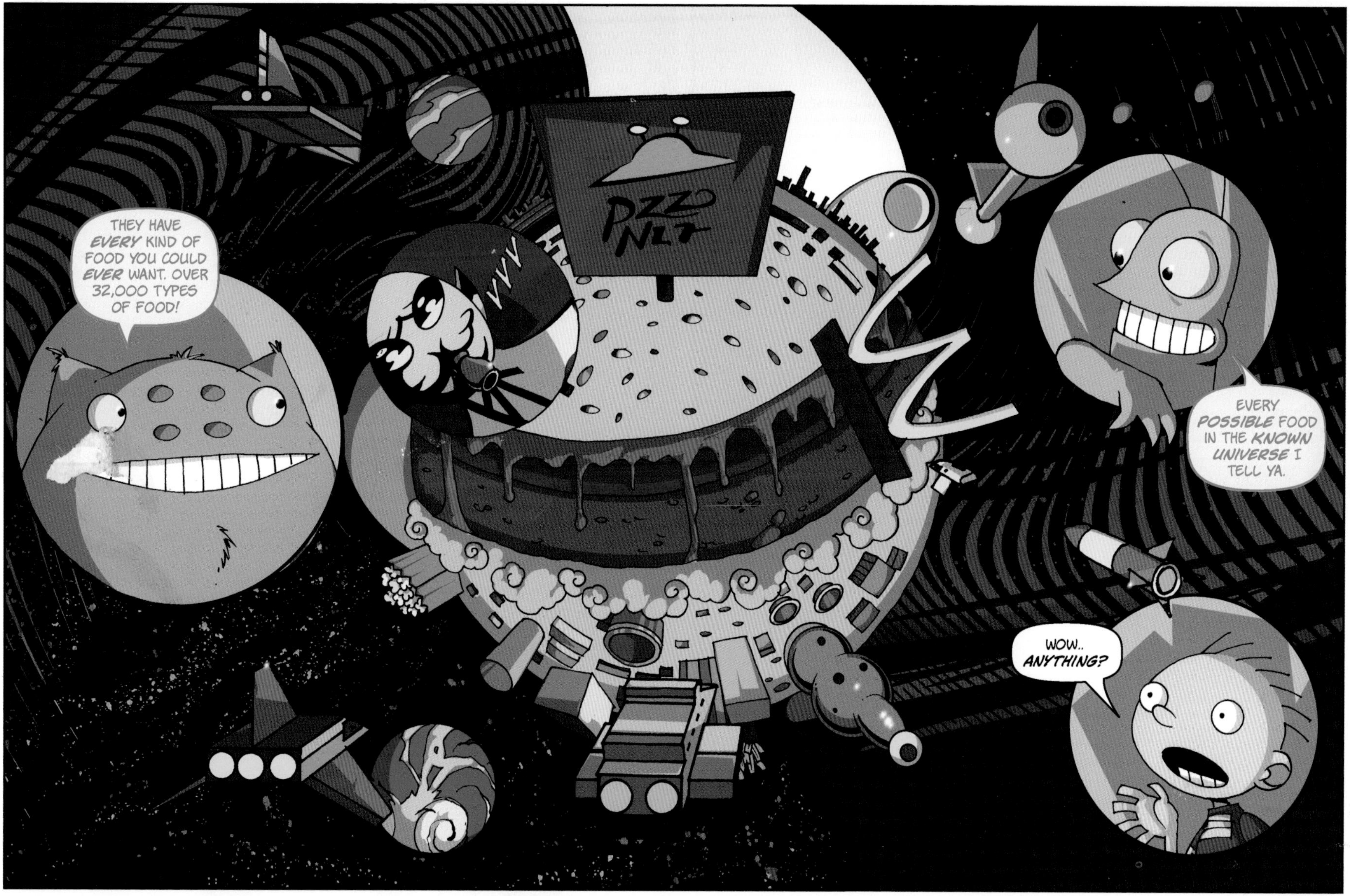
THEY HAVE EVERY KIND OF FOOD YOU COULD EVER WANT. OVER 32,000 TYPES OF FOOD!
EVERY POSSIBLE FOOD IN THE KNOWN UNIVERSE I TELL YA.
WOW.. ANYTHING?

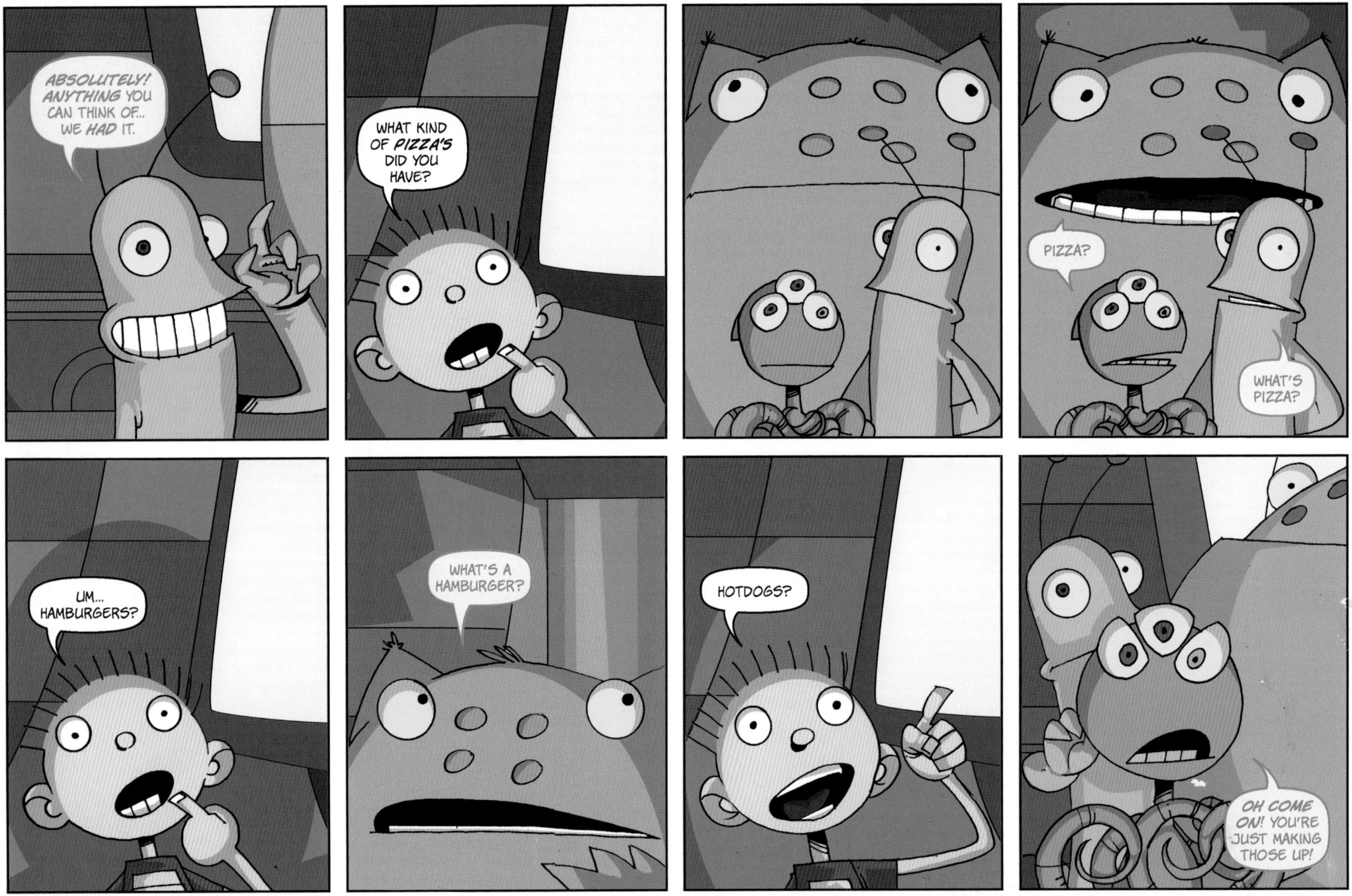
ABSOLUTELY! ANYTHING YOU CAN THINK OF... WE HAD IT.
WHAT KIND OF PIZZA'S DID YOU HAVE?
PIZZA?
WHAT'S PIZZA?
UM... HAMBURGERS?
WHAT'S A HAMBURGER?
HOTDOGS?
OH COME ON! YOU'RE JUST MAKING THOSE UP!

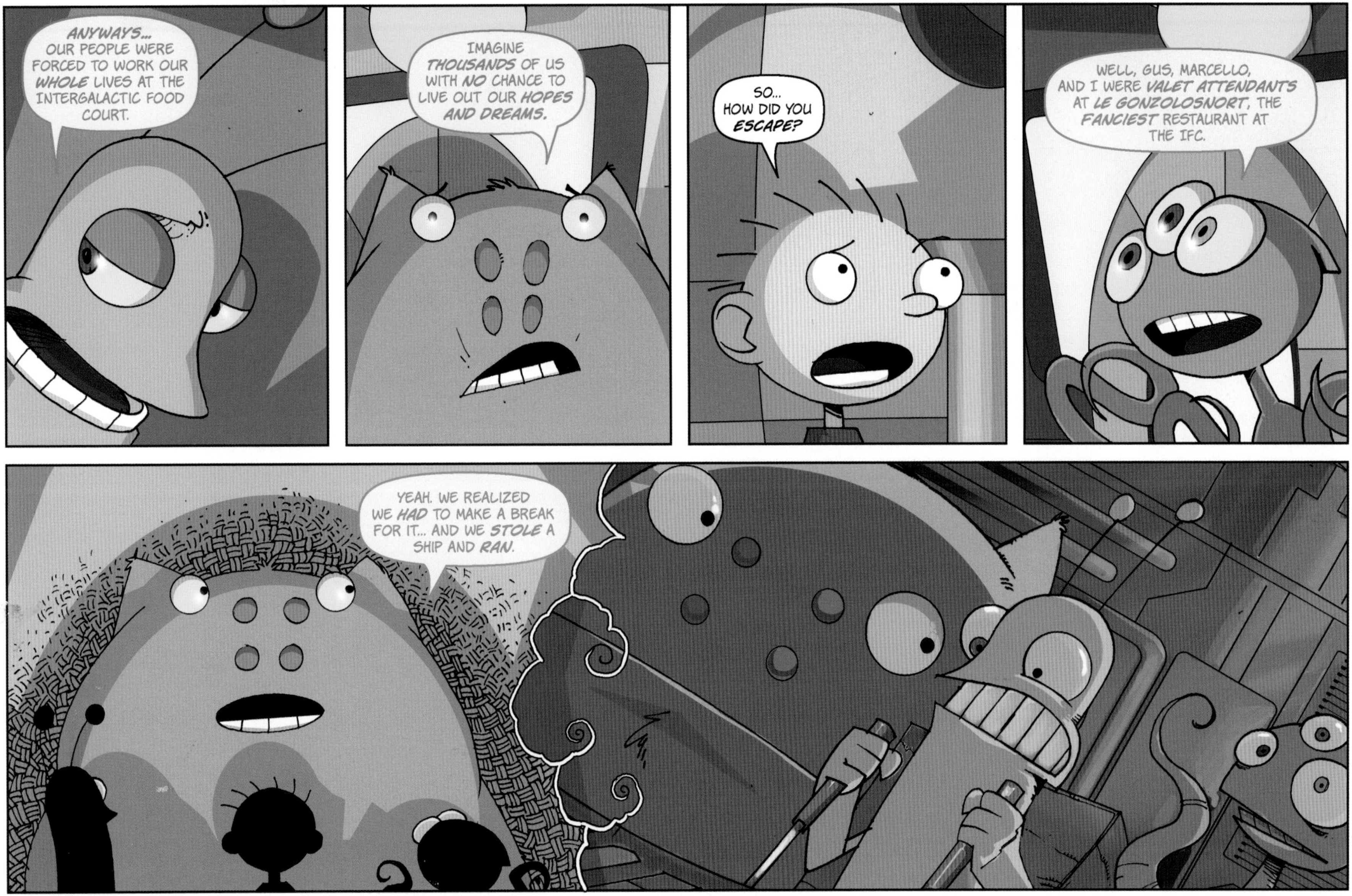
ANYWAYS... OUR PEOPLE WERE FORCED TO WORK OUR WHOLE LIVES AT THE INTERGALACTIC FOOD COURT.
IMAGINE THOUSANDS OF US WITH NO CHANCE TO LIVE OUT OUR HOPES AND DREAMS.
SO... HOW DID YOU ESCAPE?
WELL, GUS, MARCELLO, AND I WERE VALET ATTENDANTS AT LE GONZOLOSNORT, THE FANCIEST RESTAURANT AT THE IFC.
YEAH. WE REALIZED WE HAD TO MAKE A BREAK FOR IT... AND WE STOLE A SHIP AND RAN.

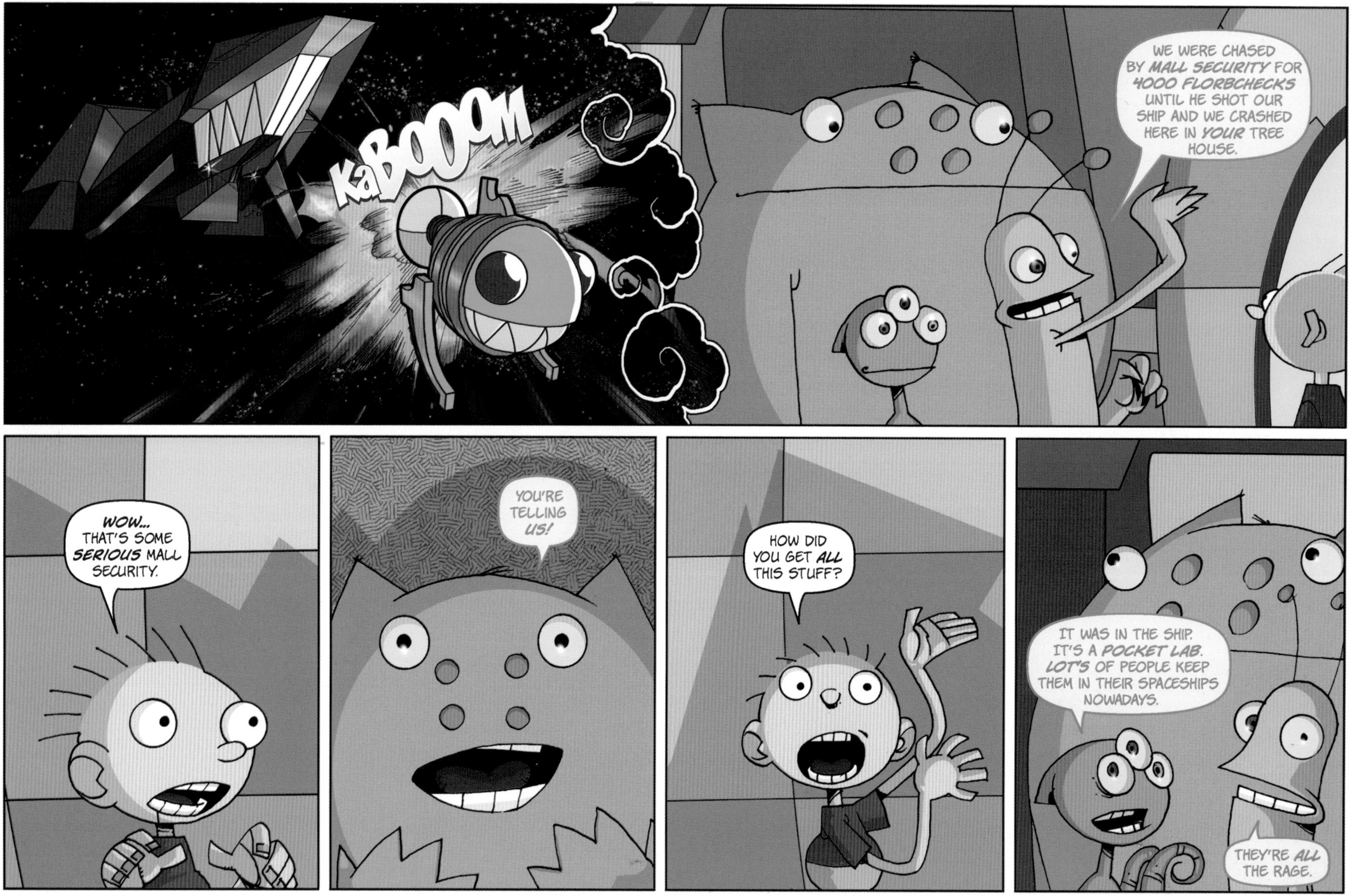
KaBOOOM
WE WERE CHASED BY MALL SECURITY FOR 4000 FLORBCHECKS UNTIL HE SHOT OUR SHIP AND WE CRASHED HERE IN YOUR TREE HOUSE.
WOW... THAT'S SOME SERIOUS MALL SECURITY.
YOU'RE TELLING US!
HOW DID YOU GET ALL THIS STUFF?
IT WAS IN THE SHIP. IT'S A POCKET LAB. LOT'S OF PEOPLE KEEP THEM IN THEIR SPACESHIPS NOWADAYS.
THEY'RE ALL THE RAGE.

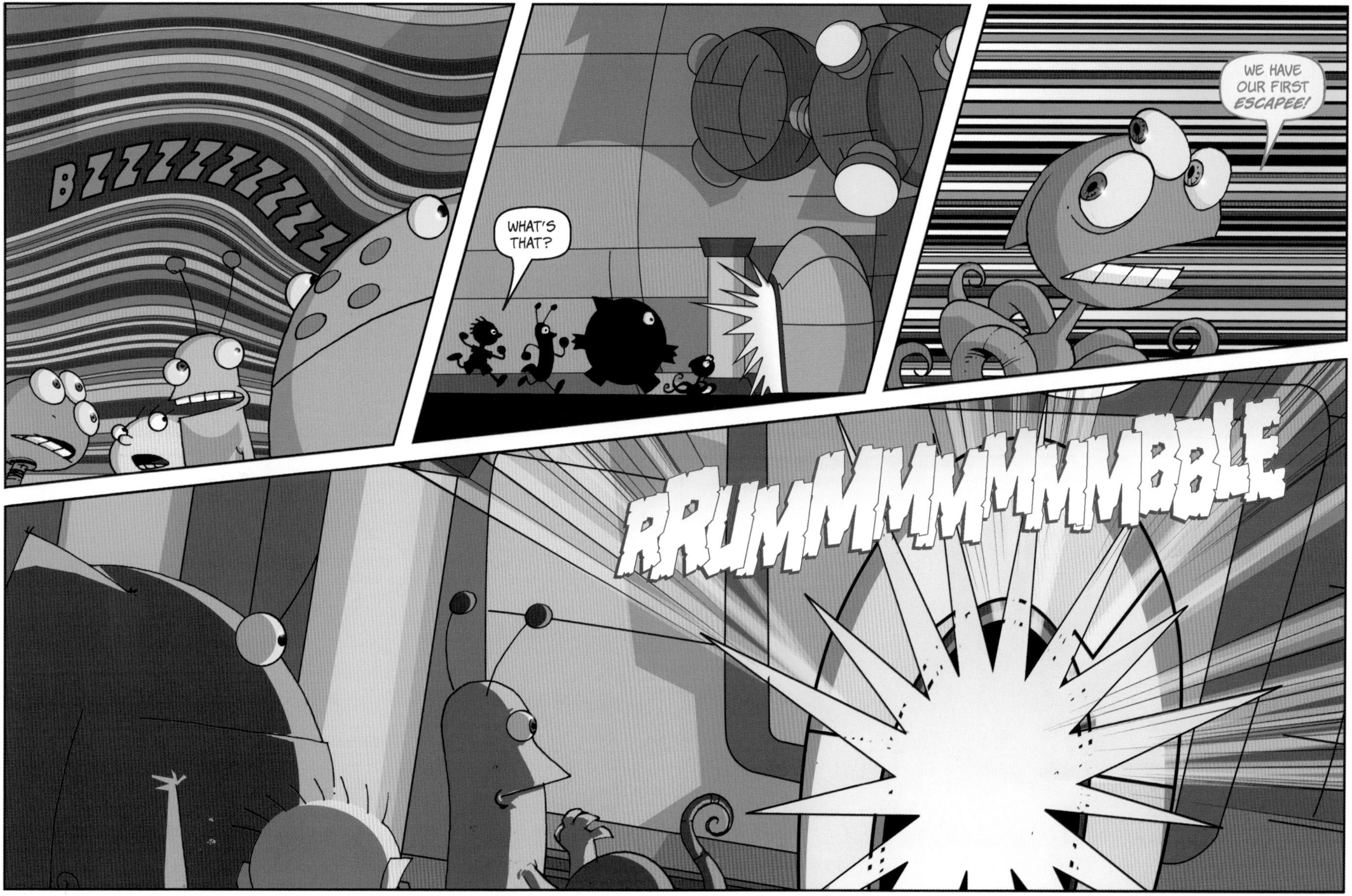
BZZZZZZZZZZ
WHAT'S THAT?
WE HAVE OUR FIRST *ESCAPEE!*
RRUMMMMMMMMMBBLE

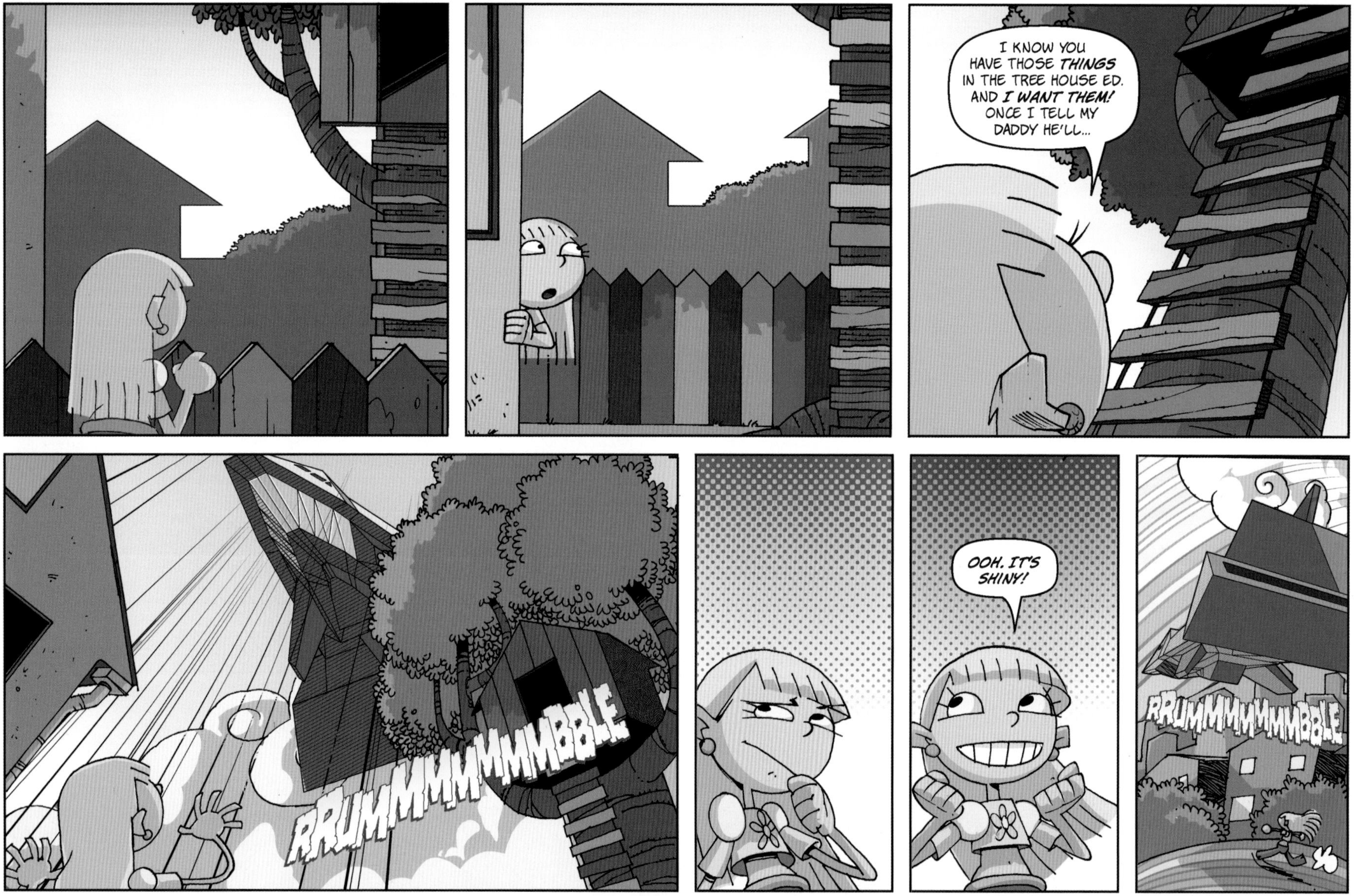
I KNOW YOU HAVE THOSE *THINGS* IN THE TREE HOUSE ED. AND *I WANT THEM!* ONCE I TELL MY DADDY HE'LL...
RRUMMMMMMMMBBLE
OOH. IT'S SHINY!
RRUMMMMMMMMBBLE

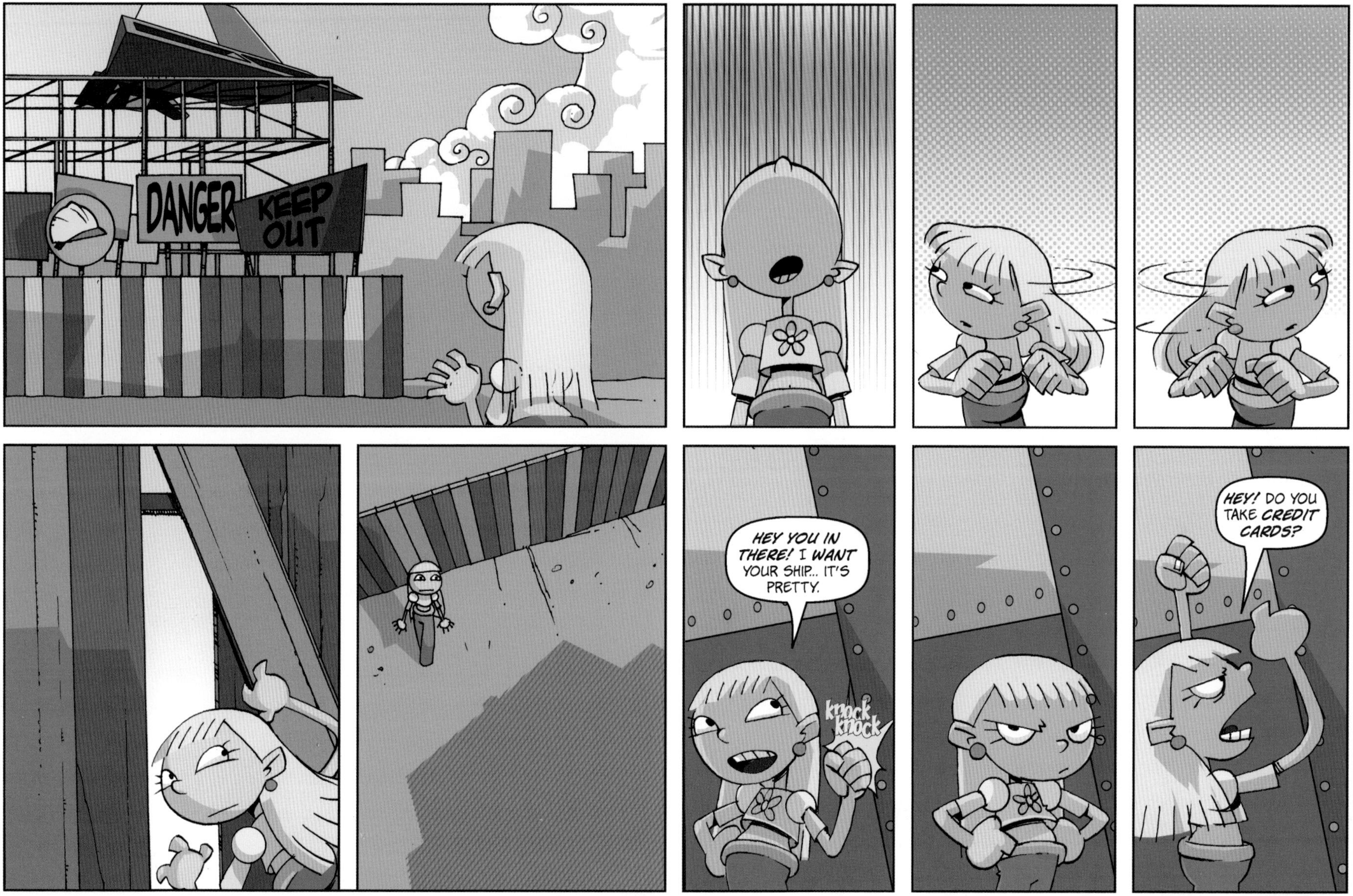
DANGER
KEEP OUT
HEY YOU IN THERE! I WANT YOUR SHIP... IT'S PRETTY.
knock knock
HEY! DO YOU TAKE CREDIT CARDS?

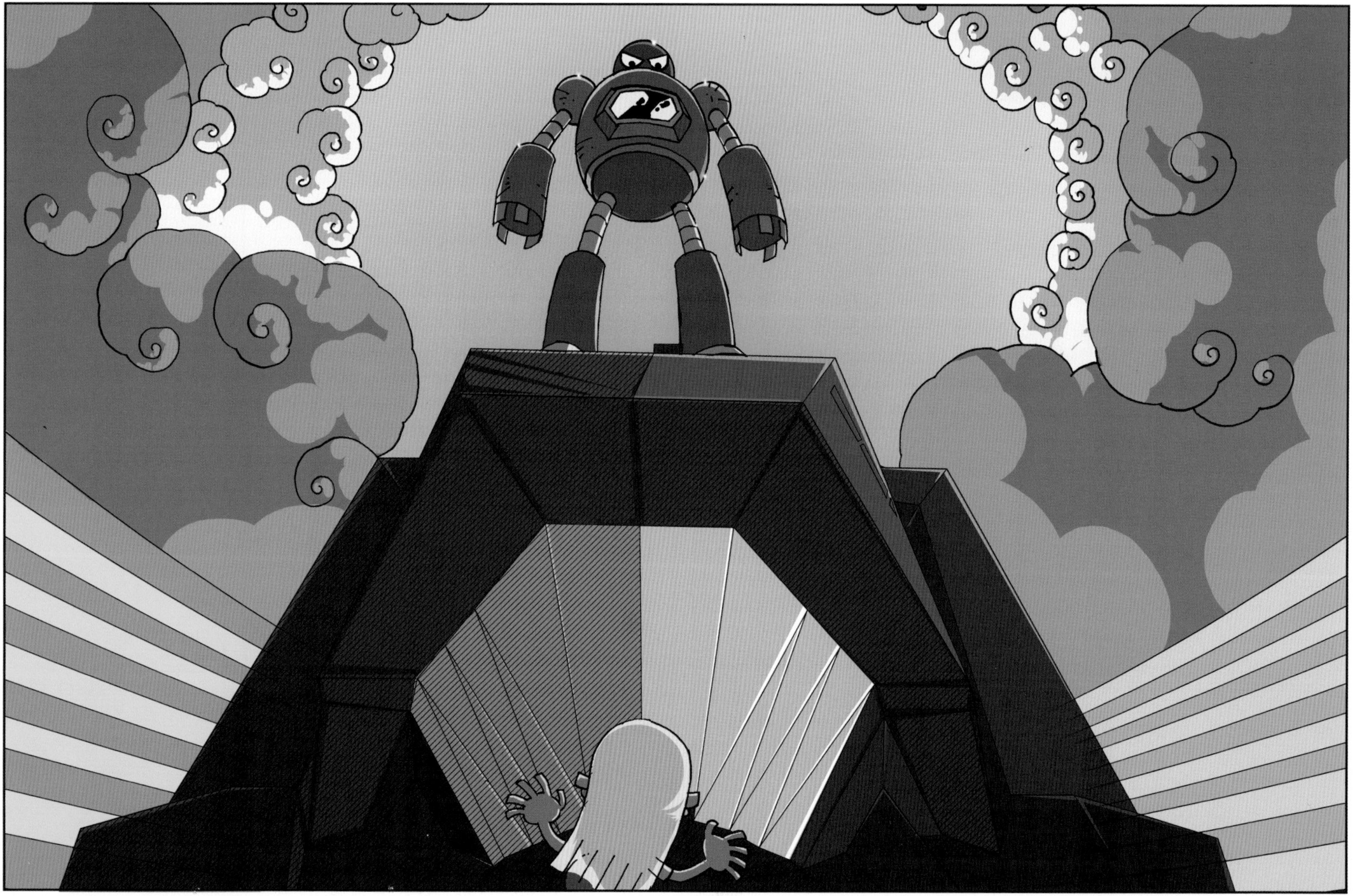

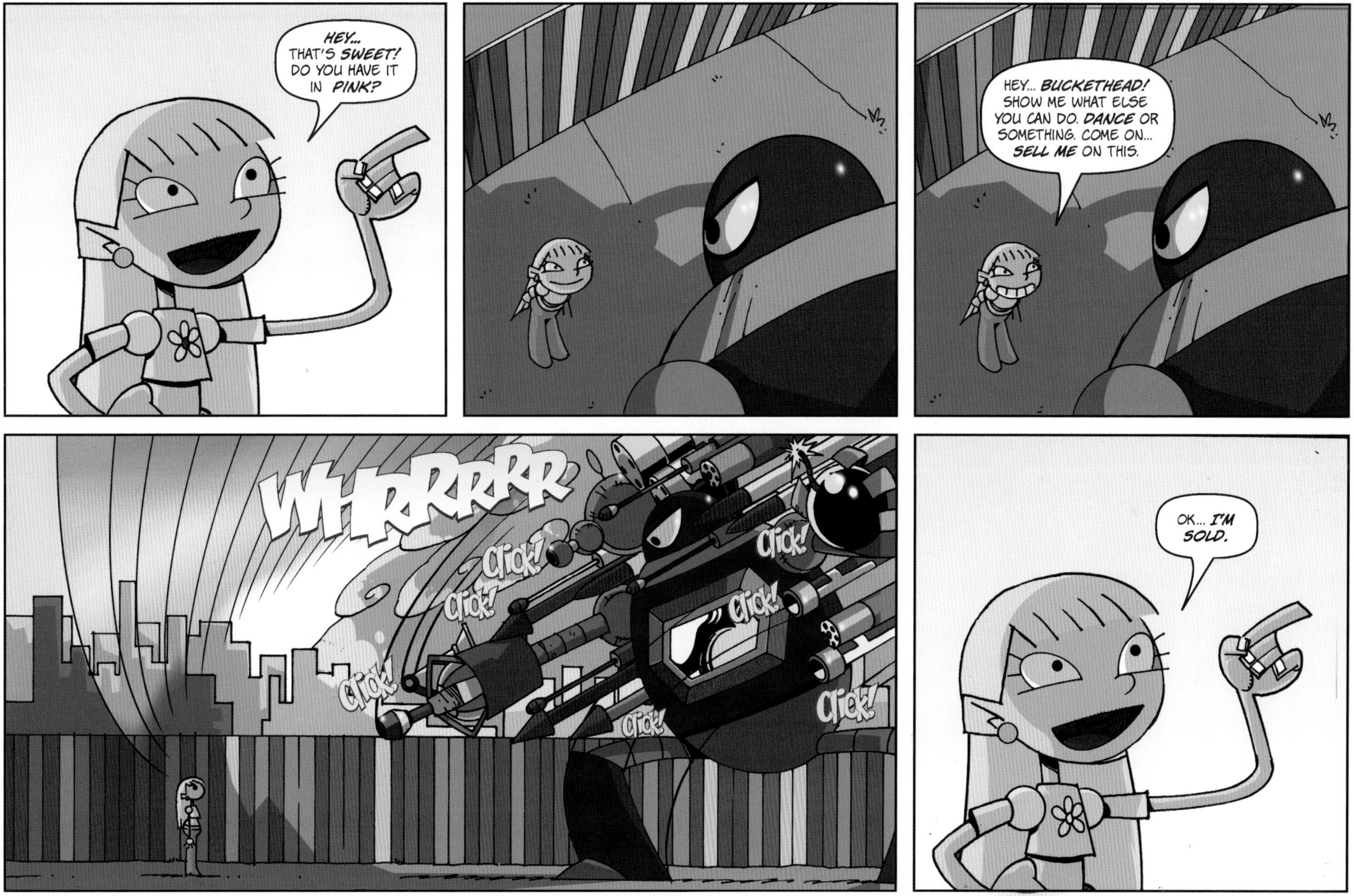
HEY... THAT'S SWEET! DO YOU HAVE IT IN PINK?
HEY... BUCKETHEAD! SHOW ME WHAT ELSE YOU CAN DO. DANCE OR SOMETHING. COME ON... SELL ME ON THIS.
WHRRRRR
CLICK!
CLICK!
CLICK!
CLICK!
CLICK!
CLICK!
CLICK!
OK... I'M SOLD.

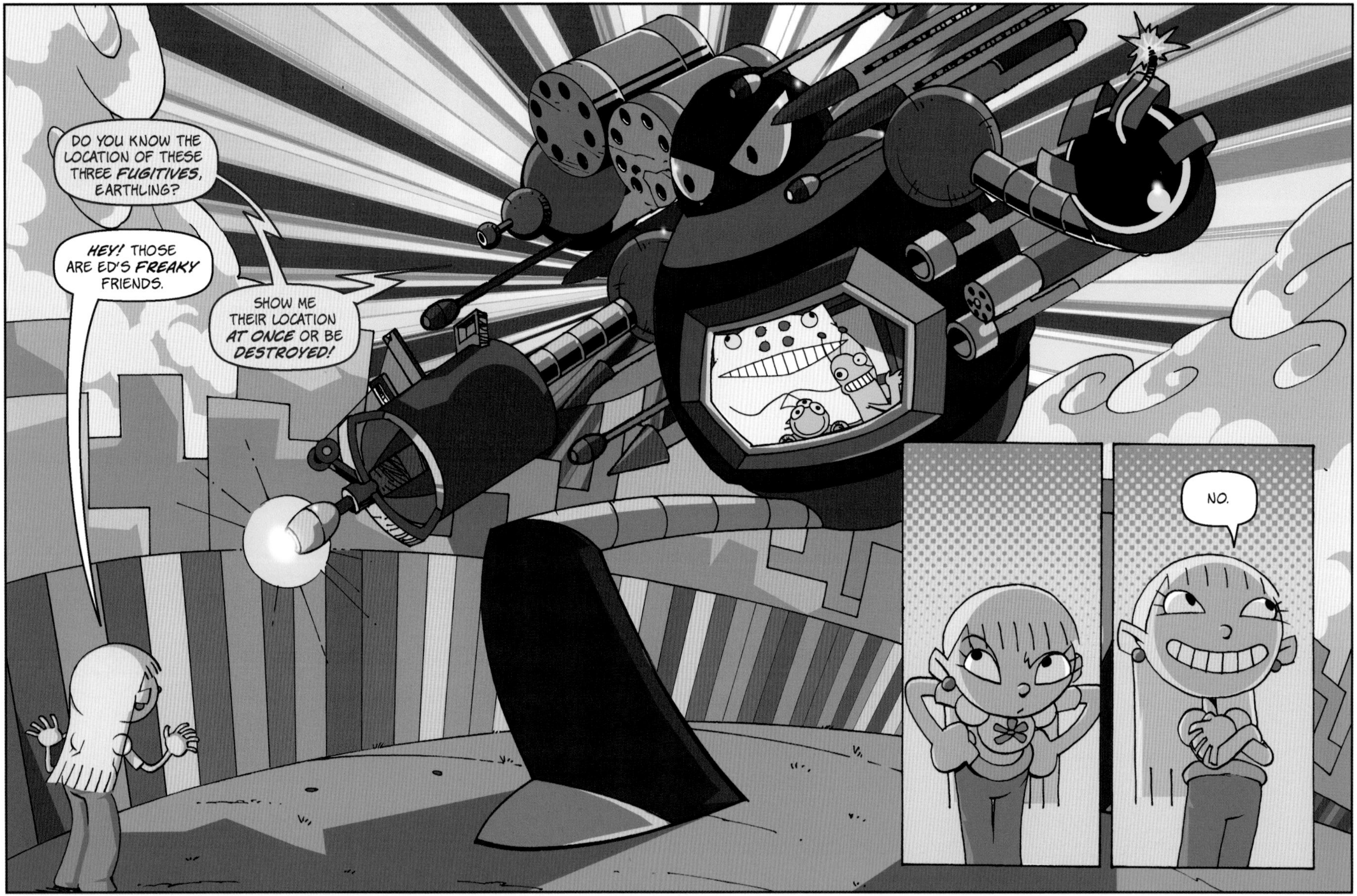
DO YOU KNOW THE LOCATION OF THESE THREE FUGITIVES, EARTHLING?
HEY! THOSE ARE ED'S FREAKY FRIENDS.
SHOW ME THEIR LOCATION AT ONCE OR BE DESTROYED!
NO.

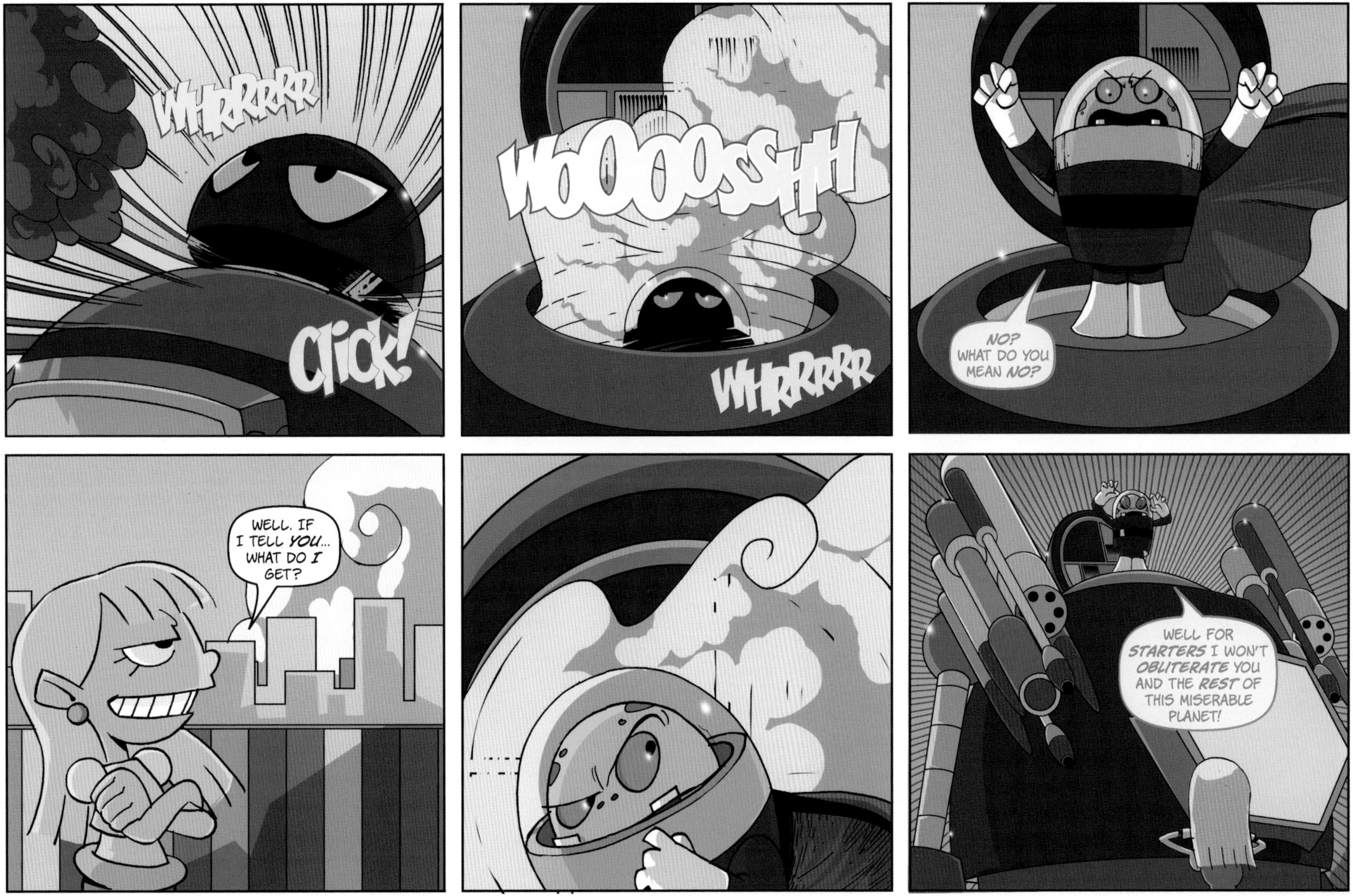
WHRRRRR
CLICK!
WOOOOSSHH
WHRRRRR
NO? WHAT DO YOU MEAN NO?
WELL. IF I TELL YOU... WHAT DO I GET?
WELL FOR STARTERS I WON'T OBLITERATE YOU AND THE REST OF THIS MISERABLE PLANET!

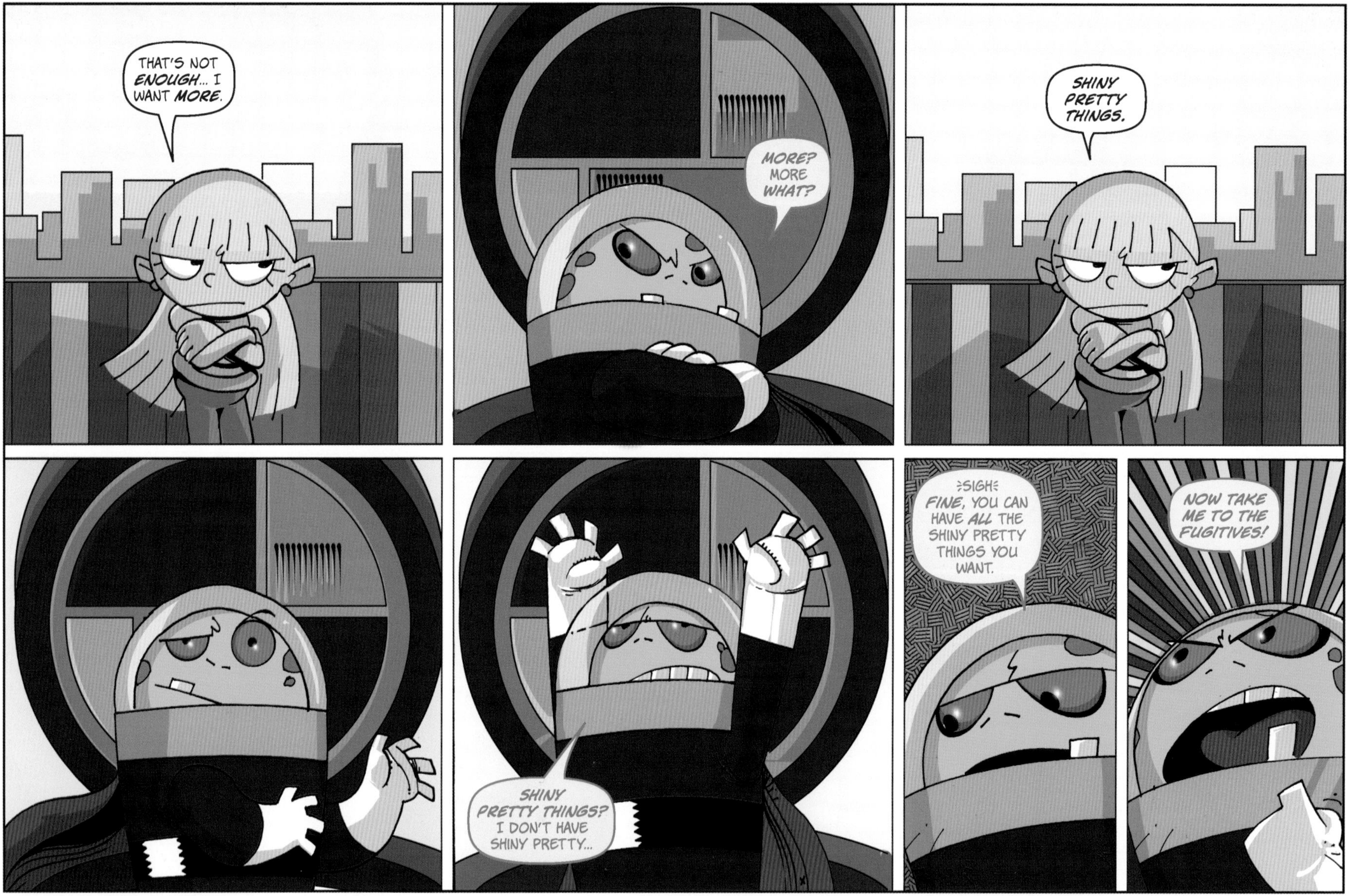
THAT'S NOT ENOUGH... I WANT MORE.
MORE? MORE WHAT?
SHINY PRETTY THINGS.
SHINY PRETTY THINGS? I DON'T HAVE SHINY PRETTY...
≈SIGH≈ FINE, YOU CAN HAVE ALL THE SHINY PRETTY THINGS YOU WANT.
NOW TAKE ME TO THE FUGITIVES!

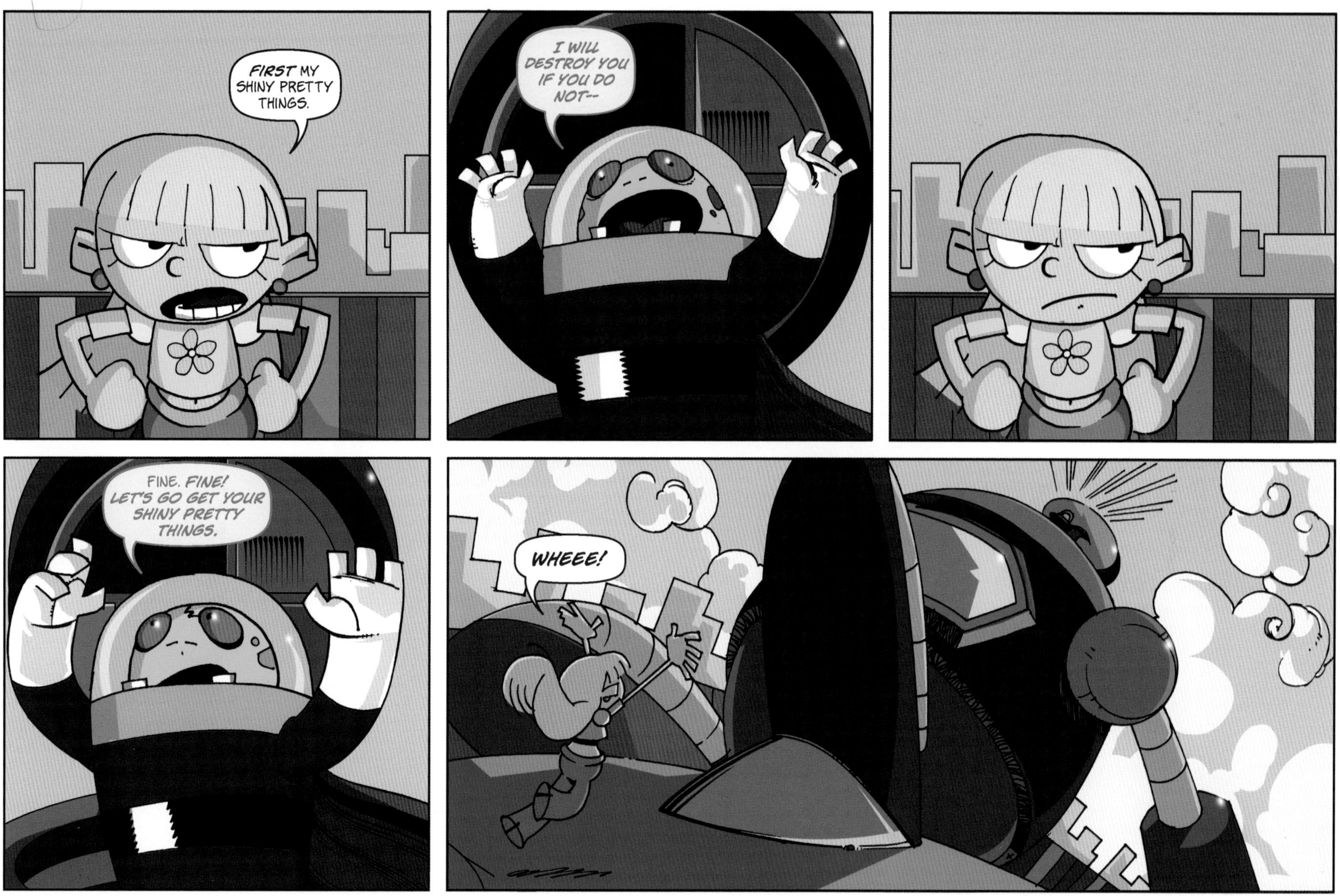

FIRST MY SHINY PRETTY THINGS.
I WILL DESTROY YOU IF YOU DO NOT--
FINE. FINE! LET'S GO GET YOUR SHINY PRETTY THINGS.
WHEEE!

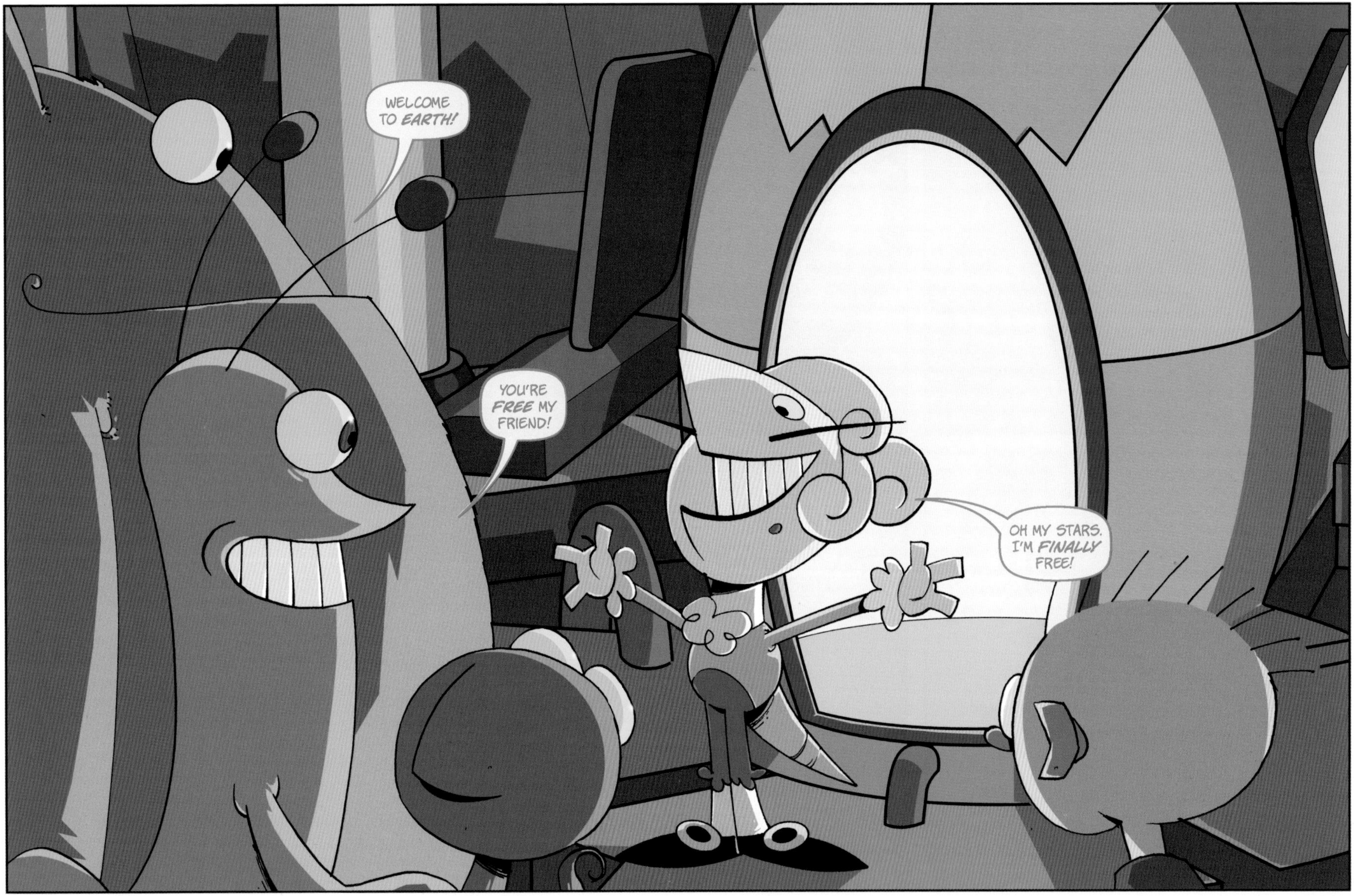
WELCOME TO EARTH!
YOU'RE FREE MY FRIEND!
OH MY STARS. I'M FINALLY FREE!

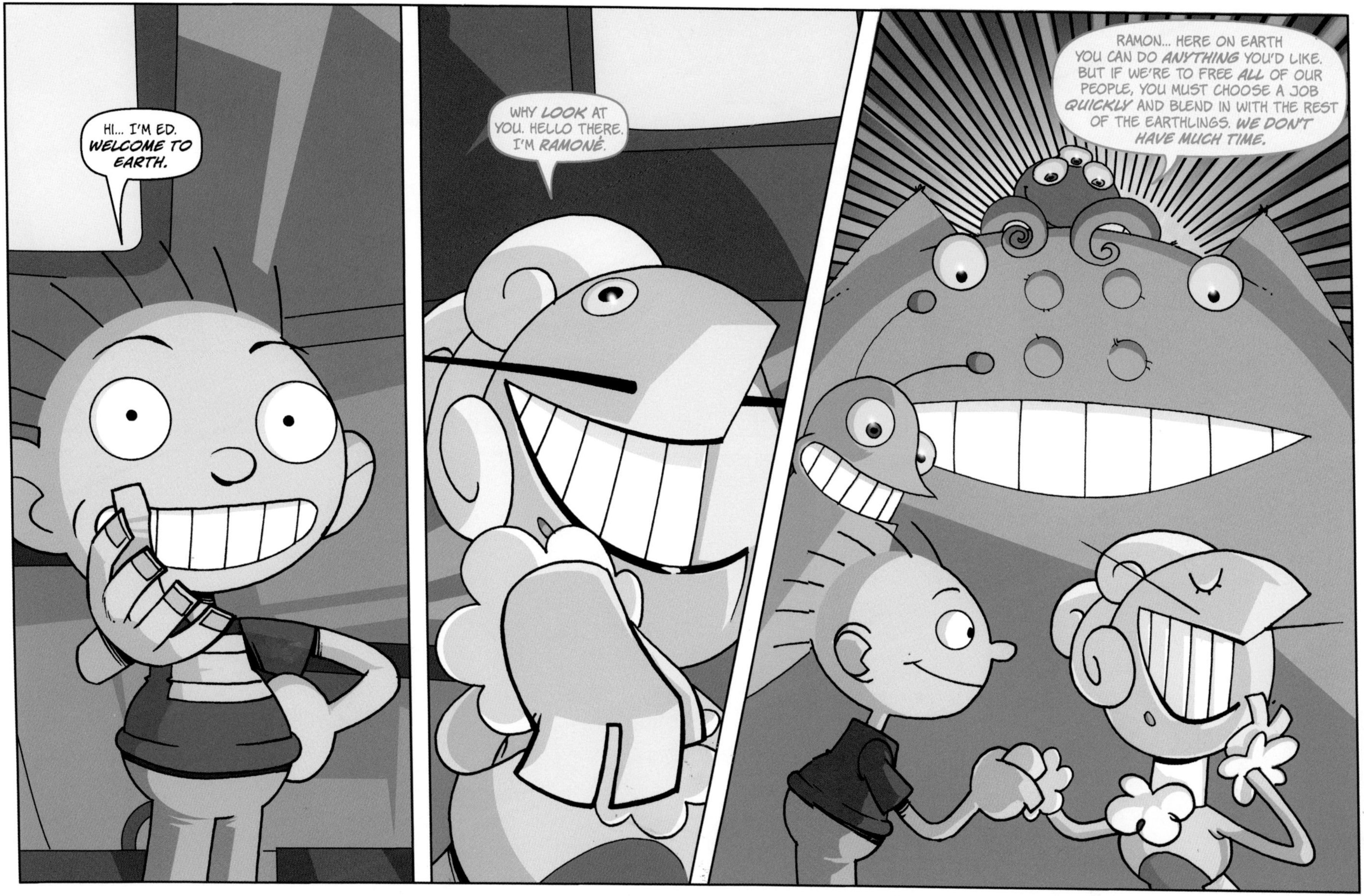
HI... I'M ED. WELCOME TO EARTH.
WHY LOOK AT YOU. HELLO THERE. I'M RAMONÉ.
RAMON... HERE ON EARTH YOU CAN DO ANYTHING YOU'D LIKE. BUT IF WE'RE TO FREE ALL OF OUR PEOPLE, YOU MUST CHOOSE A JOB QUICKLY AND BLEND IN WITH THE REST OF THE EARTHLINGS. WE DON'T HAVE MUCH TIME.

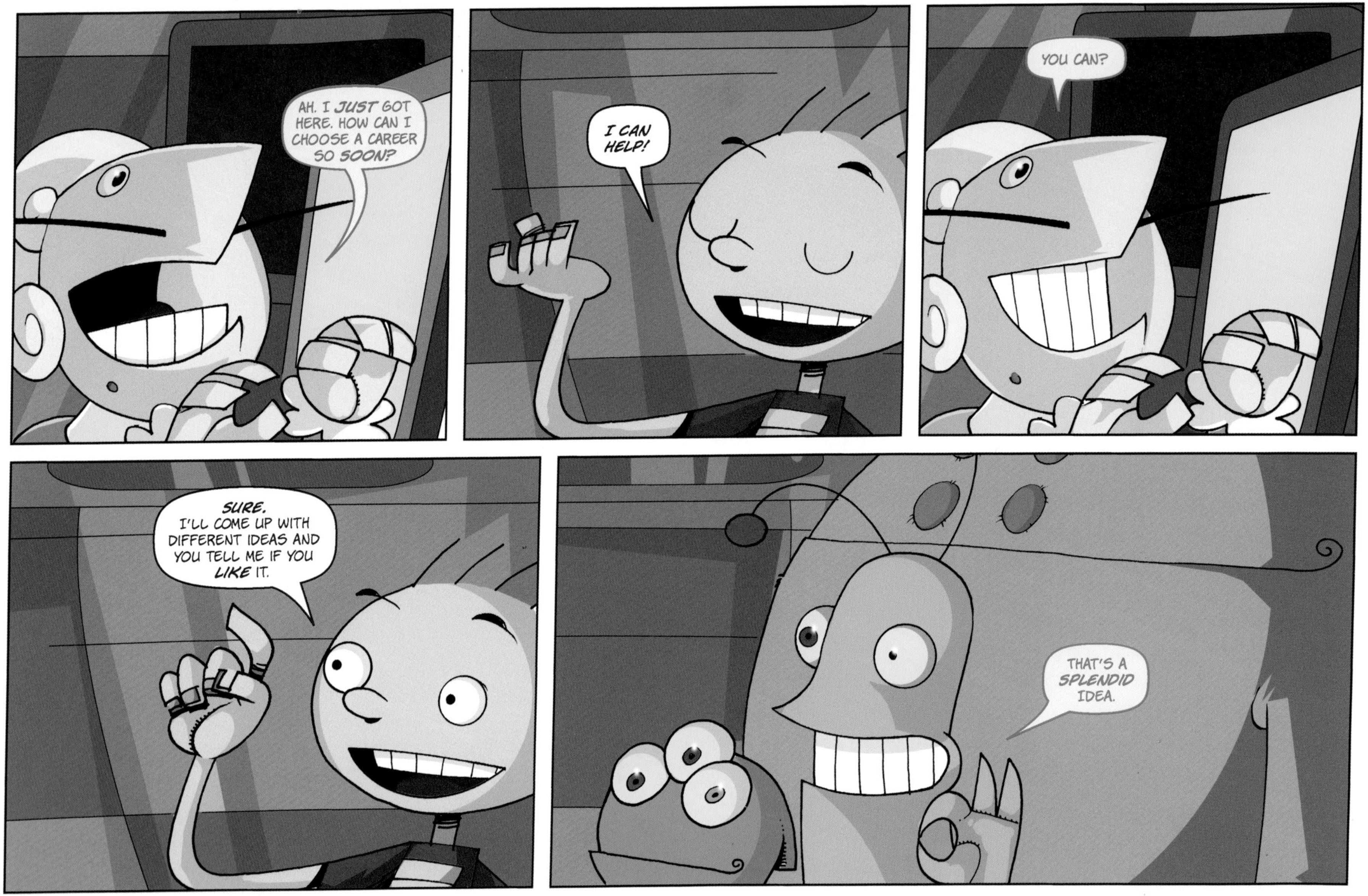
AH. I JUST GOT HERE. HOW CAN I CHOOSE A CAREER SO SOON?
I CAN HELP!
YOU CAN?
SURE. I'LL COME UP WITH DIFFERENT IDEAS AND YOU TELL ME IF YOU LIKE IT.
THAT'S A SPLENDID IDEA.

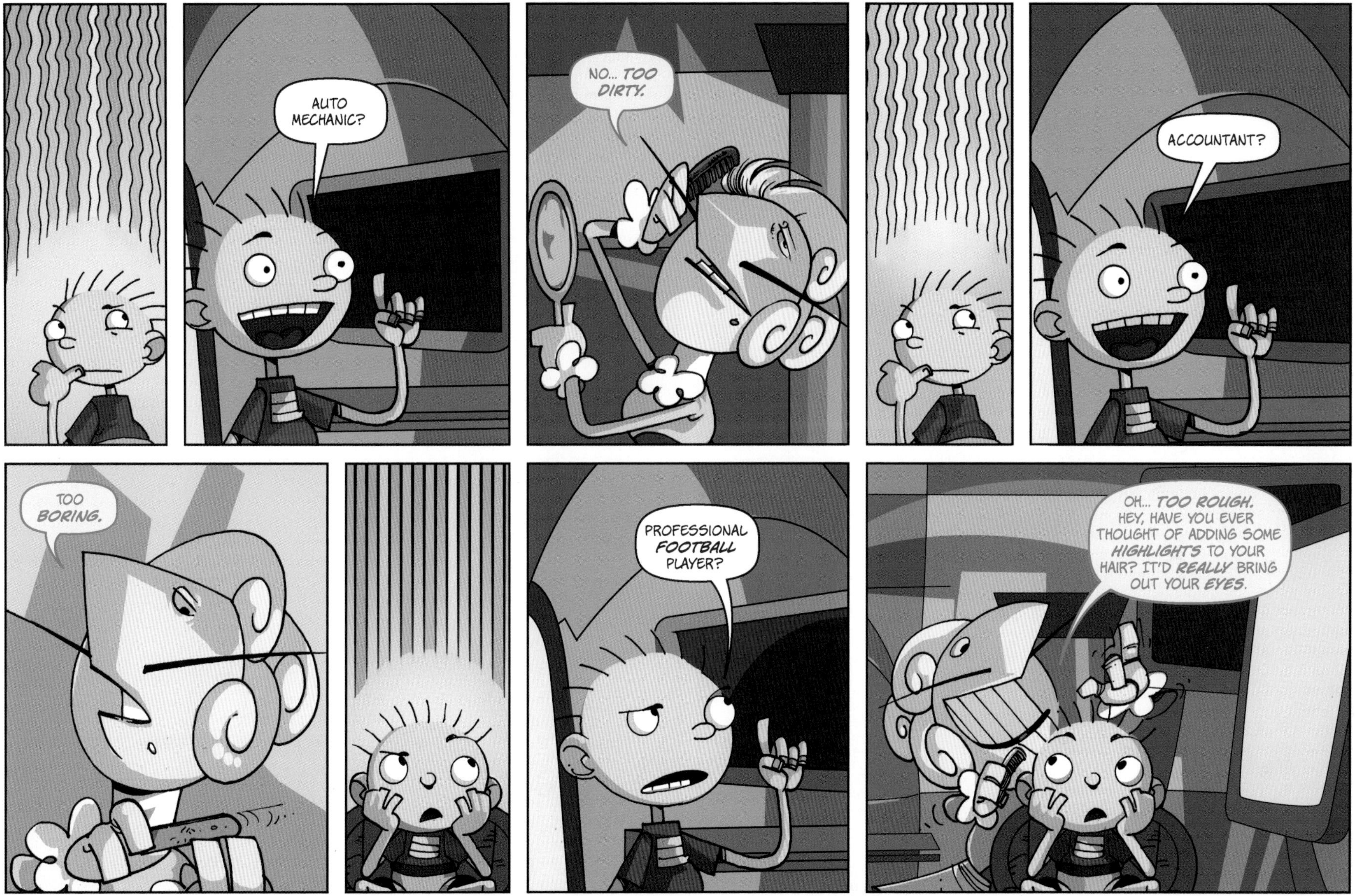
AUTO MECHANIC?
NO... *TOO DIRTY.*
ACCOUNTANT?
TOO *BORING.*
PROFESSIONAL *FOOTBALL* PLAYER?
OH... *TOO ROUGH.* HEY, HAVE YOU EVER THOUGHT OF ADDING SOME *HIGHLIGHTS* TO YOUR HAIR? IT'D *REALLY* BRING OUT YOUR *EYES.*

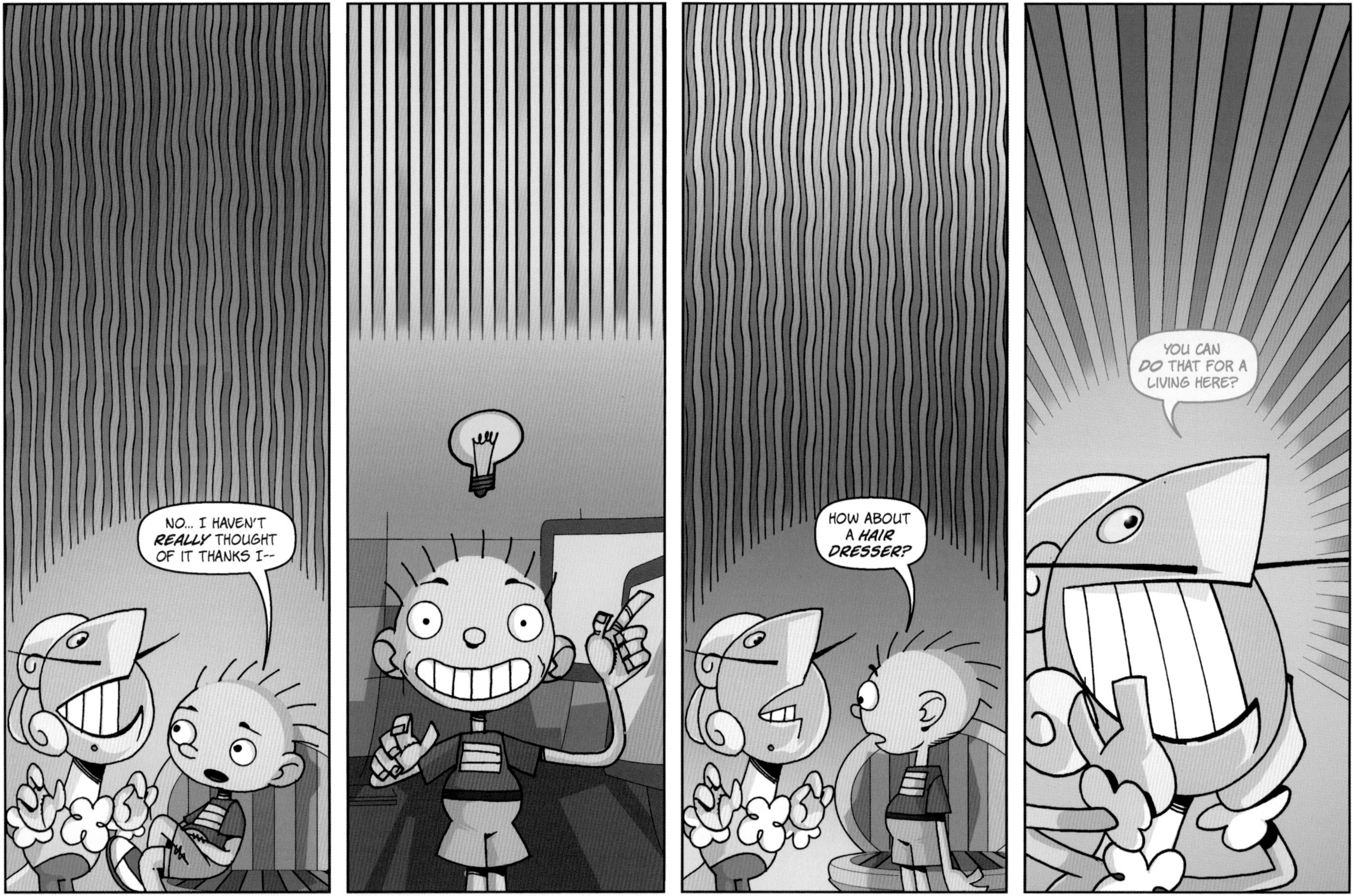
NO... I HAVEN'T REALLY THOUGHT OF IT THANKS I--
HOW ABOUT A HAIR DRESSER?
YOU CAN DO THAT FOR A LIVING HERE?

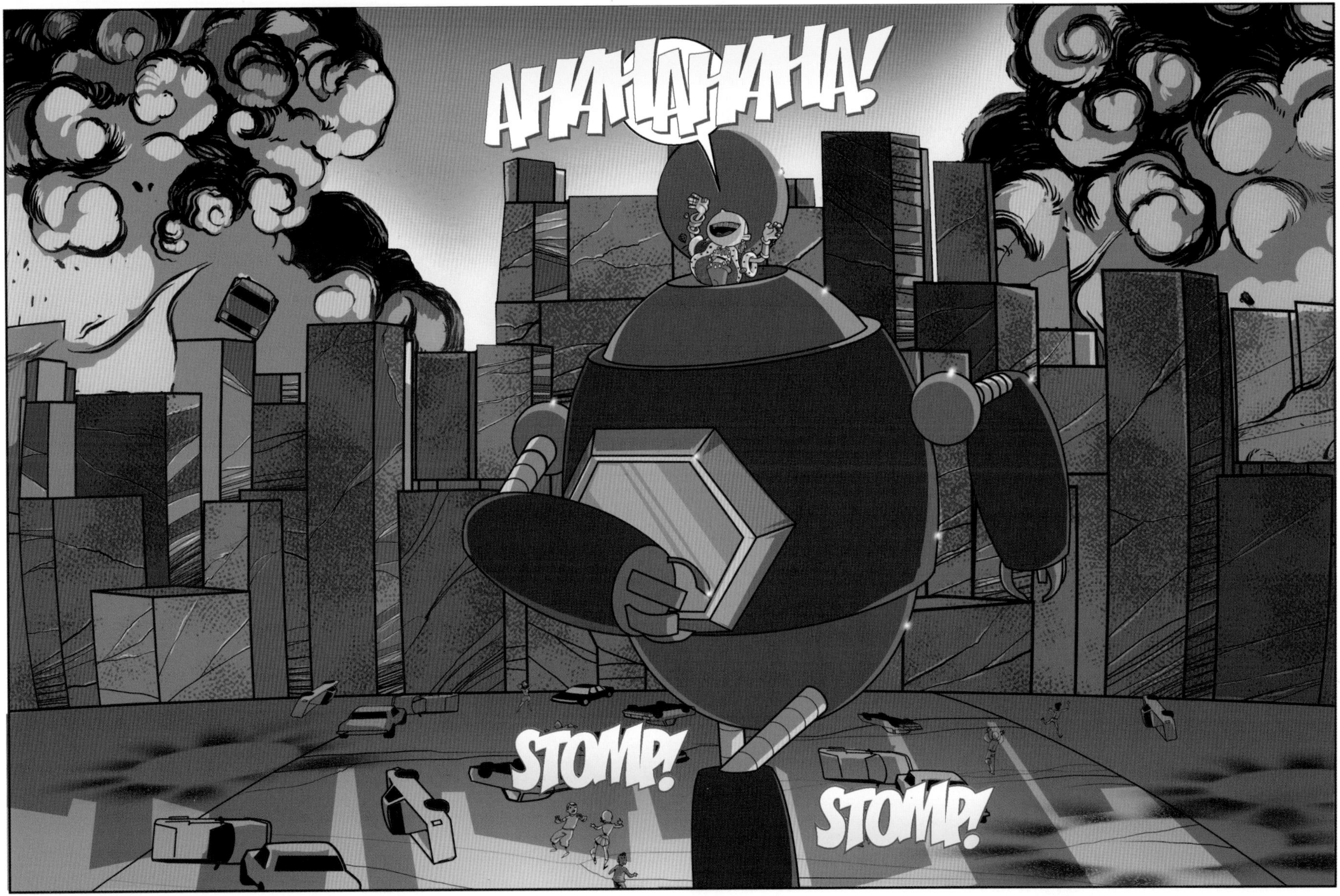
AHAHAHAHAHA!
STOMP!
STOMP!

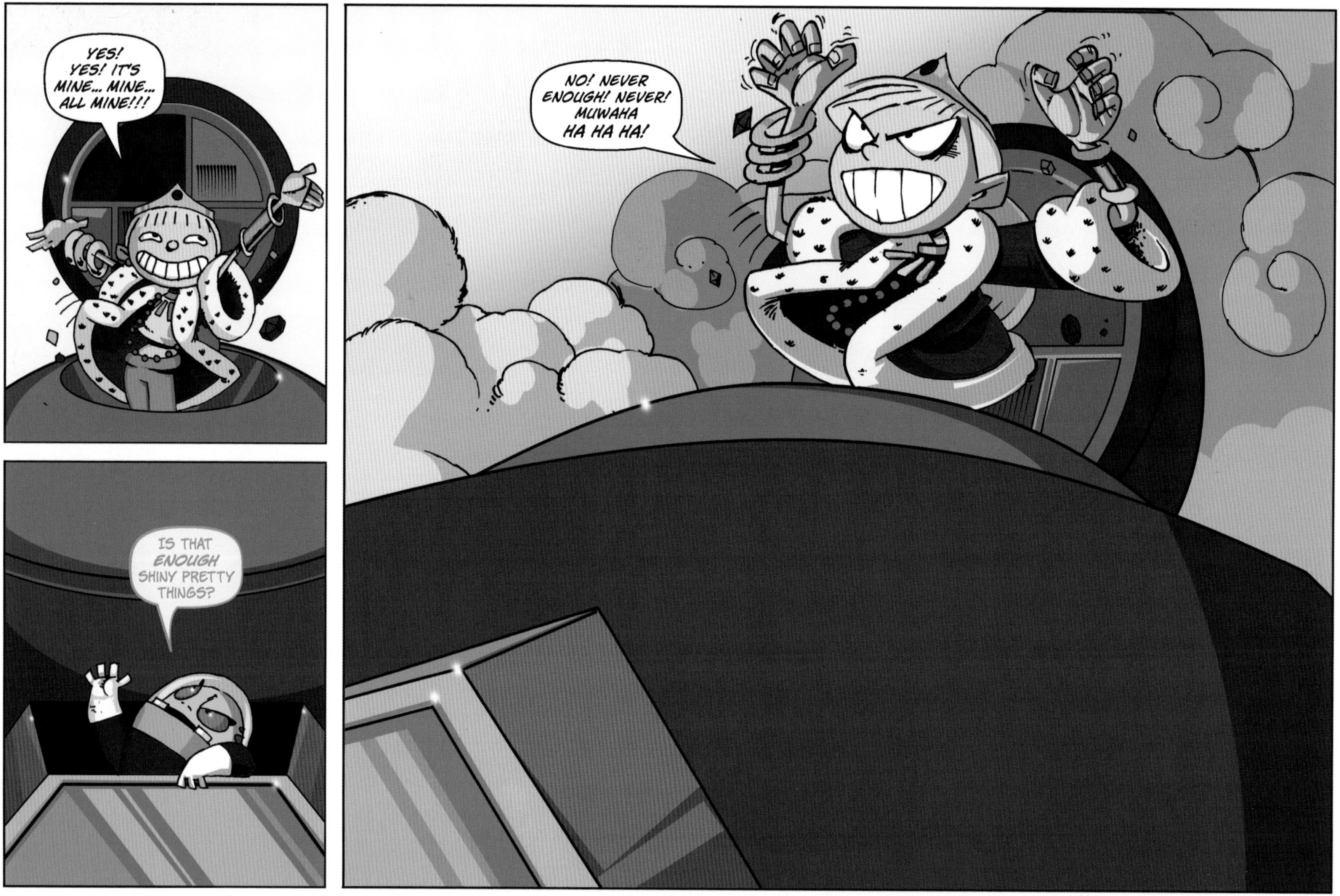
YES! YES! IT'S MINE... MINE... ALL MINE!!!
IS THAT ENOUGH SHINY PRETTY THINGS?
NO! NEVER ENOUGH! NEVER! MUWAHA HA HA HA!

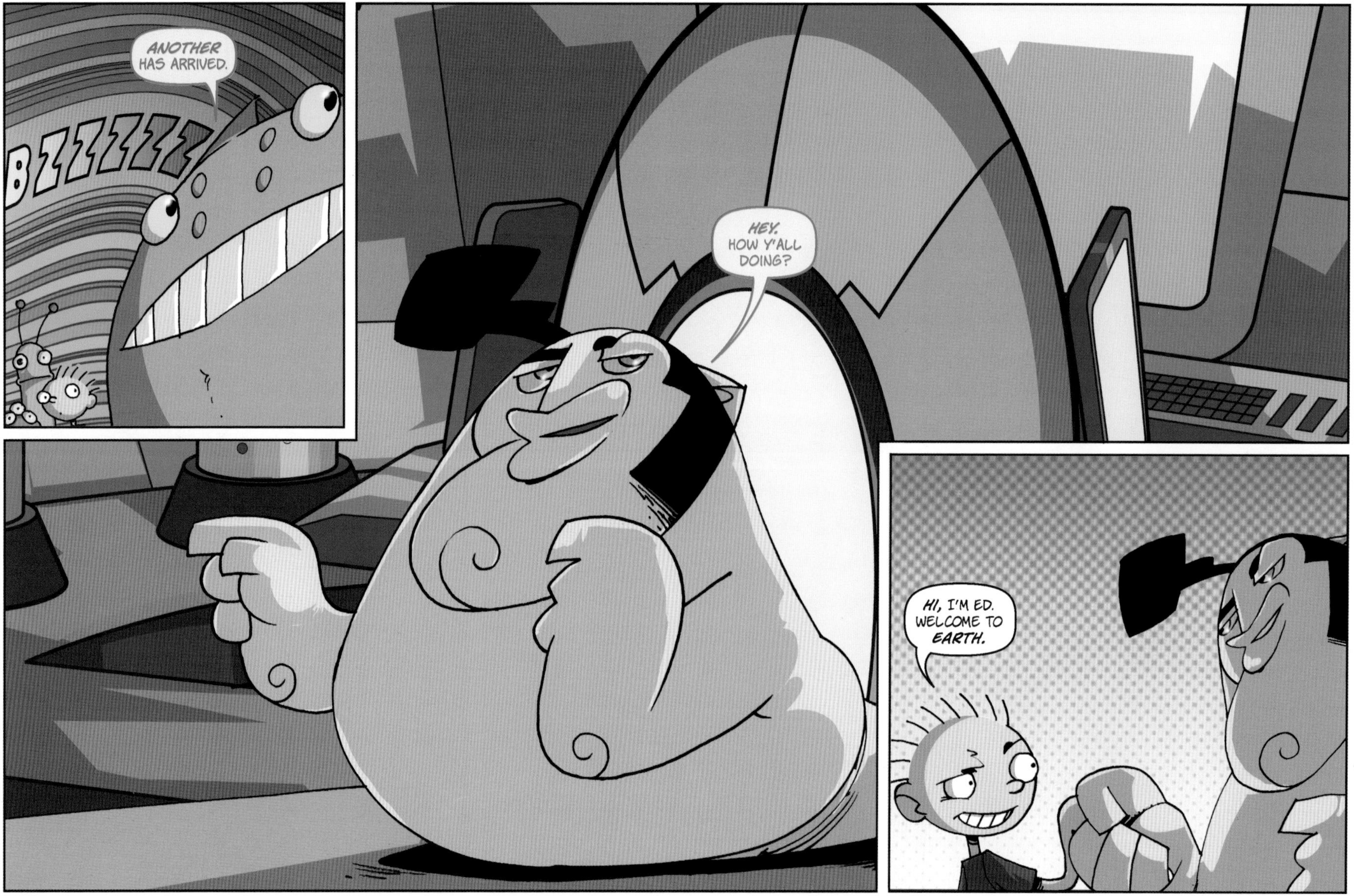

ANOTHER HAS ARRIVED.
BZZZZZZ
HEY. HOW Y'ALL DOING?
HI, I'M ED. WELCOME TO EARTH.

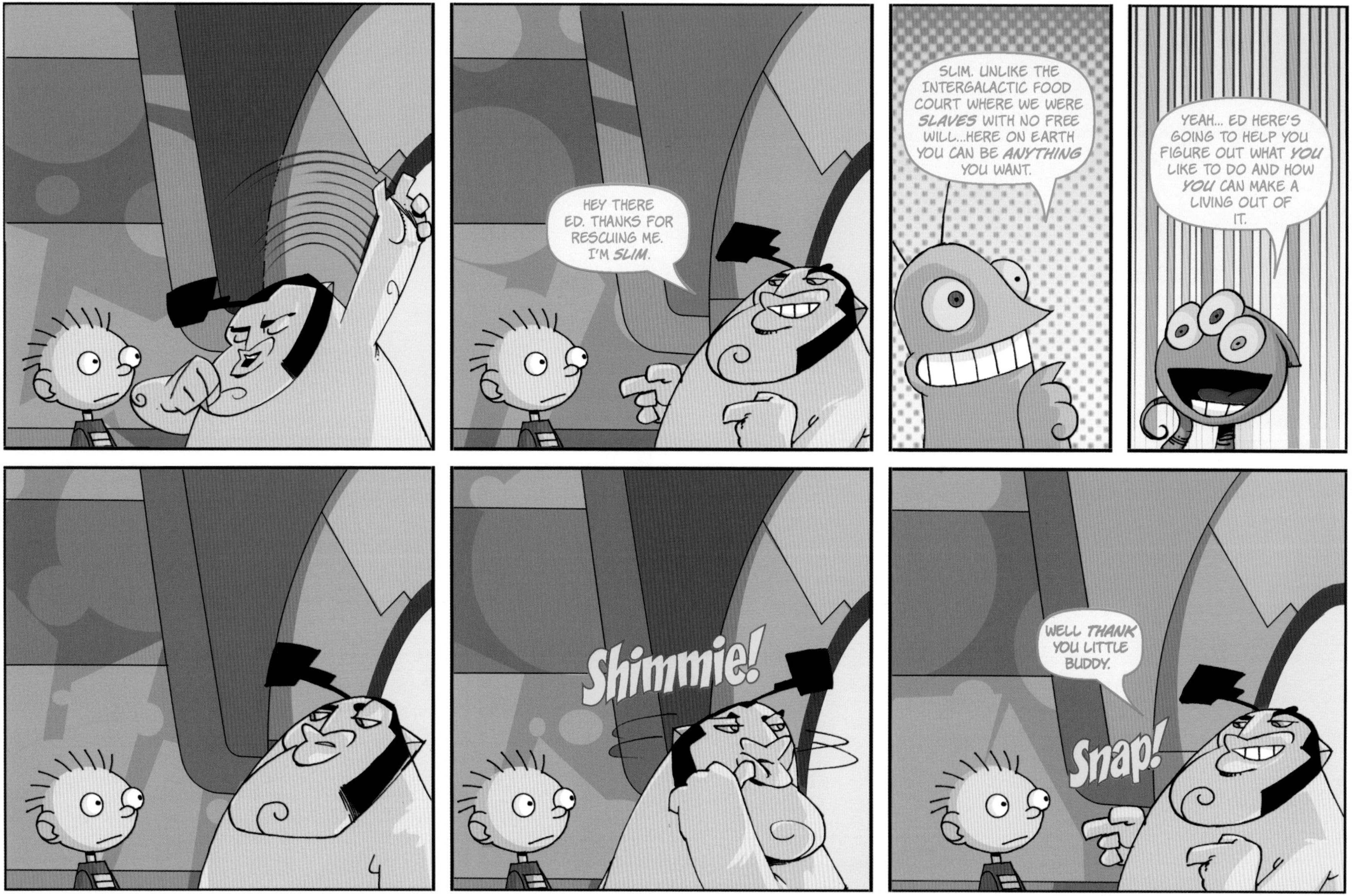
HEY THERE ED. THANKS FOR RESCUING ME. I'M SLIM.
SLIM. UNLIKE THE INTERGALACTIC FOOD COURT WHERE WE WERE SLAVES WITH NO FREE WILL...HERE ON EARTH YOU CAN BE ANYTHING YOU WANT.
YEAH... ED HERE'S GOING TO HELP YOU FIGURE OUT WHAT YOU LIKE TO DO AND HOW YOU CAN MAKE A LIVING OUT OF IT.
Shimmie!
WELL THANK YOU LITTLE BUDDY.
Snap!

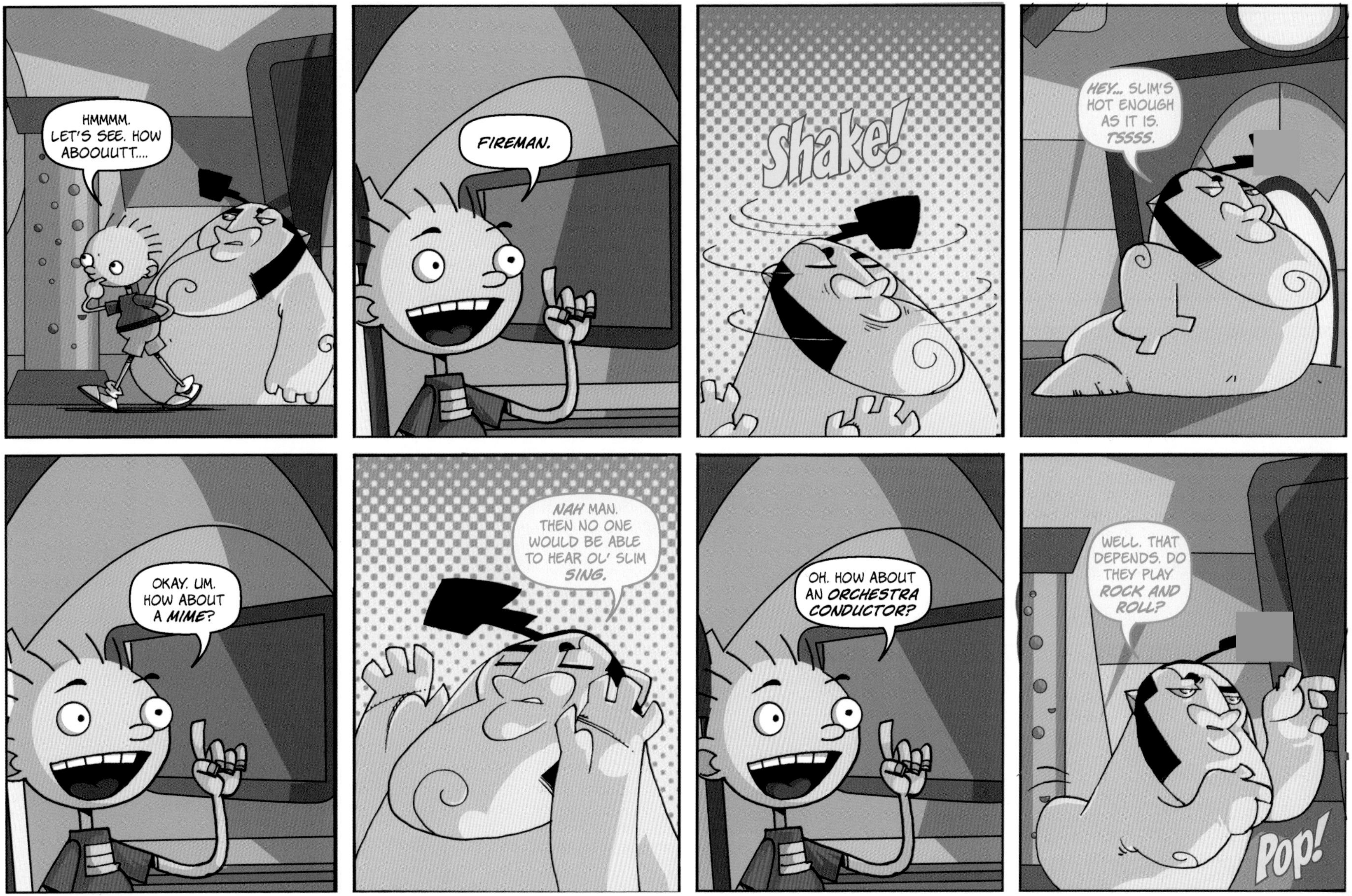
HMMMM. LET'S SEE. HOW ABOOUUTT....
FIREMAN.
Shake!
HEY... SLIM'S HOT ENOUGH AS IT IS. TSSSS.
OKAY. UM. HOW ABOUT A MIME?
NAH MAN. THEN NO ONE WOULD BE ABLE TO HEAR OL' SLIM SING.
OH. HOW ABOUT AN ORCHESTRA CONDUCTOR?
WELL. THAT DEPENDS. DO THEY PLAY ROCK AND ROLL?
POP!

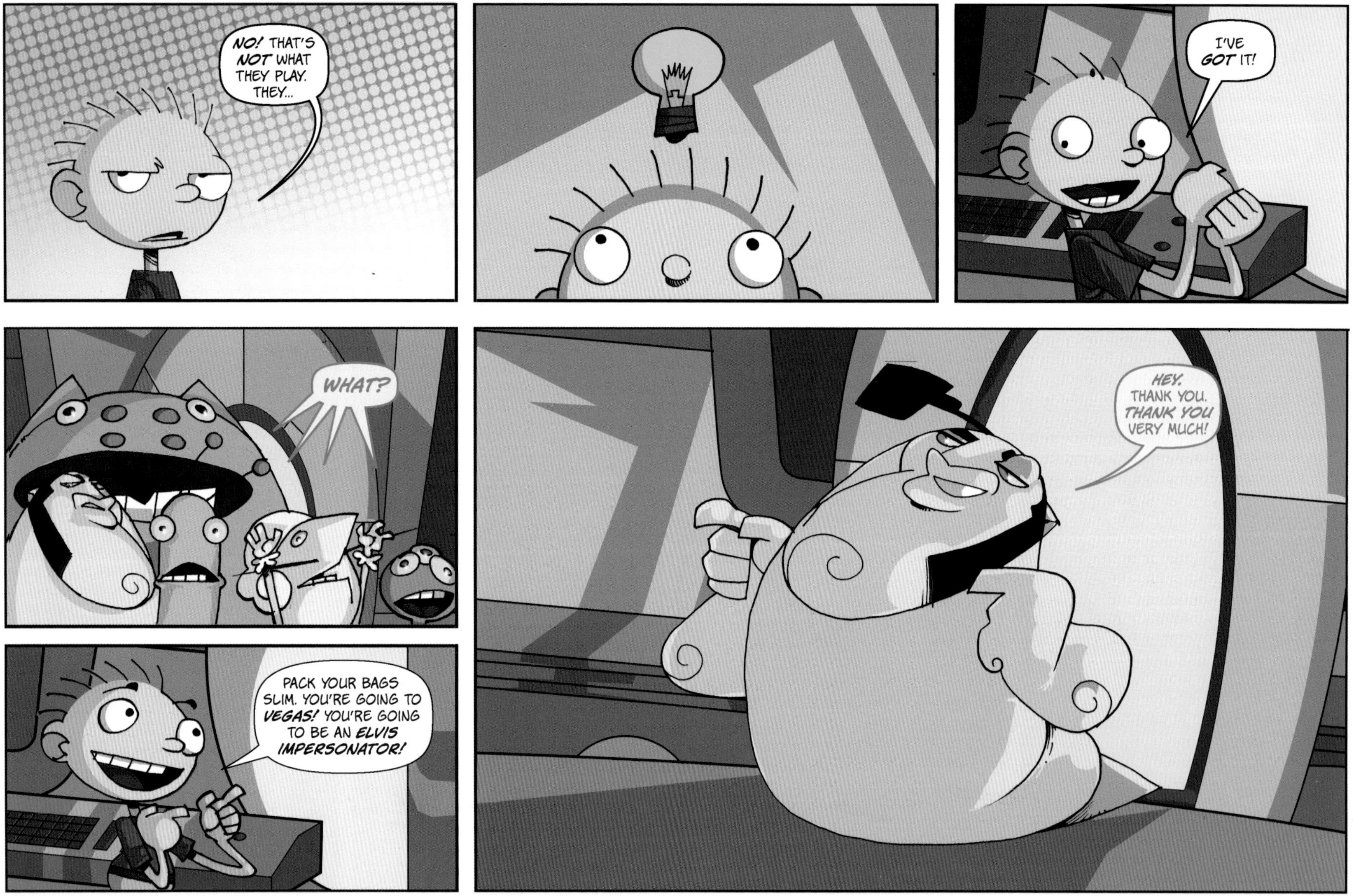

NO! THAT'S NOT WHAT THEY PLAY. THEY...
I'VE GOT IT!
WHAT?
PACK YOUR BAGS SLIM. YOU'RE GOING TO VEGAS! YOU'RE GOING TO BE AN ELVIS IMPERSONATOR!
HEY. THANK YOU. THANK YOU VERY MUCH!

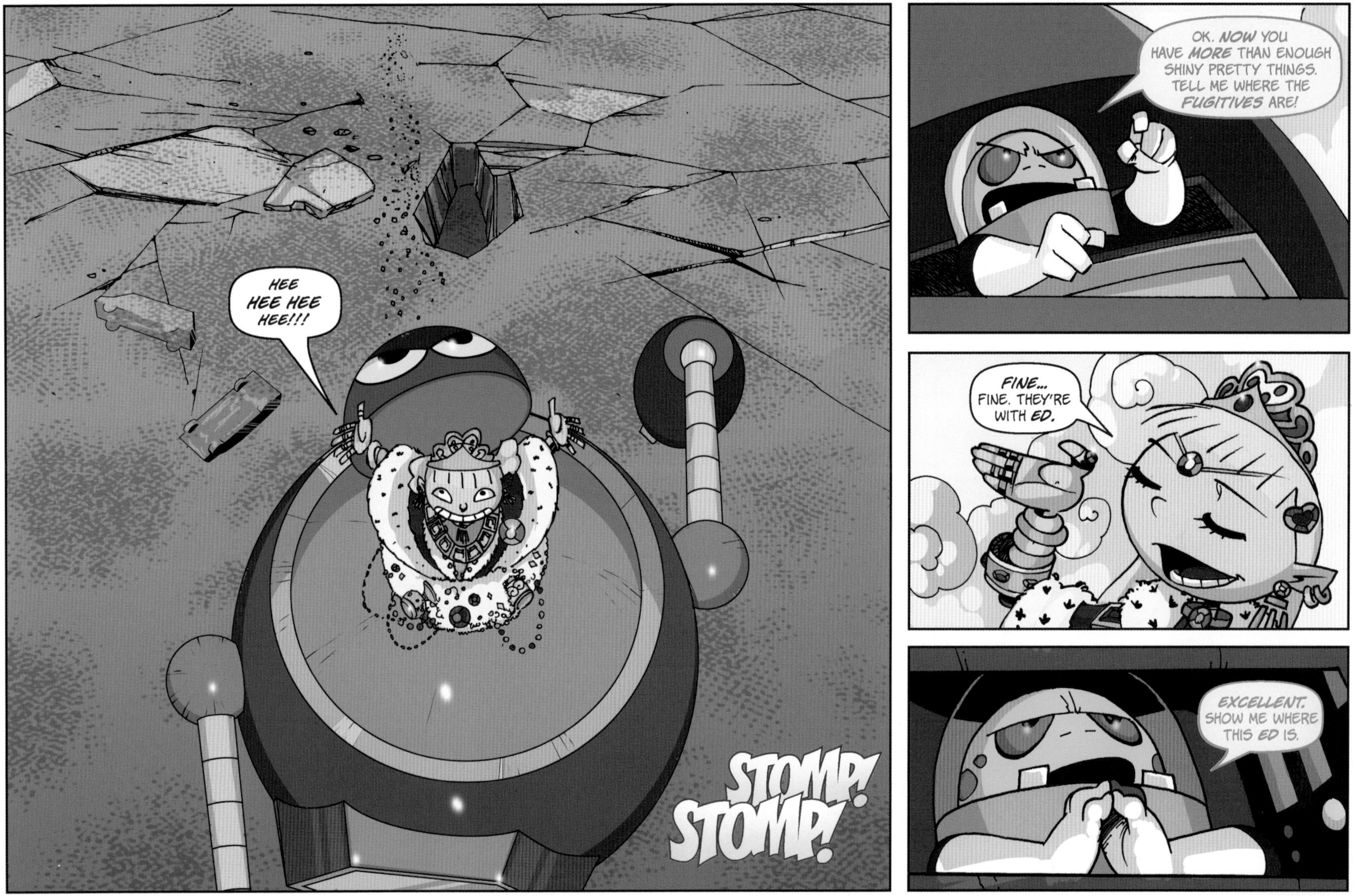
HEE HEE HEE HEE!!!
STOMP! STOMP!
OK. NOW YOU HAVE MORE THAN ENOUGH SHINY PRETTY THINGS. TELL ME WHERE THE FUGITIVES ARE!
FINE... FINE. THEY'RE WITH ED.
EXCELLENT. SHOW ME WHERE THIS ED IS.

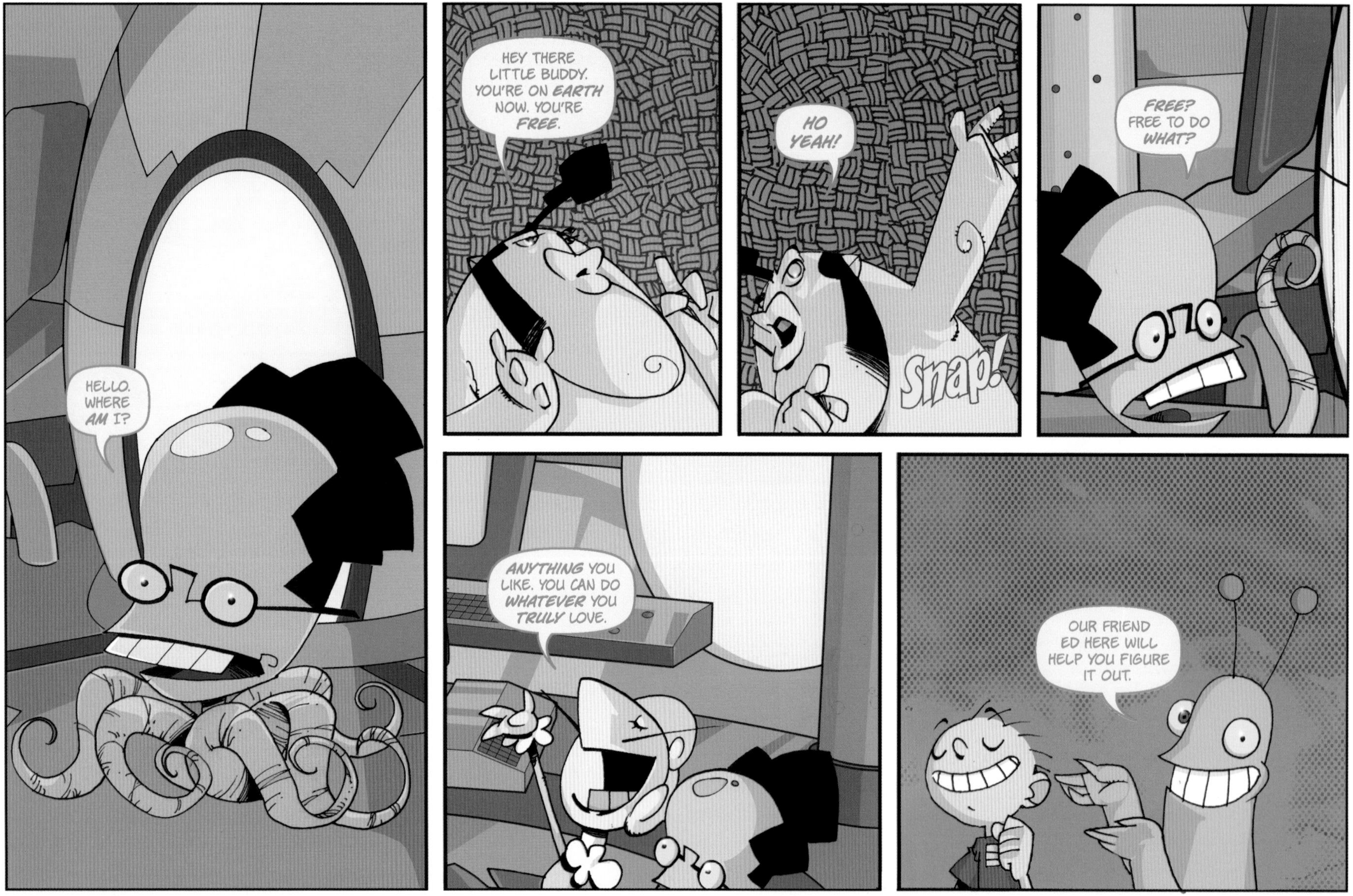
HELLO. WHERE AM I?
HEY THERE LITTLE BUDDY. YOU'RE ON EARTH NOW. YOU'RE FREE.
HO YEAH!
SNAP!
FREE? FREE TO DO WHAT?
ANYTHING YOU LIKE. YOU CAN DO WHATEVER YOU TRULY LOVE.
OUR FRIEND ED HERE WILL HELP YOU FIGURE IT OUT.

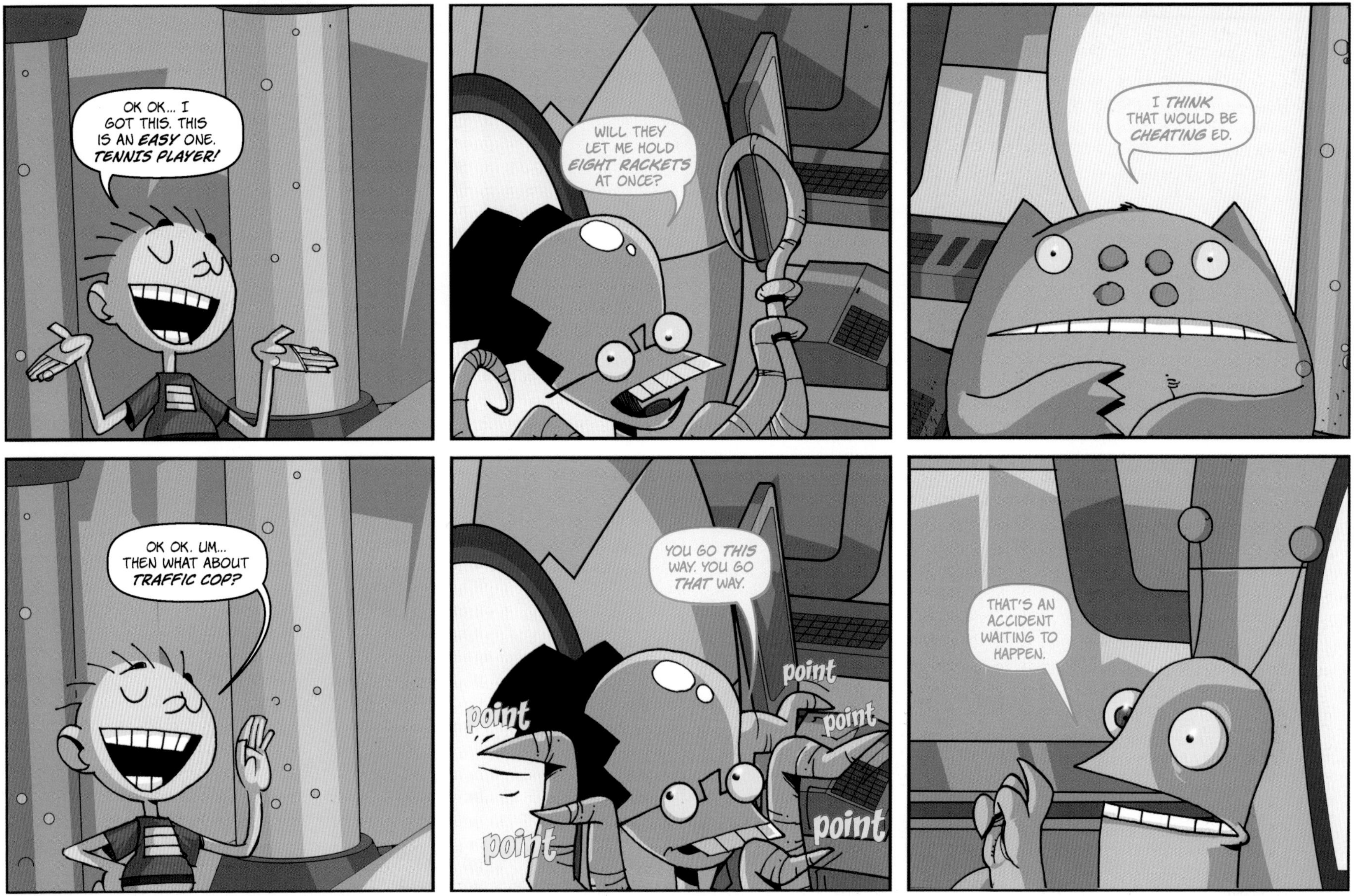
OK OK... I GOT THIS. THIS IS AN EASY ONE. TENNIS PLAYER!
WILL THEY LET ME HOLD EIGHT RACKETS AT ONCE?
I THINK THAT WOULD BE CHEATING ED.
OK OK. UM... THEN WHAT ABOUT TRAFFIC COP?
YOU GO THIS WAY. YOU GO THAT WAY.
point
point
point
point
point
THAT'S AN ACCIDENT WAITING TO HAPPEN.

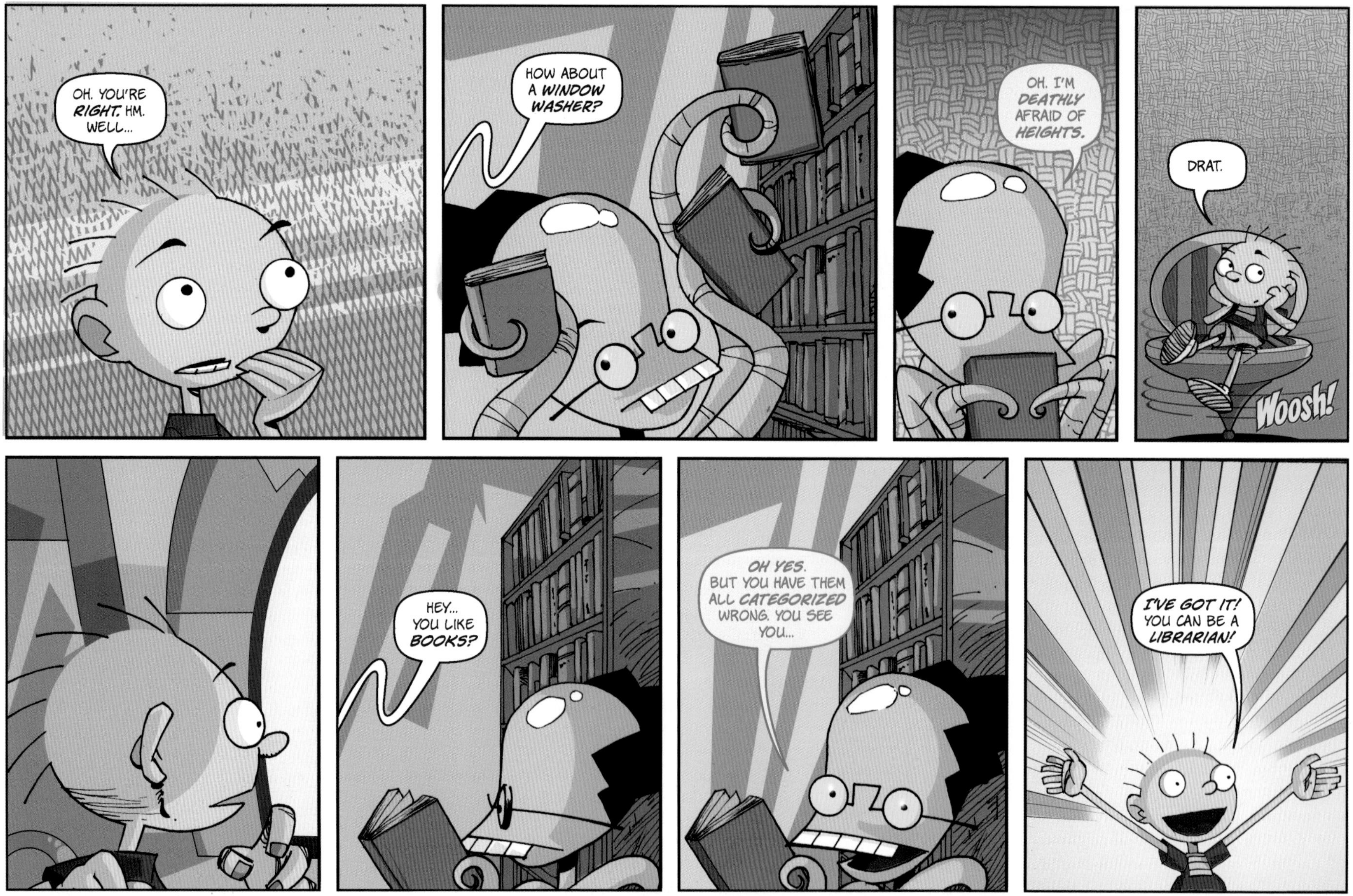
OH. YOU'RE RIGHT. HM. WELL...
HOW ABOUT A WINDOW WASHER?
OH. I'M DEATHLY AFRAID OF HEIGHTS.
DRAT.
Woosh!
HEY... YOU LIKE BOOKS?
OH YES. BUT YOU HAVE THEM ALL CATEGORIZED WRONG. YOU SEE YOU...
I'VE GOT IT! YOU CAN BE A LIBRARIAN!

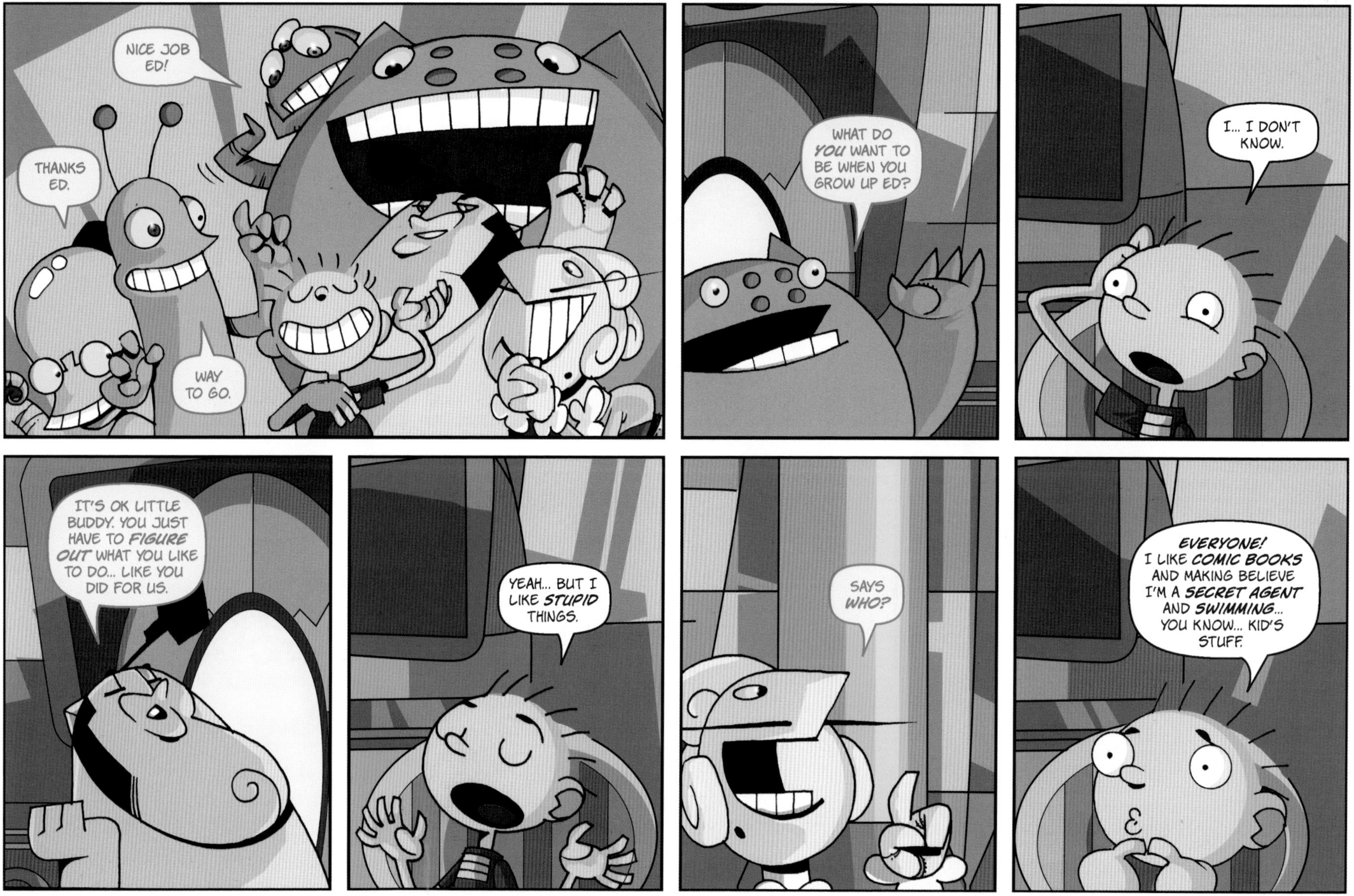
NICE JOB ED!
THANKS ED.
WAY TO GO.
WHAT DO YOU WANT TO BE WHEN YOU GROW UP ED?
I... I DON'T KNOW.
IT'S OK LITTLE BUDDY. YOU JUST HAVE TO FIGURE OUT WHAT YOU LIKE TO DO... LIKE YOU DID FOR US.
YEAH... BUT I LIKE STUPID THINGS.
SAYS WHO?
EVERYONE! I LIKE COMIC BOOKS AND MAKING BELIEVE I'M A SECRET AGENT AND SWIMMING... YOU KNOW... KID'S STUFF.

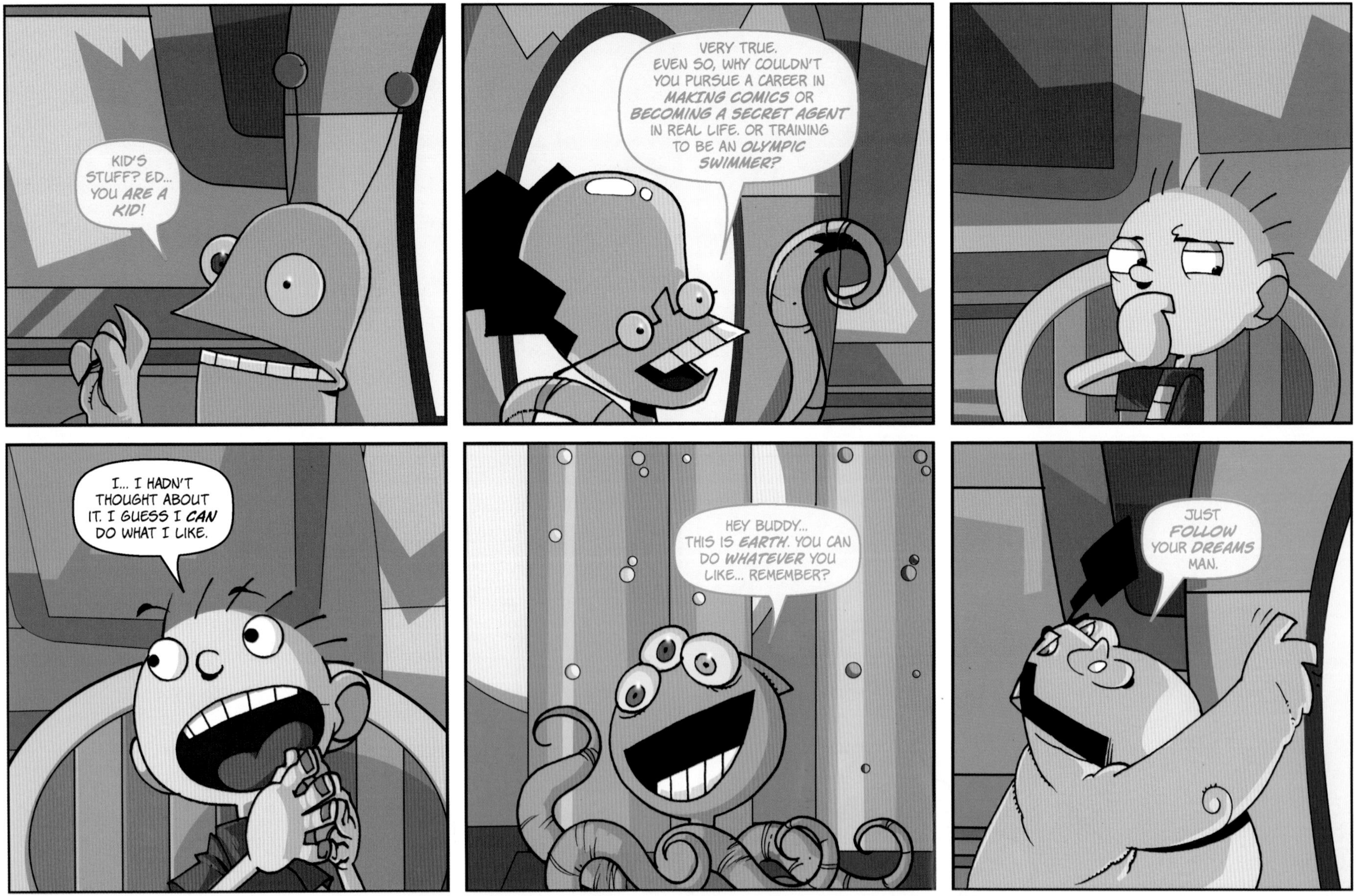
KID'S STUFF? ED... YOU ARE A KID!
VERY TRUE. EVEN SO, WHY COULDN'T YOU PURSUE A CAREER IN MAKING COMICS OR BECOMING A SECRET AGENT IN REAL LIFE. OR TRAINING TO BE AN OLYMPIC SWIMMER?
I... I HADN'T THOUGHT ABOUT IT. I GUESS I CAN DO WHAT I LIKE.
HEY BUDDY... THIS IS EARTH. YOU CAN DO WHATEVER YOU LIKE... REMEMBER?
JUST FOLLOW YOUR DREAMS MAN.

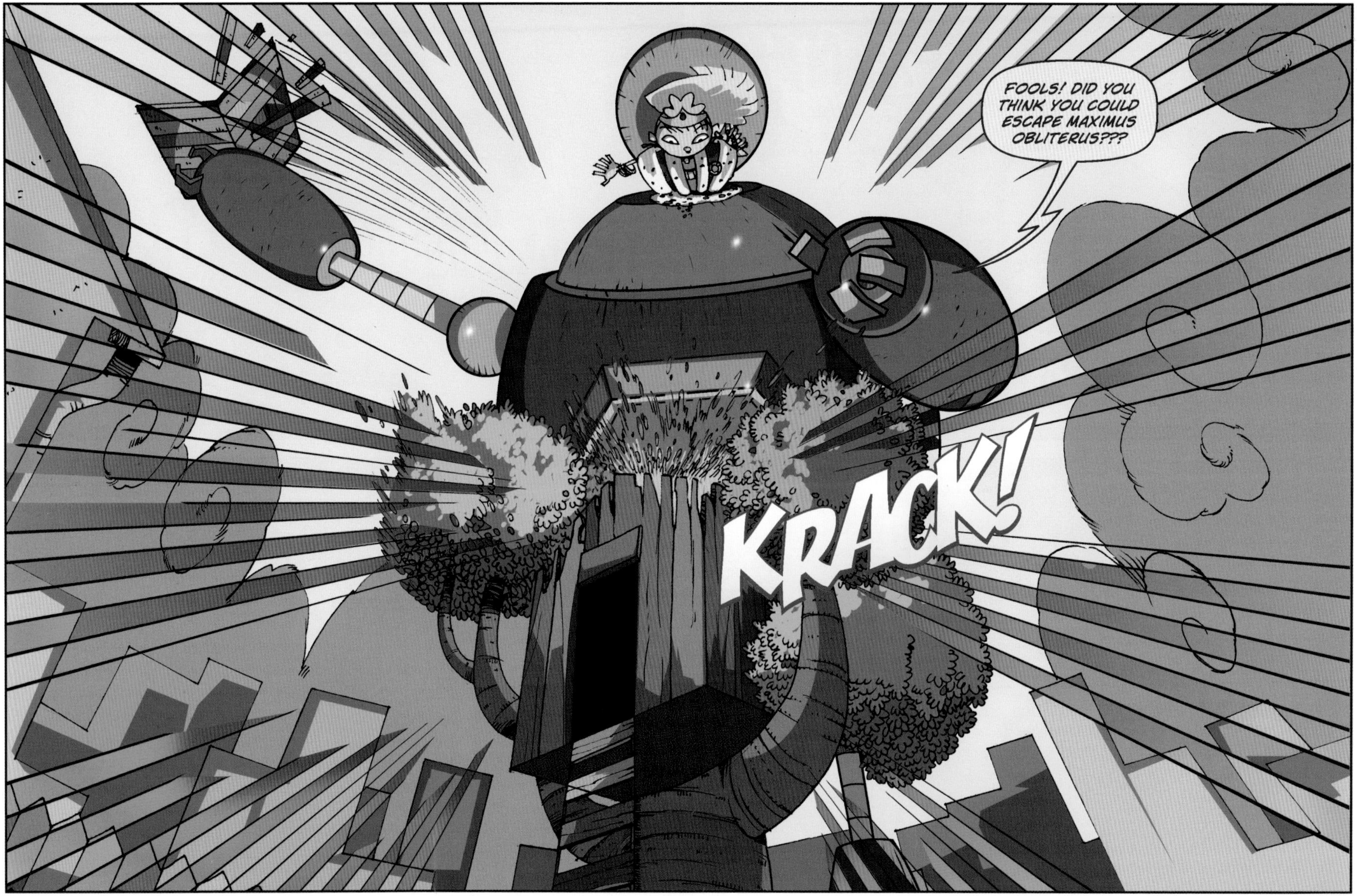
FOOLS! DID YOU THINK YOU COULD ESCAPE MAXIMUS OBLITERUS???
KRACK!

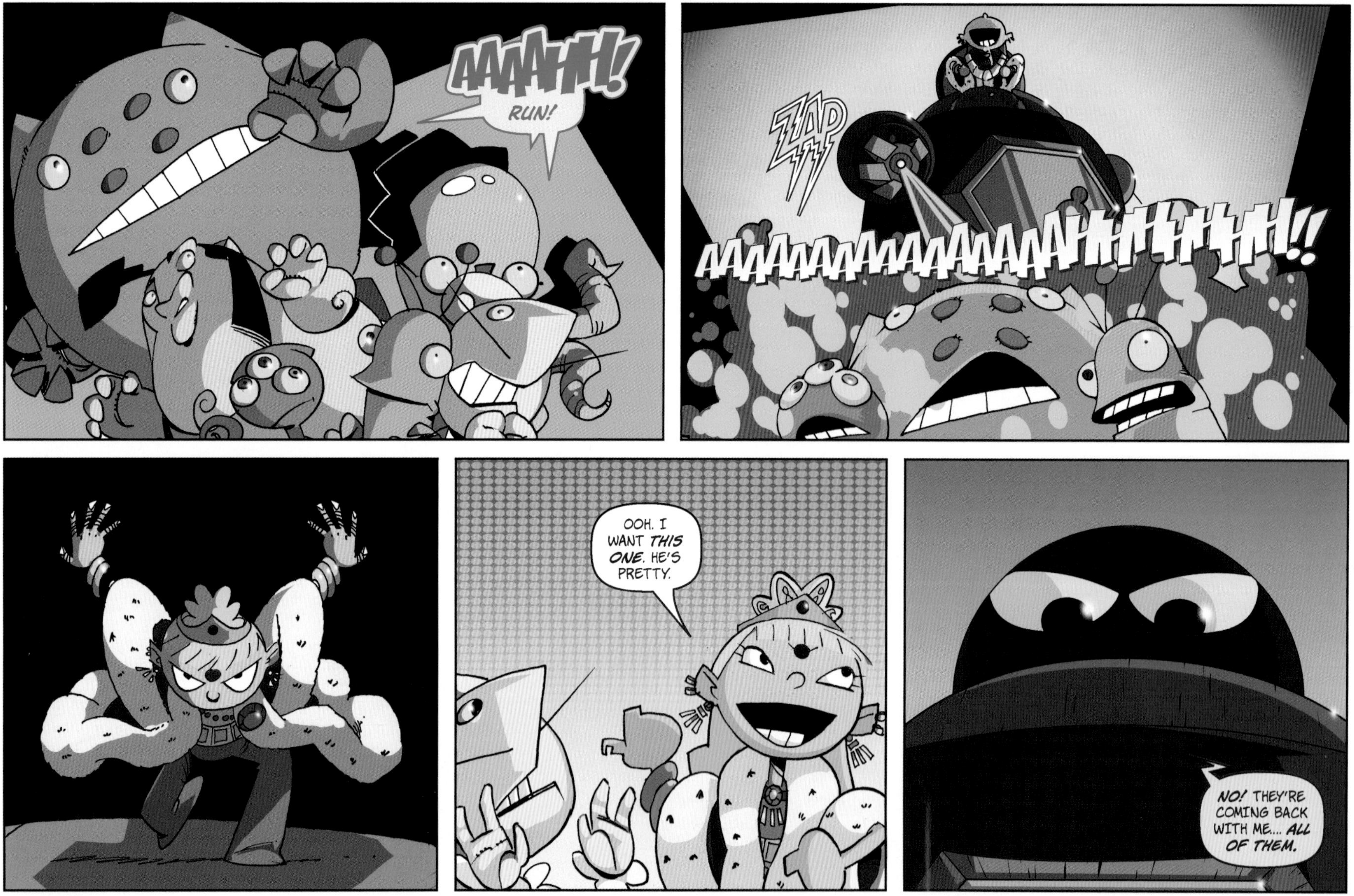
AAAAHH!
RUN!
ZAP
AAAAAAAAAAAAAAAAAAHHHHHHHHH!!
OOH. I WANT THIS ONE. HE'S PRETTY.
NO! THEY'RE COMING BACK WITH ME.... ALL OF THEM.

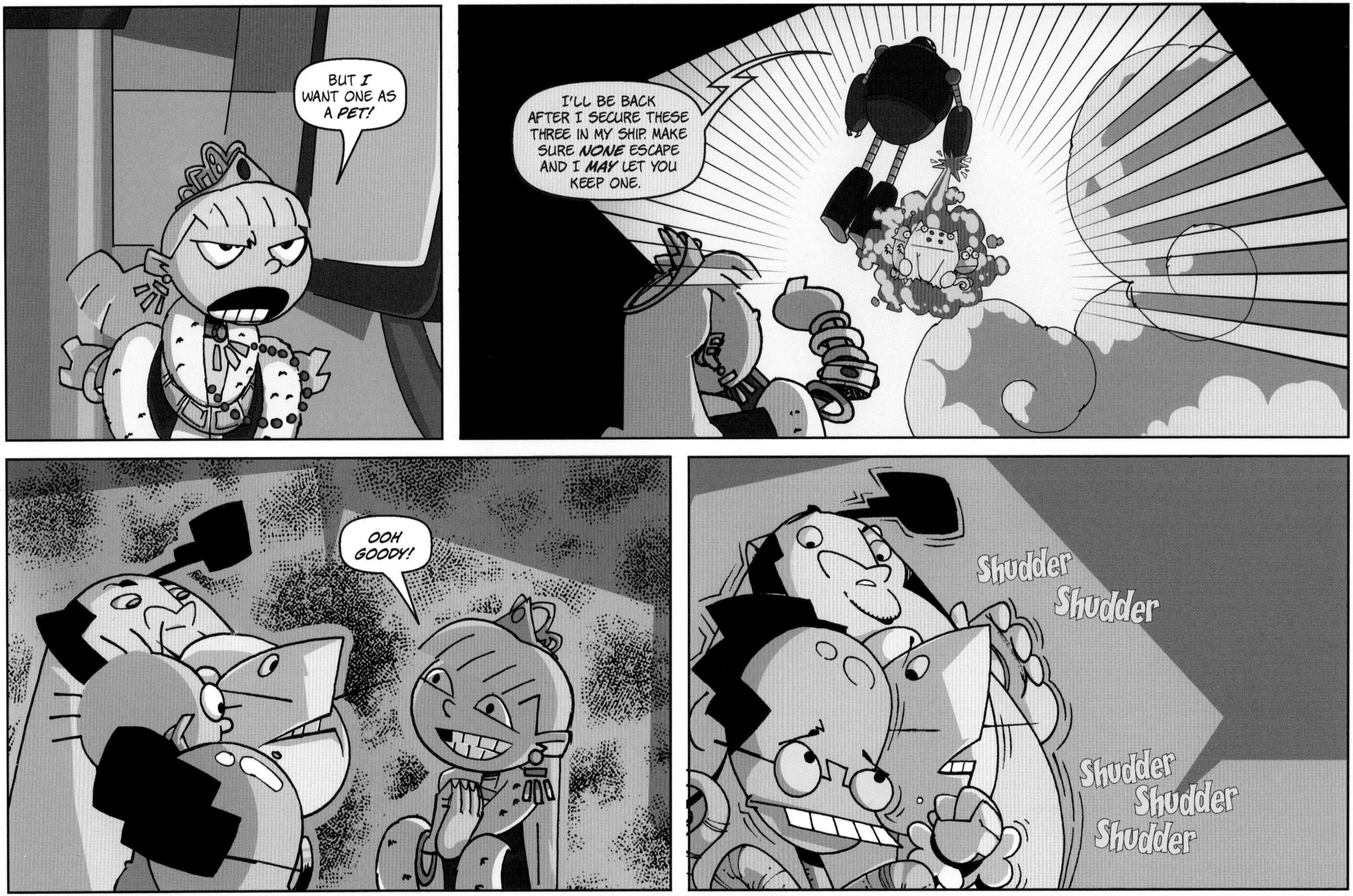
BUT *I* WANT ONE AS A *PET!*
I'LL BE BACK AFTER I SECURE THESE THREE IN MY SHIP. MAKE SURE ***NONE*** ESCAPE AND I ***MAY*** LET YOU KEEP ONE.
OOH GOODY!
Shudder
Shudder
Shudder
Shudder
Shudder

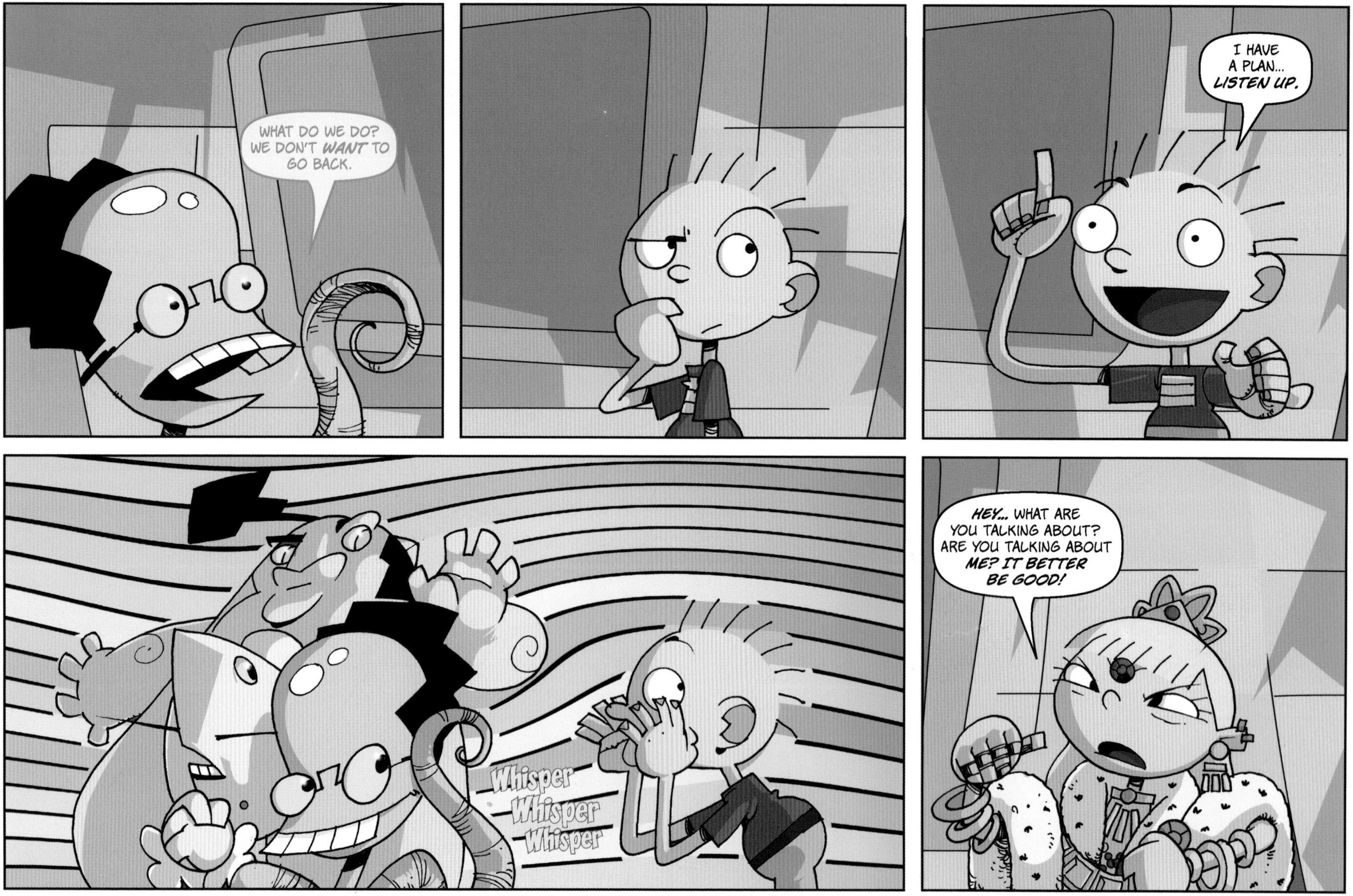
WHAT DO WE DO? WE DON'T *WANT* TO GO BACK.
I HAVE A PLAN... **LISTEN UP.**
Whisper Whisper Whisper
HEY... WHAT ARE YOU TALKING ABOUT? ARE YOU TALKING ABOUT *ME? IT BETTER BE GOOD!*

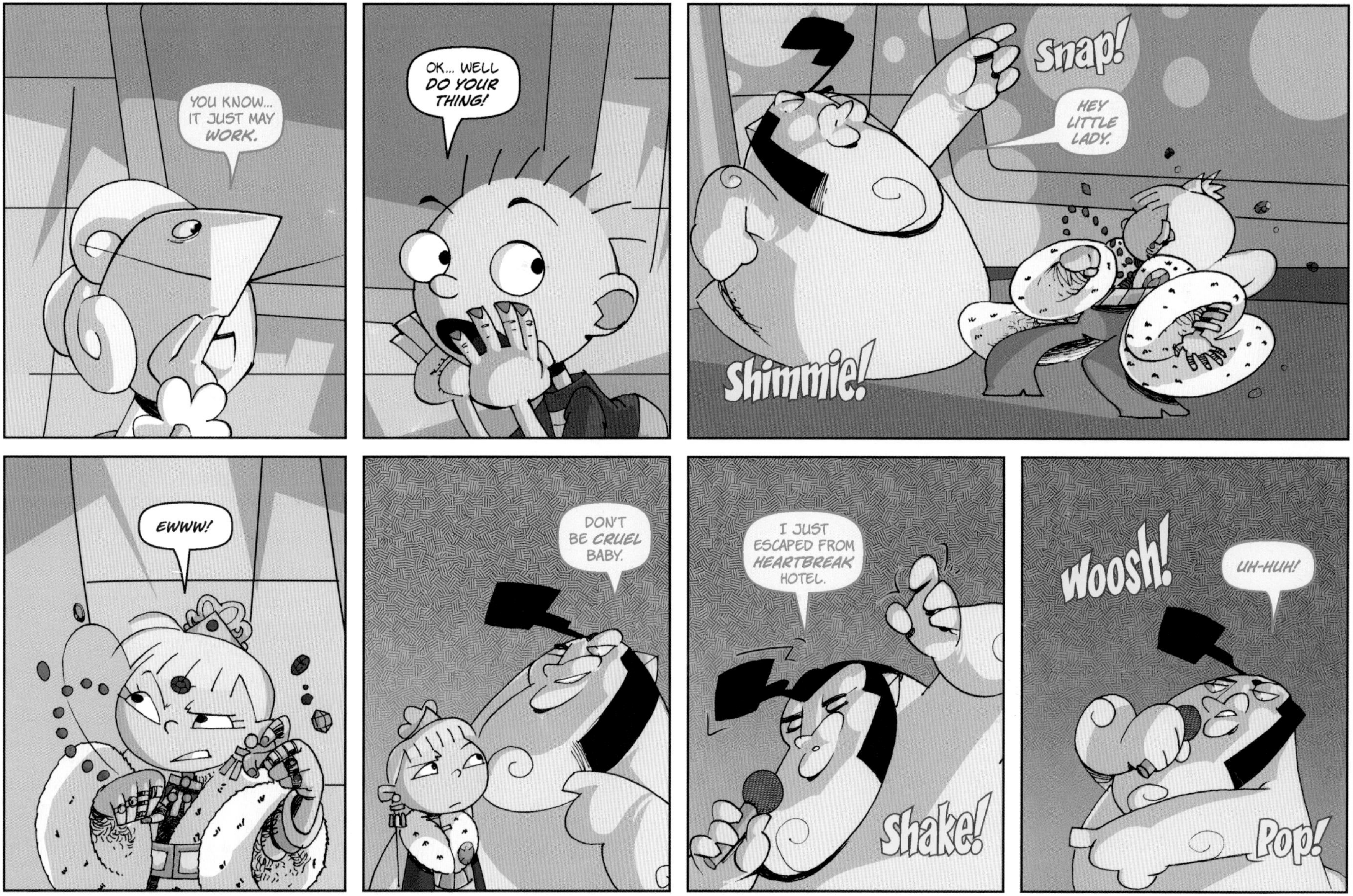

YOU KNOW... IT JUST MAY WORK.
OK... WELL DO YOUR THING!
Snap!
HEY LITTLE LADY.
Shimmie!
EWWW!
DON'T BE CRUEL BABY.
I JUST ESCAPED FROM HEARTBREAK HOTEL.
Shake!
Woosh!
UH-HUH!
Pop!

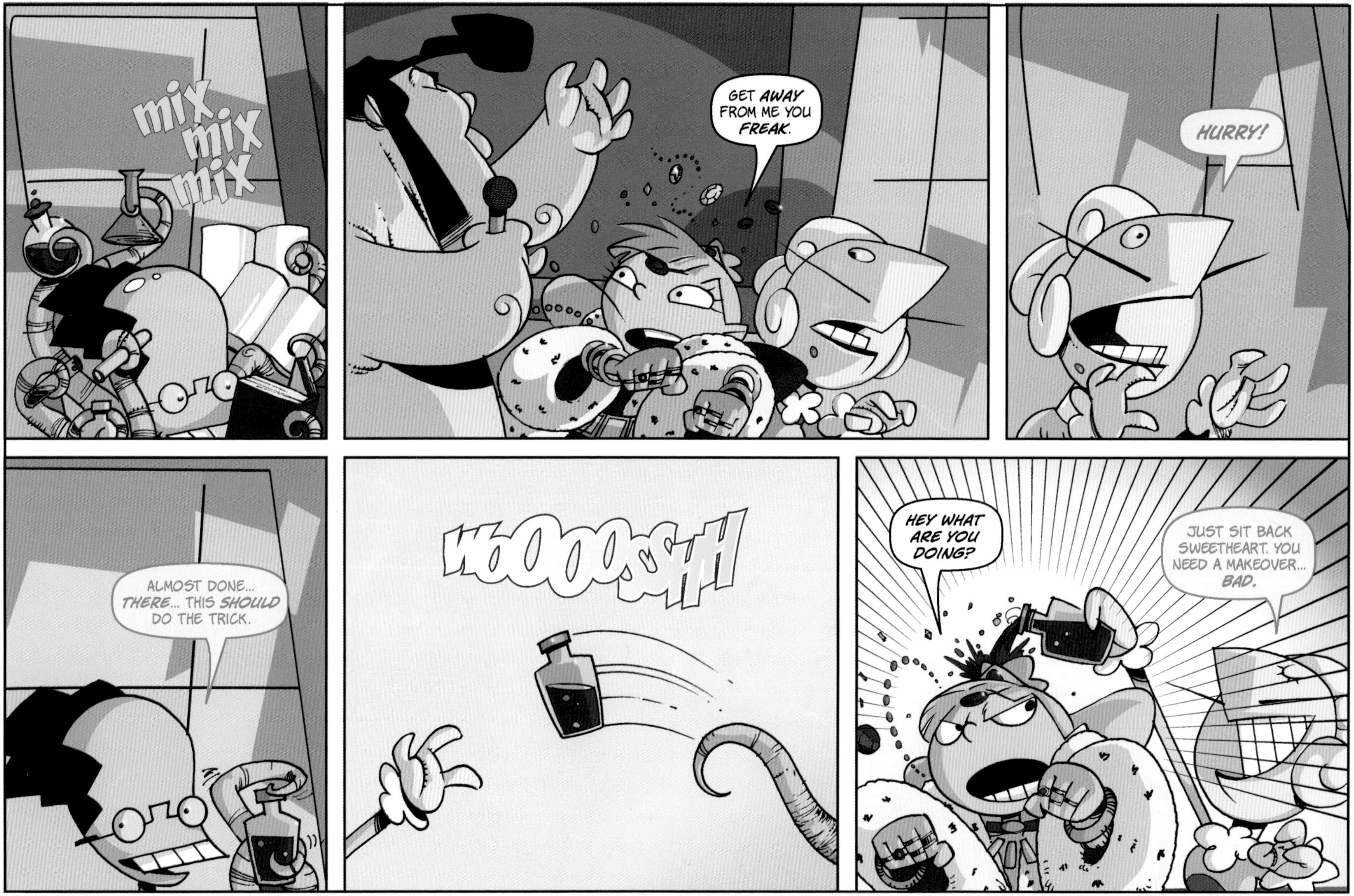

mix mix mix
GET AWAY FROM ME YOU FREAK.
HURRY!
ALMOST DONE... THERE... THIS SHOULD DO THE TRICK.
WOOOOSSHH
HEY WHAT ARE YOU DOING?
JUST SIT BACK SWEETHEART. YOU NEED A MAKEOVER... BAD.

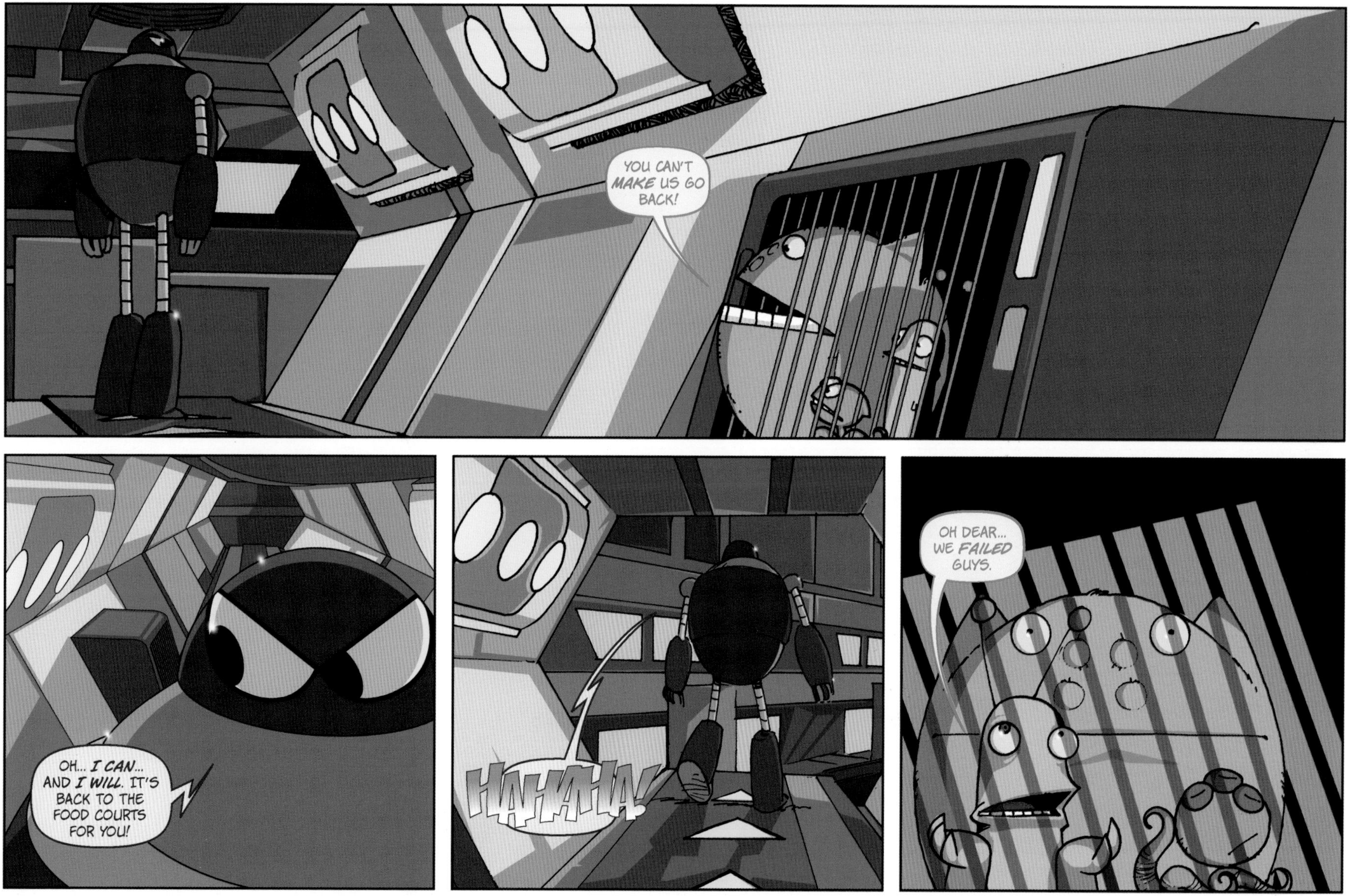
YOU CAN'T MAKE US GO BACK!
OH... I CAN... AND I WILL. IT'S BACK TO THE FOOD COURTS FOR YOU!
HAHAHA!
OH DEAR... WE FAILED GUYS.

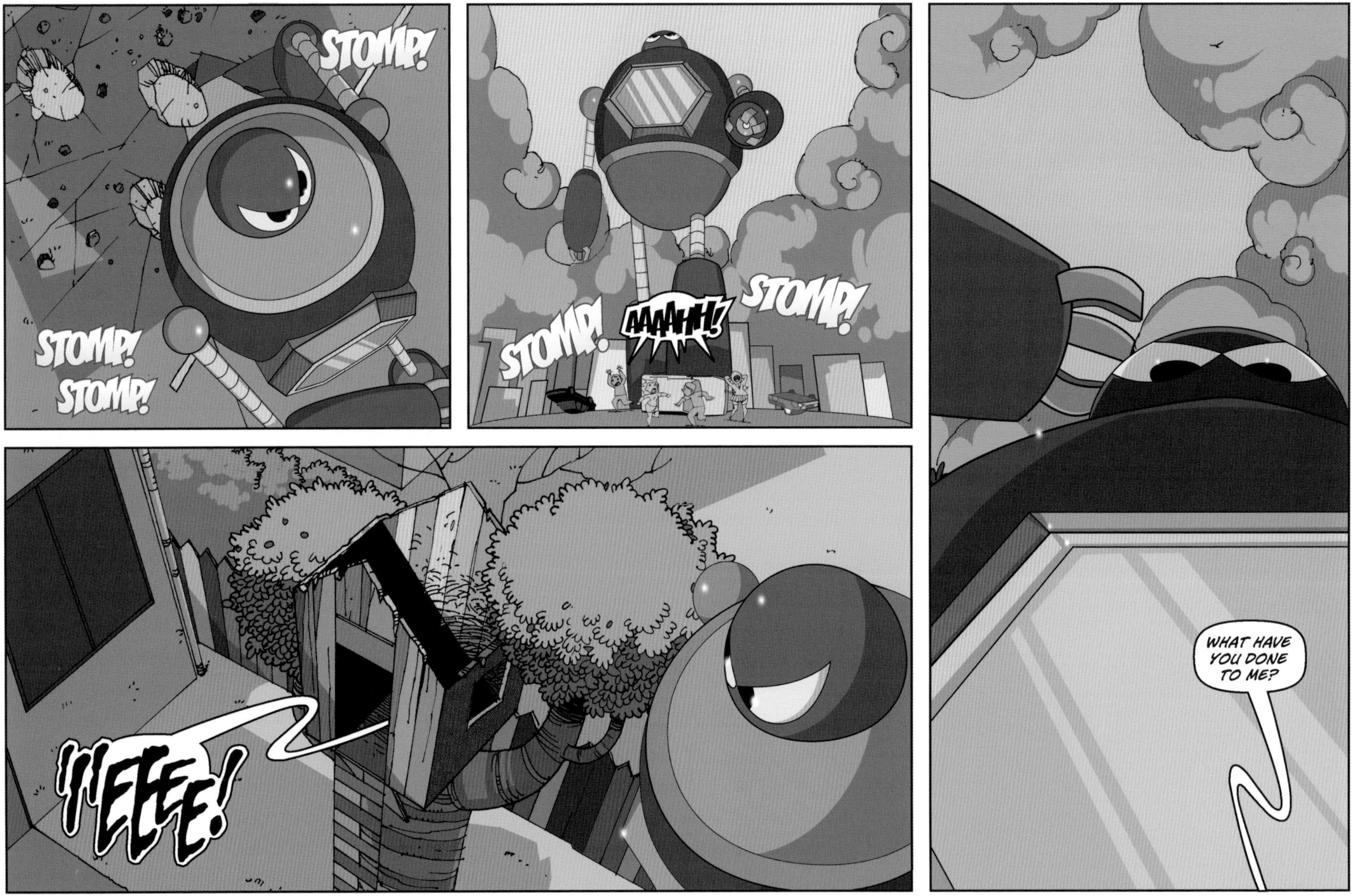
STOMP!
STOMP!
STOMP!
STOMP!
AAAAHH!
STOMP!
WHAT HAVE YOU DONE TO ME?
EEEE!

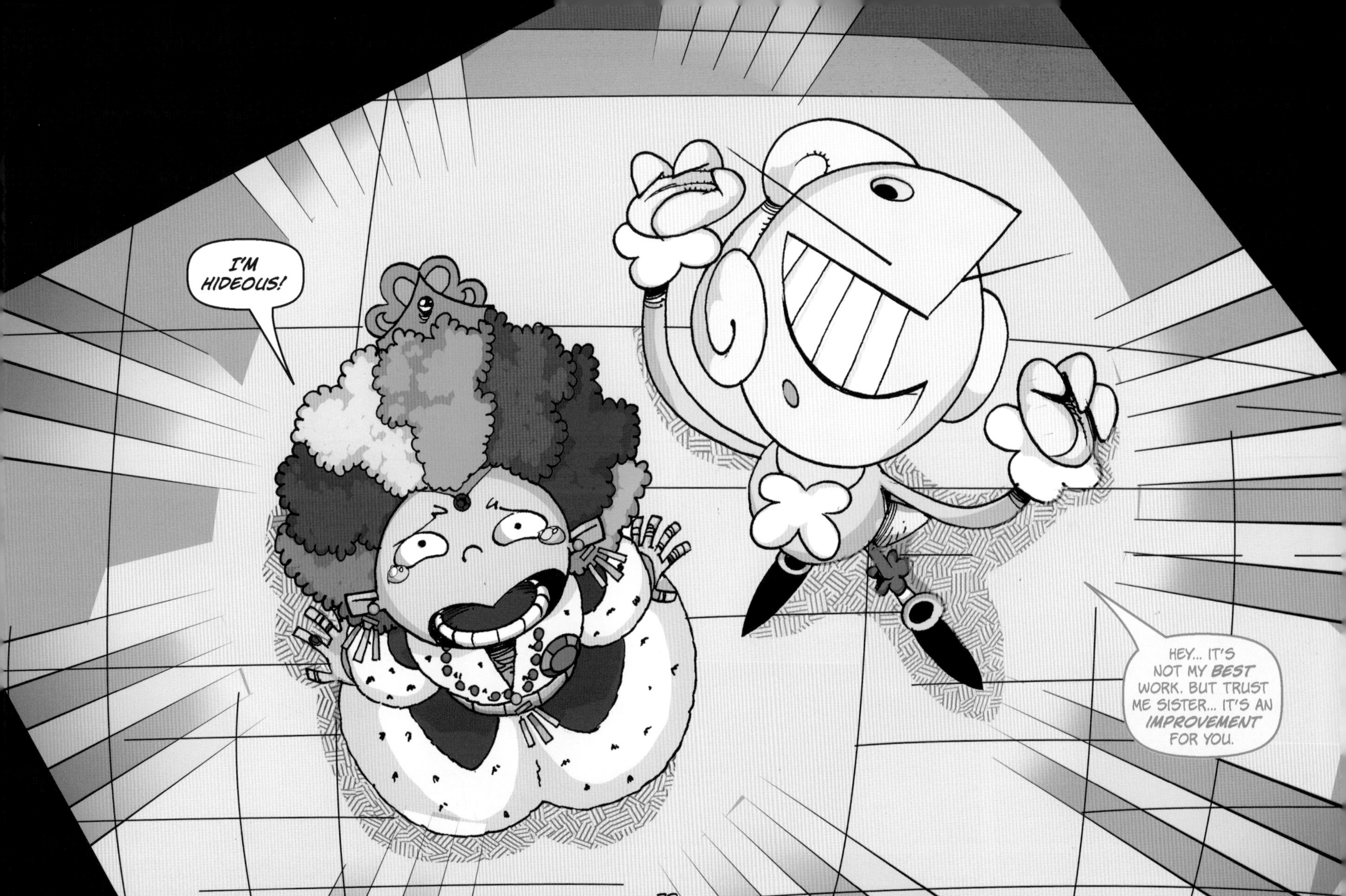
I'M HIDEOUS!
HEY... IT'S NOT MY BEST WORK. BUT TRUST ME SISTER... IT'S AN IMPROVEMENT FOR YOU.

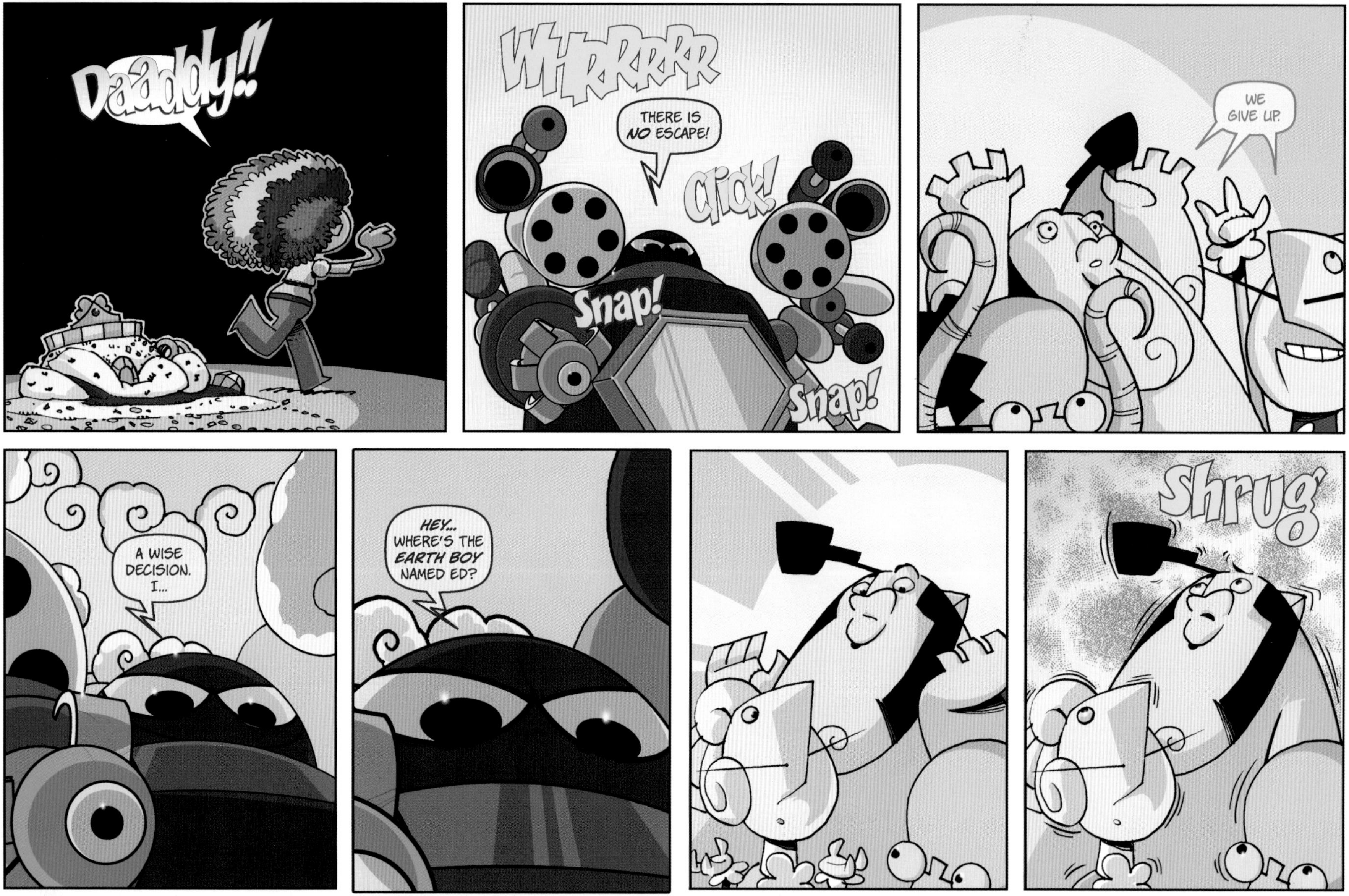
Daaddy!!
WHRRRRR
THERE IS NO ESCAPE!
Click!
Snap!
Snap!
WE GIVE UP.
A WISE DECISION. I...
HEY... WHERE'S THE EARTH BOY NAMED ED?
Shrug

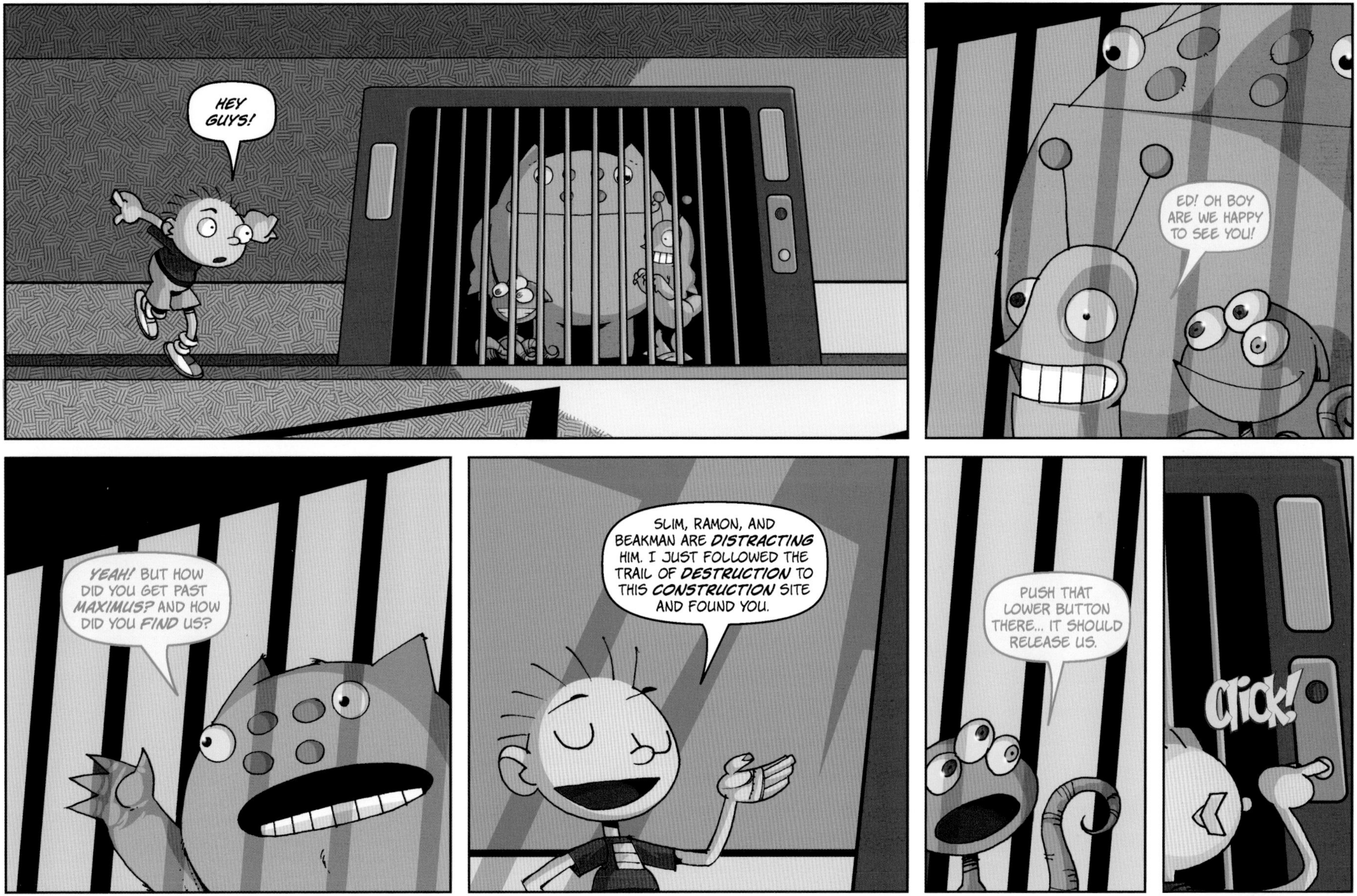
HEY GUYS!
ED! OH BOY ARE WE HAPPY TO SEE YOU!
YEAH! BUT HOW DID YOU GET PAST MAXIMUS? AND HOW DID YOU FIND US?
SLIM, RAMON, AND BEAKMAN ARE DISTRACTING HIM. I JUST FOLLOWED THE TRAIL OF DESTRUCTION TO THIS CONSTRUCTION SITE AND FOUND YOU.
PUSH THAT LOWER BUTTON THERE... IT SHOULD RELEASE US.
CLICK!

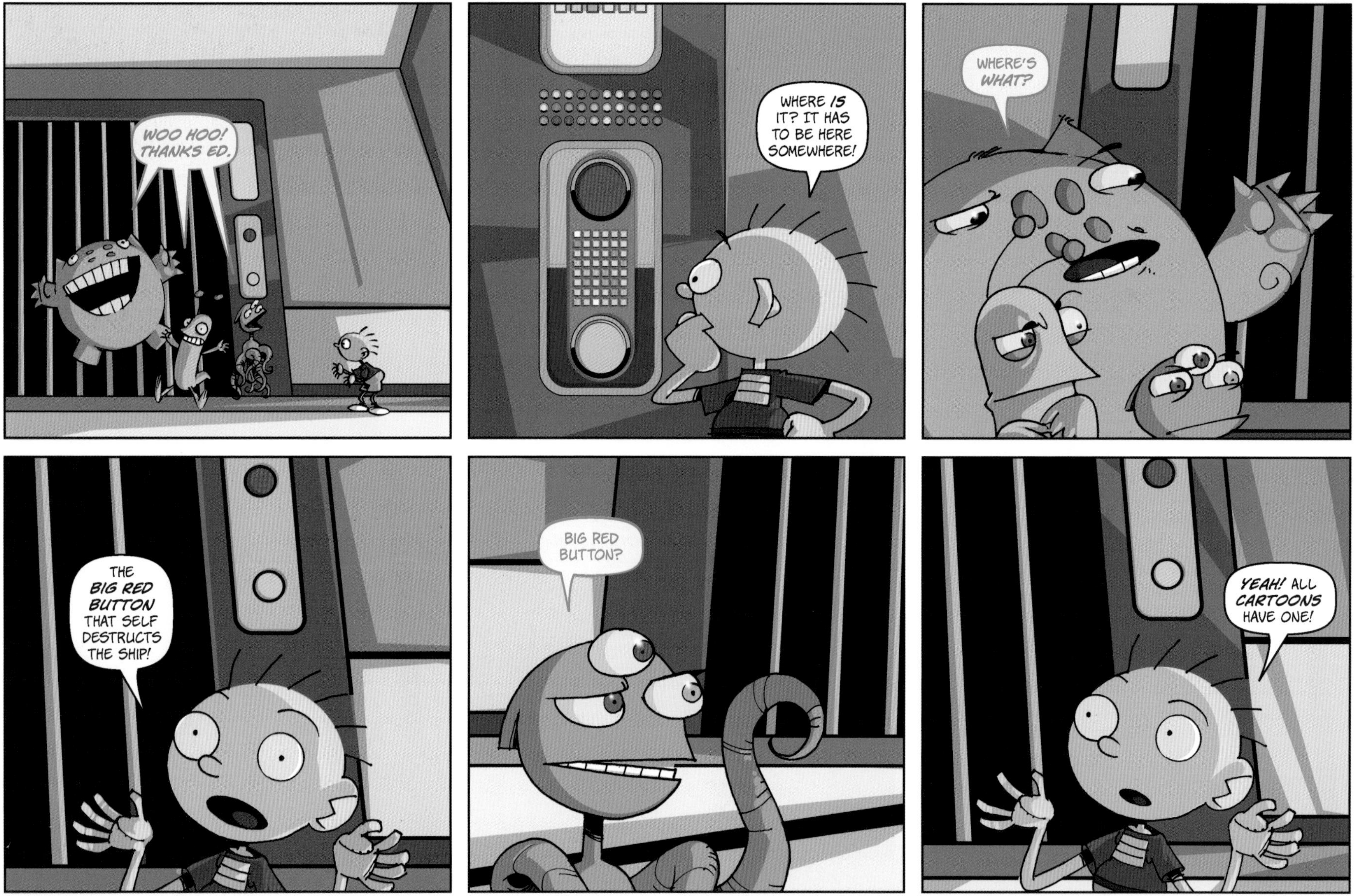
WOO HOO! THANKS ED.
WHERE IS IT? IT HAS TO BE HERE SOMEWHERE!
WHERE'S WHAT?
THE BIG RED BUTTON THAT SELF DESTRUCTS THE SHIP!
BIG RED BUTTON?
YEAH! ALL CARTOONS HAVE ONE!

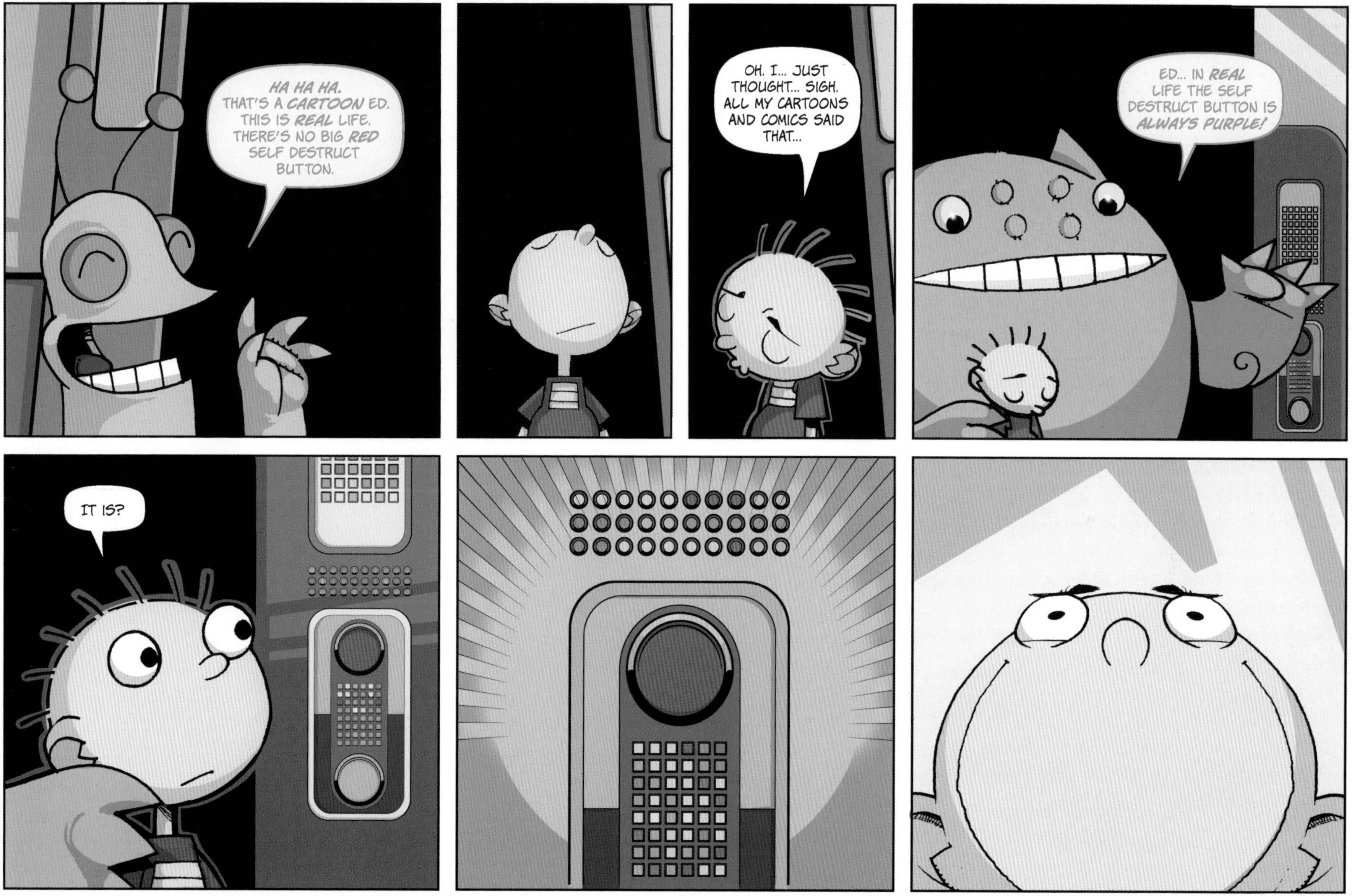
HA HA HA. THAT'S A CARTOON ED. THIS IS REAL LIFE. THERE'S NO BIG RED SELF DESTRUCT BUTTON.
OH. I... JUST THOUGHT... SIGH. ALL MY CARTOONS AND COMICS SAID THAT...
ED... IN REAL LIFE THE SELF DESTRUCT BUTTON IS ALWAYS PURPLE!
IT IS?

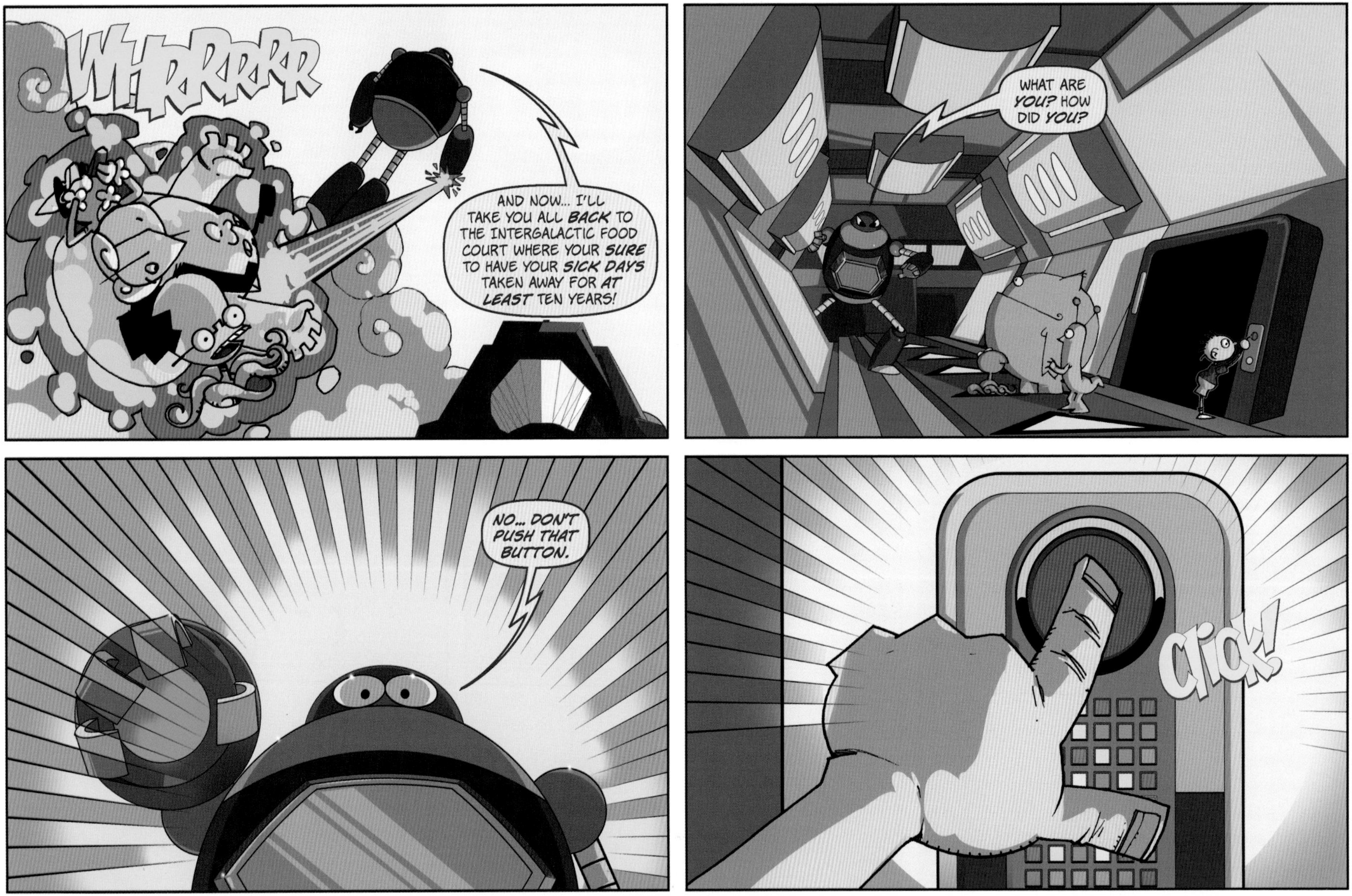
WHRRRRRR
AND NOW... I'LL TAKE YOU ALL BACK TO THE INTERGALACTIC FOOD COURT WHERE YOUR SURE TO HAVE YOUR SICK DAYS TAKEN AWAY FOR AT LEAST TEN YEARS!
WHAT ARE YOU? HOW DID YOU?
NO... DON'T PUSH THAT BUTTON.
CLICK!

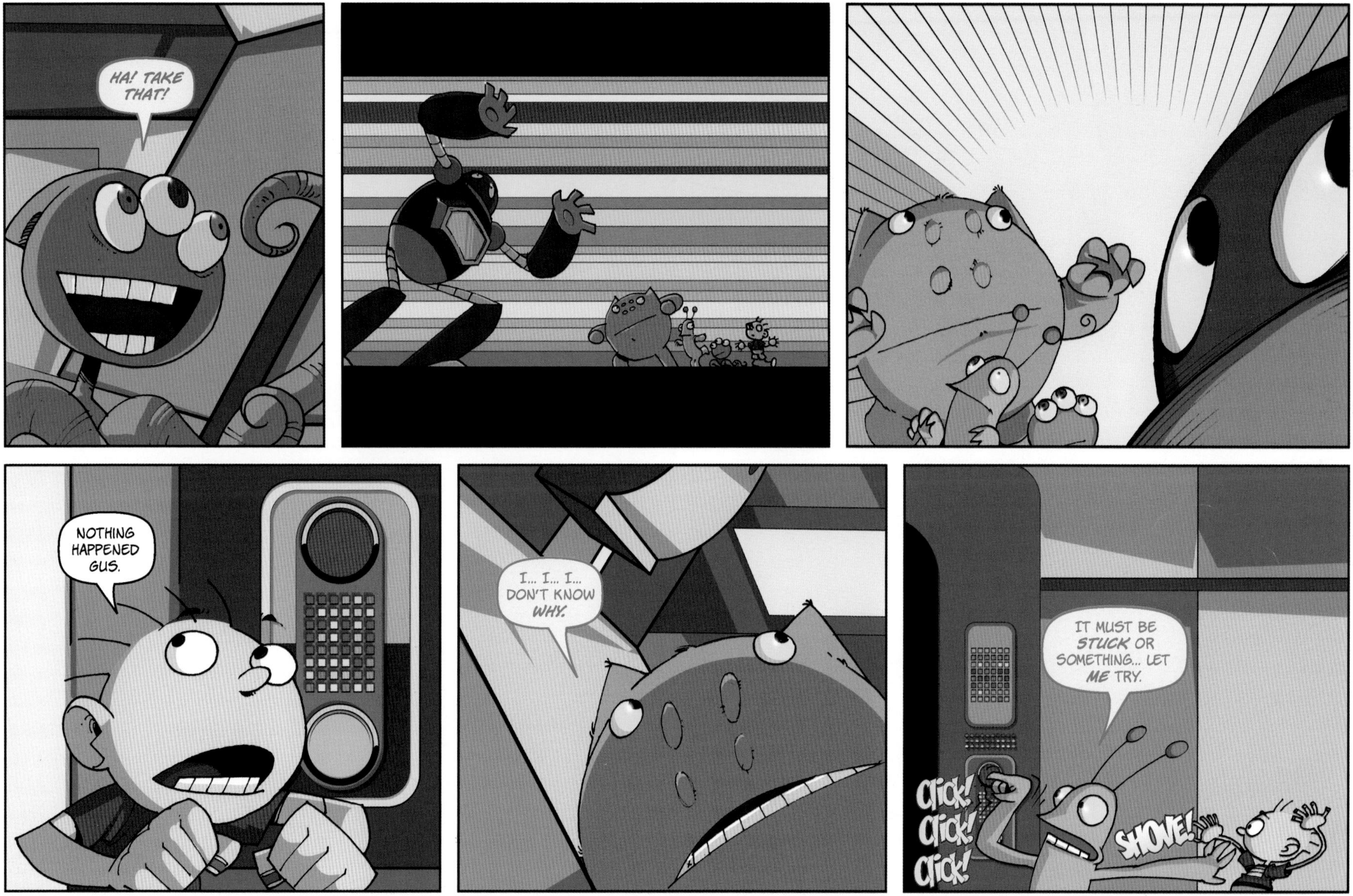
HA! TAKE THAT!
NOTHING HAPPENED GUS.
I... I... I... DON'T KNOW WHY.
IT MUST BE STUCK OR SOMETHING... LET ME TRY.
CLICK! CLICK! CLICK!
SHOVE!

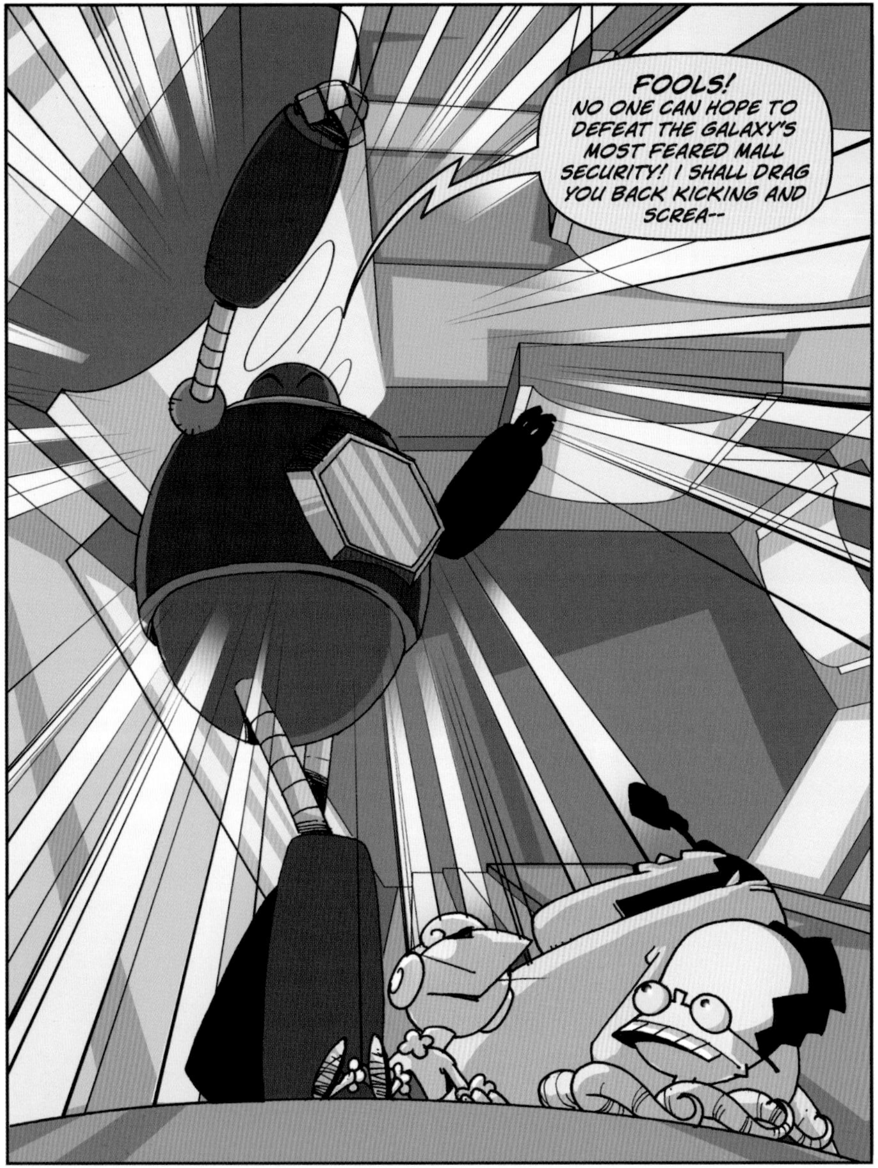
FOOLS!
NO ONE CAN HOPE TO DEFEAT THE GALAXY'S MOST FEARED MALL SECURITY! I SHALL DRAG YOU BACK KICKING AND SCREA--

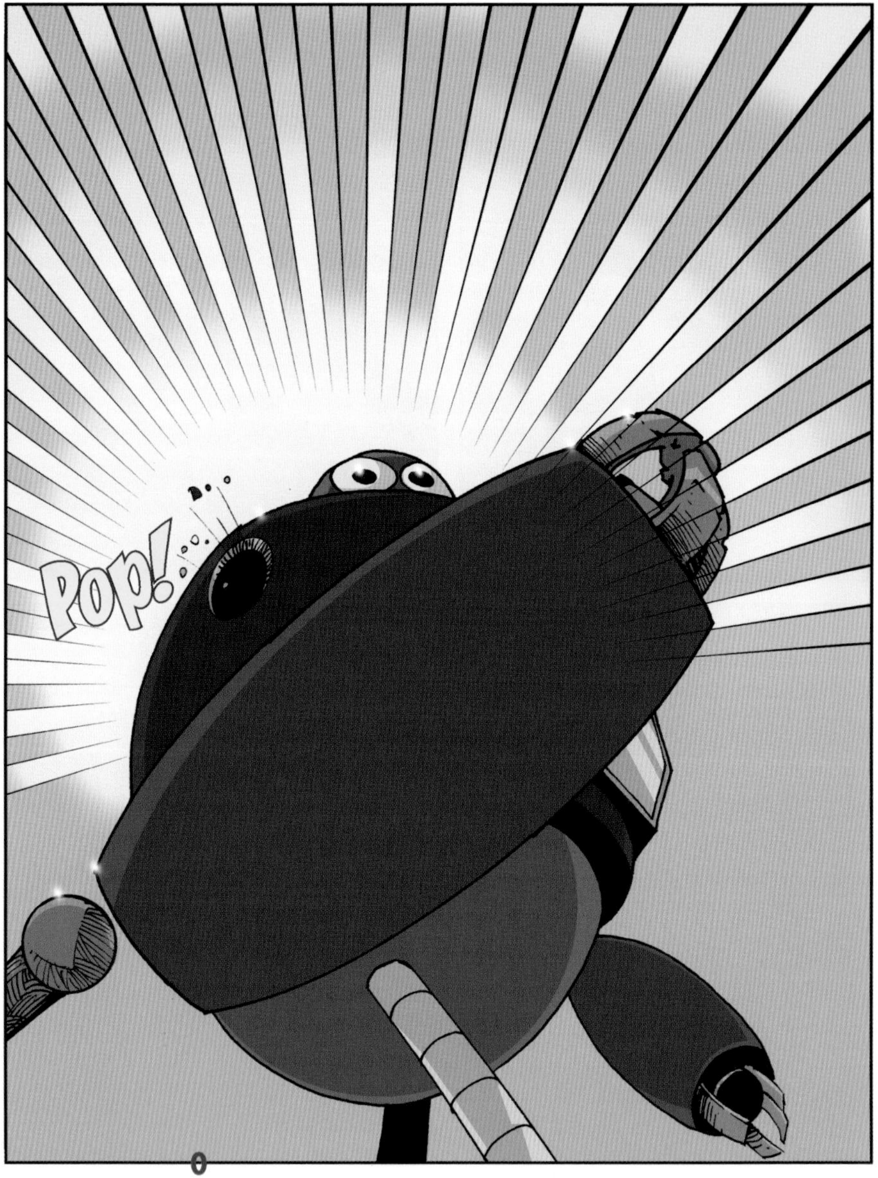
POP!

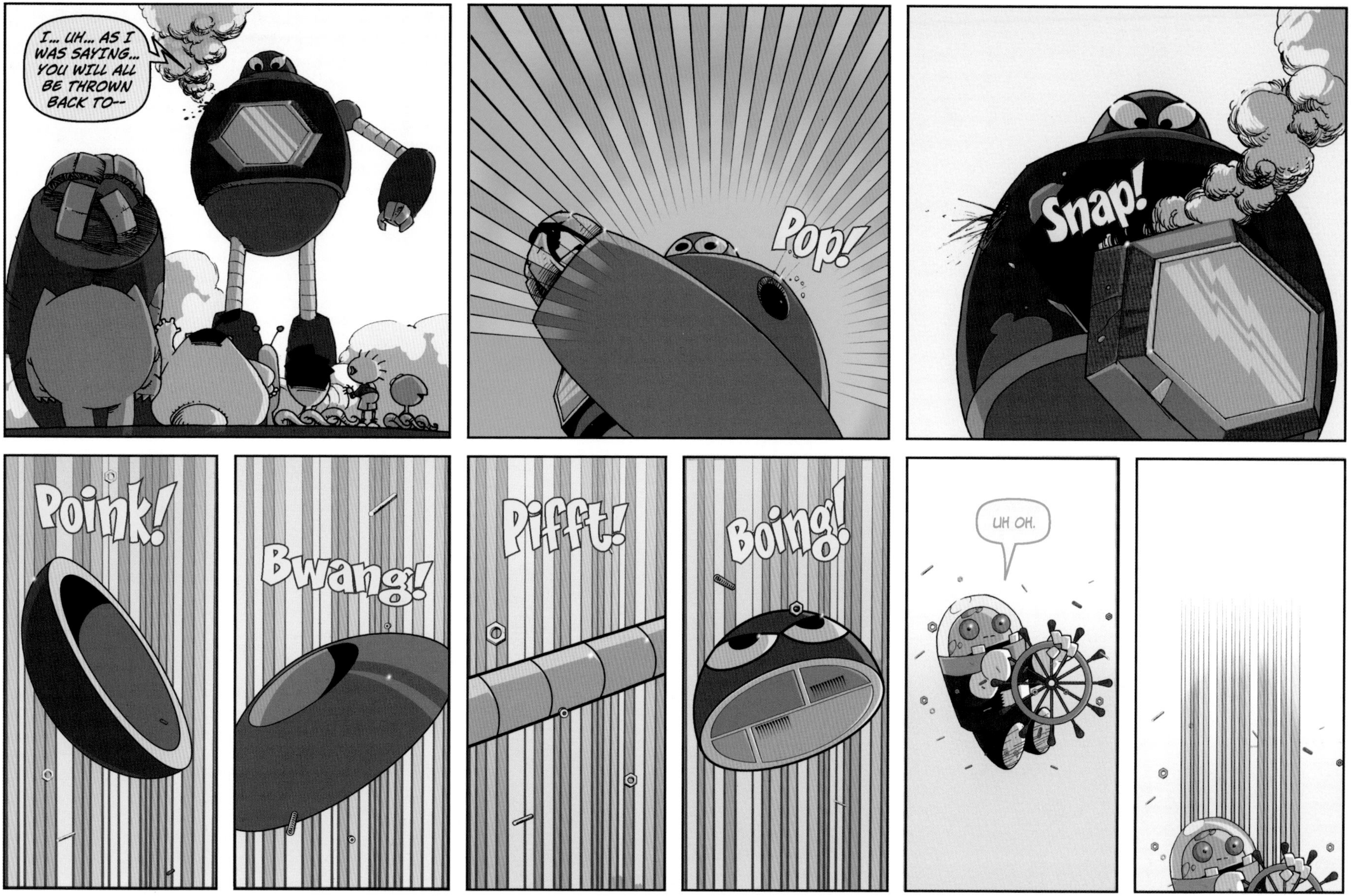
I... UH... AS I WAS SAYING... YOU WILL ALL BE THROWN BACK TO--
Pop!
Snap!
Poink!
Bwang!
Pifft!
Boing!
UH OH.

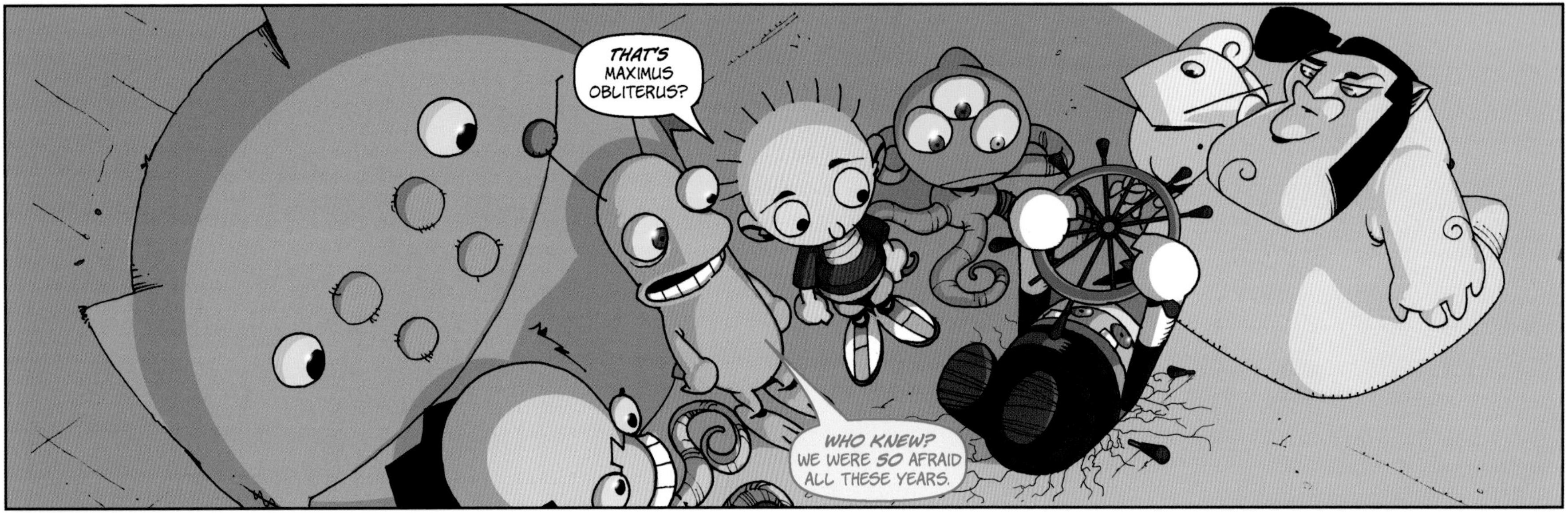
THAT'S MAXIMUS OBLITERUS?
WHO KNEW? WE WERE SO AFRAID ALL THESE YEARS.

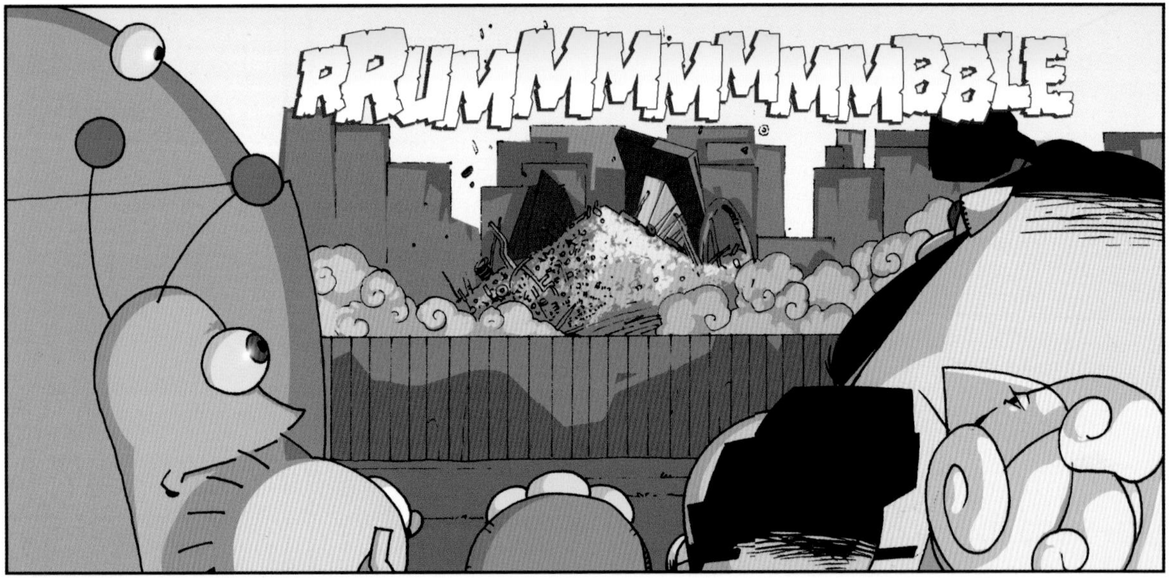
rRUMMMMMMMMMBBLE

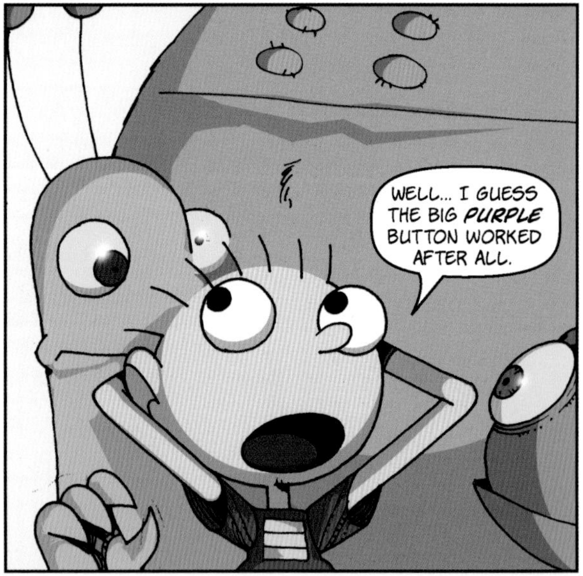
WELL... I GUESS THE BIG PURPLE BUTTON WORKED AFTER ALL.

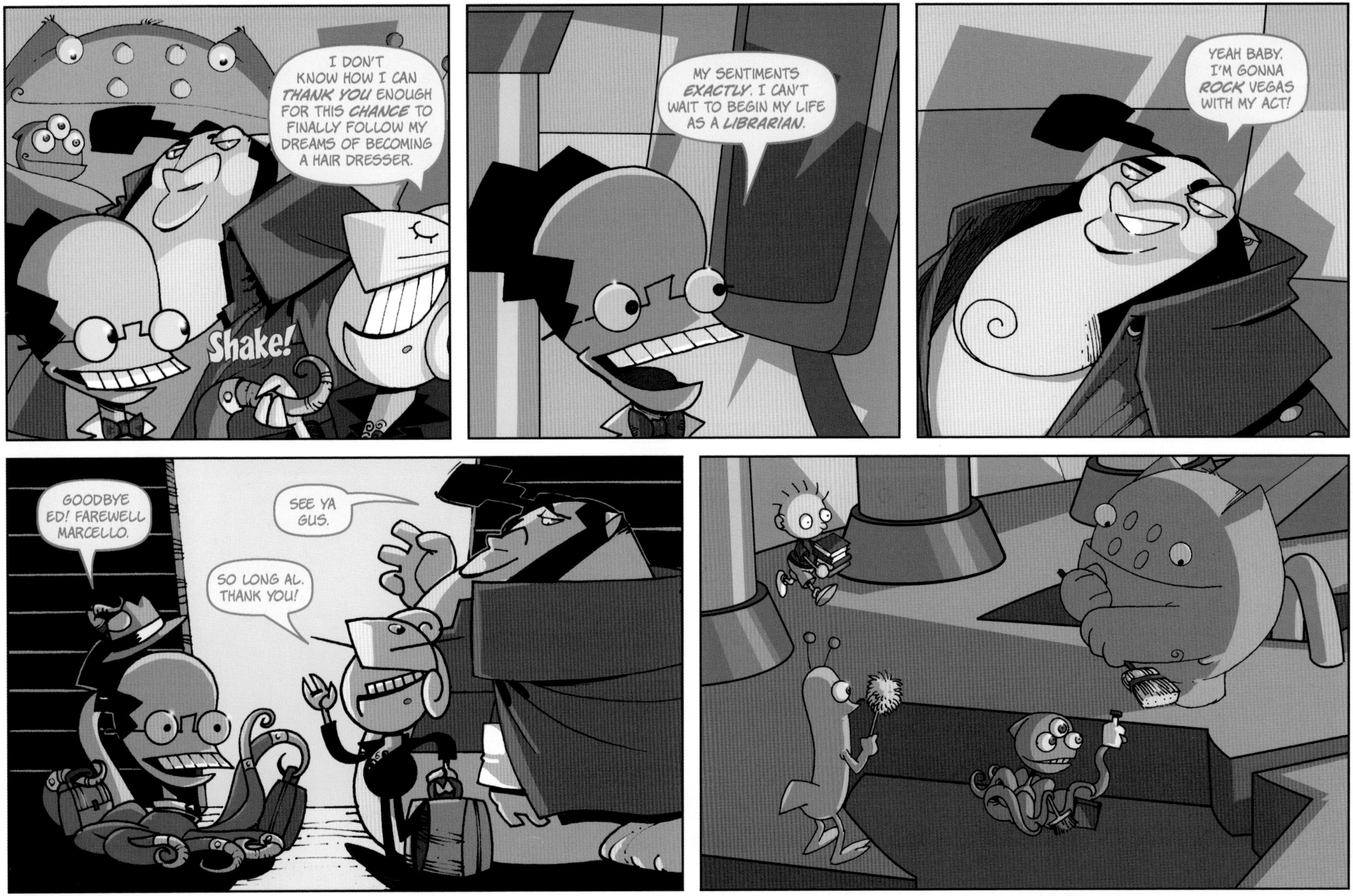

I DON'T KNOW HOW I CAN THANK YOU ENOUGH FOR THIS CHANCE TO FINALLY FOLLOW MY DREAMS OF BECOMING A HAIR DRESSER.
Shake!
MY SENTIMENTS EXACTLY. I CAN'T WAIT TO BEGIN MY LIFE AS A LIBRARIAN.
YEAH BABY. I'M GONNA ROCK VEGAS WITH MY ACT!
GOODBYE ED! FAREWELL MARCELLO.
SEE YA GUS.
SO LONG AL. THANK YOU!

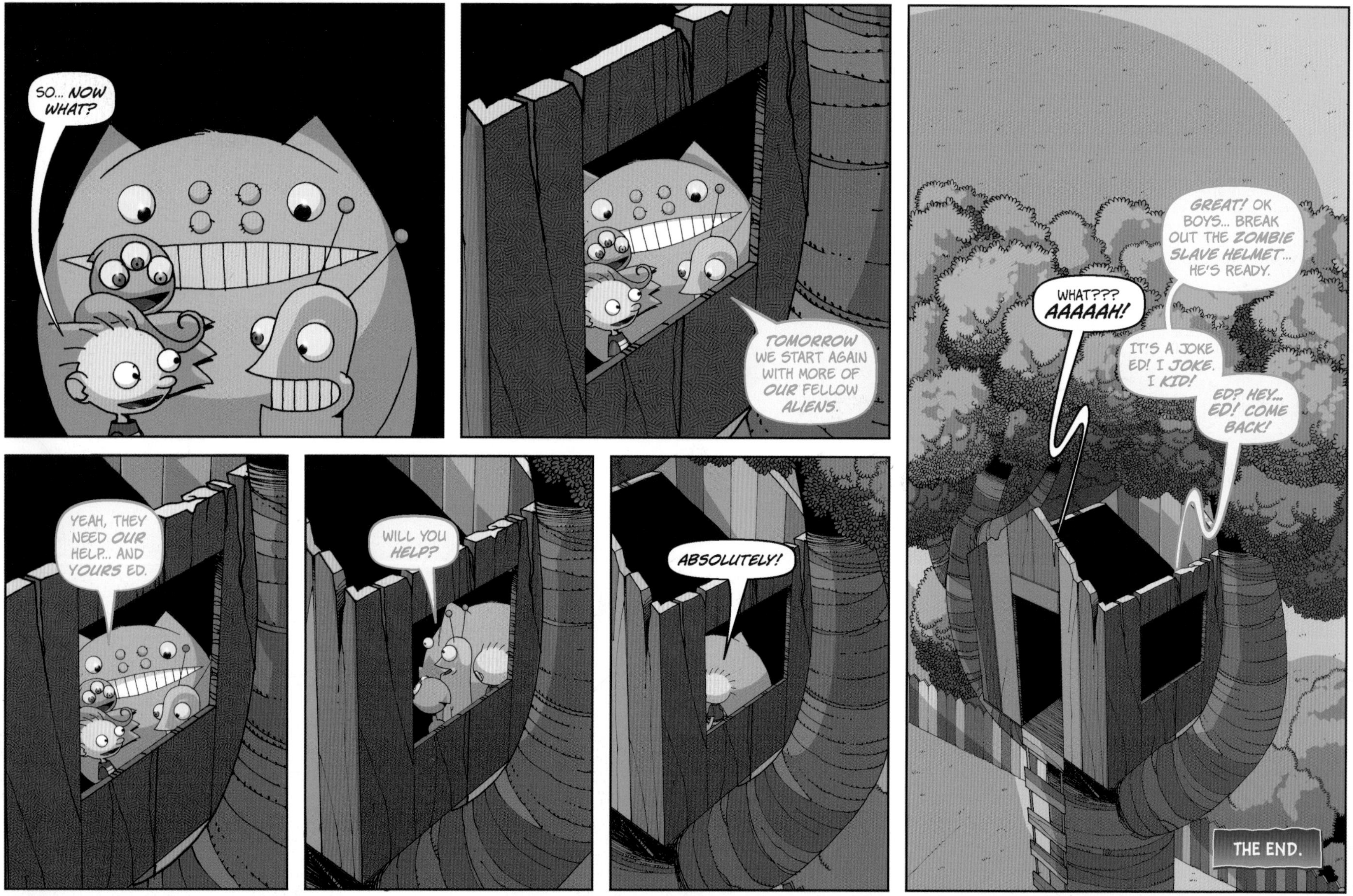
SO... NOW WHAT?
TOMORROW WE START AGAIN WITH MORE OF OUR FELLOW ALIENS.
YEAH, THEY NEED OUR HELP... AND YOURS ED.
WILL YOU HELP?
ABSOLUTELY!
GREAT! OK BOYS... BREAK OUT THE ZOMBIE SLAVE HELMET... HE'S READY.
WHAT??? AAAAAH!
IT'S A JOKE ED! I JOKE. I KID!
ED? HEY... ED! COME BACK!
THE END.

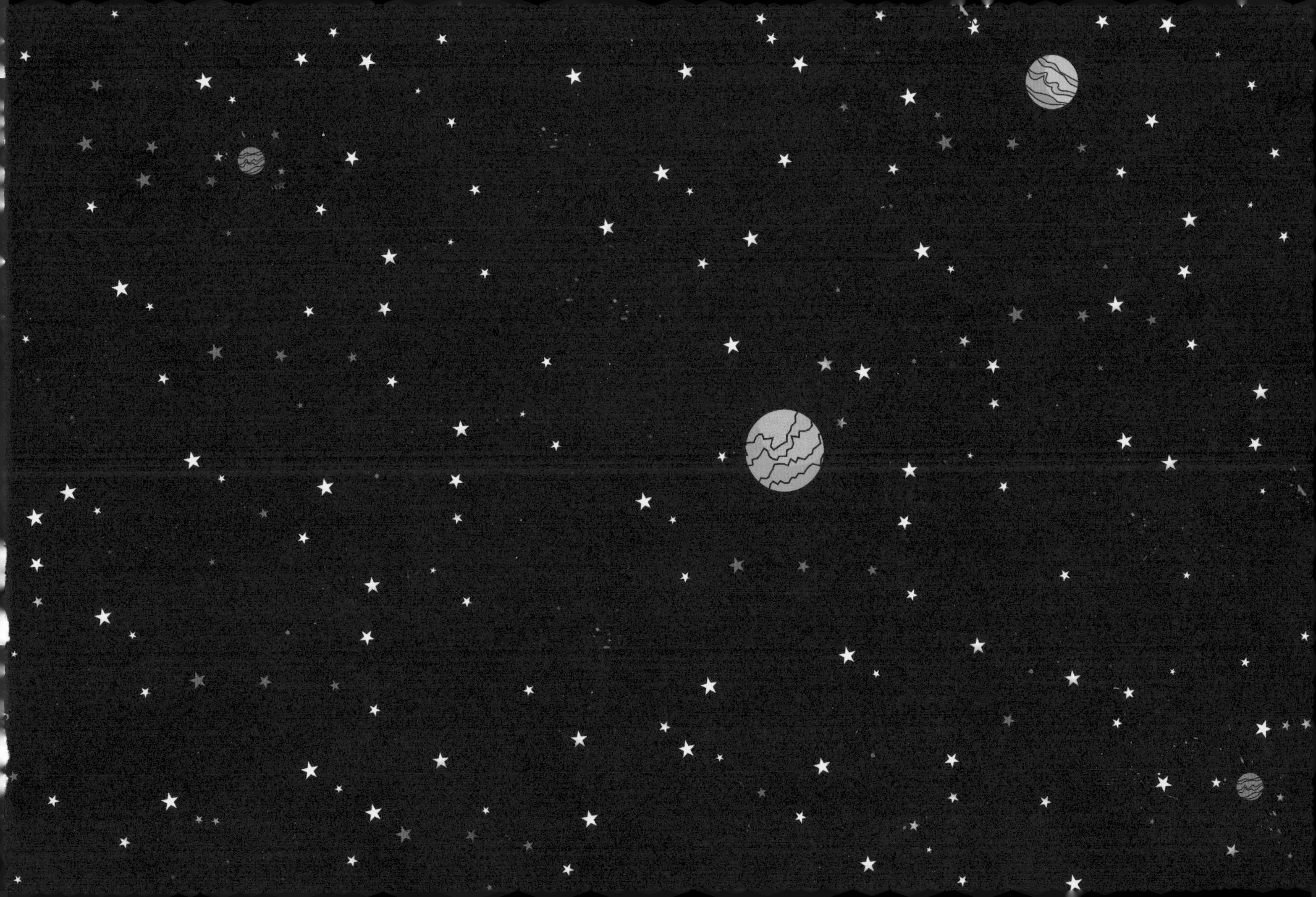

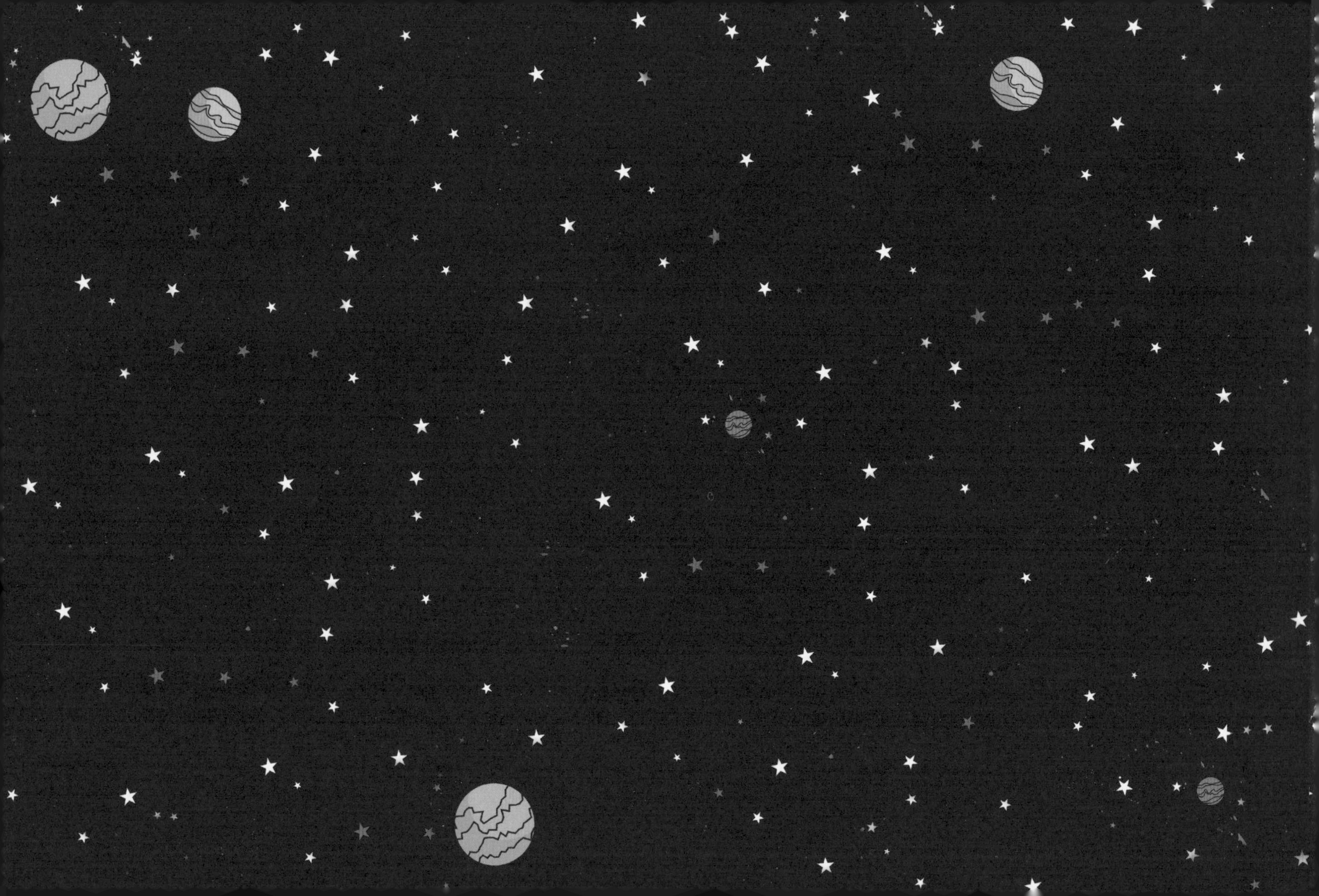